Forever Verse

written by ANTHONY FARINA
illustrated by JACKIE NICKLE

A Traitmarker Book

Forever Verse

written by ANTHONY FARINA
illustrated by JACKIE NICKLE

A Traitmarker Book

Robbie Grayson
2984 Del Rio Pike
Franklin, TN 37069

Ordering Information for Quantity Sales:
Special discounts are available on quantity purchases by corporations, asso-ciations, and others. For details, contact the publisher at the address above.

Attributions:
Interior Text Font: Harrington
Interior Title Fonts: Moonlight Shadow
Editor: Sharilyn Grayson
Typesetter: Robbie Grayson
Illustrator: Jackie Nickle
Website Design & Layout: Sara Elisabeth Olsen (www.ForeverVerse.com)
Cover Design: Andrew Macarthur (www.drewone.com)

Book Publishing Information:
ForeverVerse
ISBN: 978-1-684-338-7

Published by Traitmarker Books (traitmarkerbooks.com)
To contact the Publisher: traitmarker@gmail.com

Printed in the United States of America

Contents

D E D I C A T I O N

...

To my daughter, Darby Paige -
There is no easy way for a father to show or
tell his daughter that he loves her, because it
must be done a thousand times and in a
thousand ways. May you know by this book
just one of those many ways.

Dad

iii

CHAPTER I

The Kingdom of St. Mein

KING Salvatore looked up from his pacing to see Cleric Jeremy walking solemnly toward him across the throne room. Jeremy bowed and spoke the words King Salvatore had both dreaded and anticipated for years. "It has begun. Prince Samuel is born, my king."

"And the wizard?" the king asked swiftly.

"He has no knowledge of it," Jeremy assured him. "The blessings from the creator are keeping Ablewis bound in chains for the present. He will be moved out of the dungeon and placed into the wilderness within the hour. I have called on certain powers within the forest to guard him, never allowing him to return and do harm. As long as the prince does not enter the wilderness, he will be safe from the wizard."

The king paused before asking the next question. He feared from Jeremy's solemn face that he already knew the answer. "And Queen Kathleen?"

"She died during childbirth; you will be left to care for the prince," Jeremy answered gently.

King Salvatore nodded and turned away. Jeremy left him to his thoughts, knowing that no words could soothe the pain the king had to bear.

When the king turned back to Cleric Jeremy, he was calm; after all, he had grieved before today. Ever since Cleric Jeremy had told King Salvatore and Queen Kathleen the prophecy about the child that was to come, the royal couple had accepted the hard fate that lay in store for them. King Salvatore merely continued the conversation he and Cleric Jeremy had been having for months.

"The boy must not know of the prophecy. He must meet his fate without the knowledge that he has been chosen. As you will supervise his education, I look to you to do your duty by keeping him unaware of what waits in store for him. Prepare him, but do not inform him."

Cleric Jeremy bowed. "You have my word, my king."

King Salvatore shook his head and sighed. "Honestly, what chance does the world have to survive the madness that the prophecy describes? No matter how well you prepare Samuel, I find it hard to believe that he can turn aside such a flood of evil."

Placing a reassuring hand on the king's arm, Cleric Jeremy said, "Neither you nor I can say for sure whether Samuel will succeed as the prophecy foretells. We must wait and see who he becomes as he grows. But he is the last of your bloodline, my king.

Should he fail, we will all suffer a dark, eternal fate at the hands of a dangerous wizard. As I must choose either to hope in his abilities or fear Ablewis, I choose to hope until Samuel meets his trials."

King Salvatore gazed sadly out the windows of the throne room. After suffering his queen's death, he was not in a mood to hope. "I want the boy watched at all times. He needs to grow up in the kingdom, far from the wilderness that keeps the wizard. And as you educate him, he must learn the ways of the sword. Excellent swordsmanship will be one gift that I can leave him should he ever have to fight the wizard alone."

"I will ensure that he is trained in the arts of war and made aware of the dangers in this world," Jeremy promised, but he frowned. "Remember, my king, we cannot hide him from all danger. He will have to face certain obstacles himself if he is to ever grow into a true defender of the crown of the Kingdom of St. Mein."

"You will have every asset you need, Cleric," King Salvatore vowed. "There is not one thing you shall lack concerning my son's welfare. As soon as he can walk, I want him holding a sword. As soon as he can speak, I want him to learn how to read. He is a prince, after all."

"Yes, my king," Jeremy acknowledged, rubbing his tired eyes and stifling a yawn. The birth had taken a long time, and he was exhausted in body, mind, and spirit. "Do you need anything else from me before I retire for the night?"

"One last thing, Jeremy," King Salvatore said

mournfully, tears welling in his eyes. "Pray for hope. Mine is gone."

...

Six years passed – six years that saw the prince grow sturdy and strong and smart. He spent his days either at Cleric Jeremy's side, learning from the thick, dusty books in the library all the clerics shared, or in the castle courtyard, learning to fight from Captain Steven, head of King Salvatore's army.

The prince rarely spent time with his father, who always seemed sad or angry when Samuel appeared. Samuel did not know why his father seemed to dislike him. He loved his father with all of his heart.

When Samuel asked Cleric Jeremy about his father's dark mood, Cleric Jeremy would only say, "Your father has lost much in the fight against evil. He still grieves, and that grief clouds his love for you. Be patient with him, little prince." Samuel did his very best to obey Jeremy and be patient with his father, but it was hard for him. He sometimes felt very lonely.

In the center of the Kingdom of St. Mein, the castle stood very close to a monastery. So Prince Samuel was usually busy in one place or the other. Far away in the distance, a vast wilderness grew. Samuel was curious about the wilderness, but he was too busy to explore it. Besides, he had no way to travel so far.

Samuel spent long hours each day outside in the

courtyard of the castle with the captain of the guard, Captain Steven. Captain Steven trained Samuel in knife fighting, wrestling, and swordsmanship. Samuel's grandfather, King Harold of St. Mein, had trained Captain Steven when he was only a boy. The captain, who had fought many battles for the kingdom, was King Harold's most trusted advisor. Long after the sad passing of the great King Harold, Captain Steven was left to carry on and train all future kings of St. Mein.

Usually, Samuel's studies with Cleric Jeremy and exercises with Captain Steven tired him out so thoroughly that he slept soundly all night, but from time to time, a vision intruded on his dreams.

Swinging diligently with careful bloodlust, he swung hard and fast, slicing through the air so quickly that the enemy could not help but pause with awe at the ferocity of this one man who stood against many. Knowing he was vastly outnumbered, the prince continued to fight for his life and that of the princess.

In the dream, Samuel was both the warrior and himself, a child of six, watching the warrior. Sometimes he watched through the man's eyes and felt the ache in his arms from wielding the sword. Sometimes he watched through his own eyes from the shelter of the circling trees. But always Samuel knew that the child and the man were both himself.

Cleric Jeremy was at his side, fighting off continuous waves of attackers. The old cleric had never seen close combat with evil. Today was different, a day he'd long awaited. Samuel could see the grim

13

satisfaction on his face.

Blasting away at the unsightly creatures, two fairies focused their might on the minions who approached Samuel and Jeremy from their blind side. Samuel looked back to a small house in the middle of a clearing in the woods. There he saw the princess, the most beautiful woman he had ever seen. Though he had never met her before in his waking life, he knew that she was dearer to him than anyone else in the world.

The princess looked hopefully at Samuel, who smiled at her and went back to fighting. This hope ignited a unique feeling deep within her. In a state of reverie, she found herself being drawn to the middle of the dangerous ground where the prince stood.

Descending the steps of the cabin, she kept her eyes only on him, disregarding the danger to herself. But as she stepped off the cabin porch, a group of winged foes began to form a circle around her. Snapping out of the trance, she realized she was not on the cabin steps anymore; she was in the middle of all the chaos!

Screaming in fear, she caught the prince's attention. Samuel quickly turned around to see the princess surrounded by evil forces. Leaving Jeremy's side without hesitation, he rushed right into the crowd of foes who were harassing the princess and placed himself into the center of the circle amidst the chaos.

"What do we do?" the princess cried.

"Grab my hand!" Samuel ordered, extending his

own.

"What?"

"Trust me!"

The princess grabbed his hand. He broke through the crowd of attackers, pulling her with him and thrashing heroically at those who would do his true love harm. Guiding the princess back onto the porch of the cabin, he shouted, "Get back inside!"

As the prince was shouting to the princess, one of the creatures seized the moment to sneak up behind Samuel. The beast came close, and as the prince was about to turn, the creature dealt a blow to the back of the prince's head with a wooden club. The prince lost consciousness immediately; knees first, then chest and finally his head, Samuel slammed into the dirt, sword flying from hand. Now Samuel the child watched from the trees, terrified.

Turning toward the shimmer of light, the princess saw Samuel the warrior, lying face-down on the ground. She could not contain herself as she cried out his name for all creation to hear.

Viewing the dream from within his mind, the child prince looked into her eyes and saw a place where time had no meaning and only memories existed. A quiet time in his life appeared to him, a time of peace and youth, a time of young love. Samuel began to see scenes from his life flash through his mind.

A hand on his shoulder brought him back to himself, a child on the edge of a forest in a dream. Samuel whirled around to see the owner of the hand: a tall man with a twisted smile and an evil gleam in his eyes. Samuel shouted in fear and shook the hand loose, running deep into the forest to escape the horrible man. But he could not escape. The man was right behind him. The cold hand was reaching, reaching, reaching – it almost had him...

Awaking in his bed, shaking and looking about frantically in his room, Samuel sat straight up, his eyes wide open. He was breathing deeply, his little chest expanding and collapsing quickly, almost more than the boy's body could handle. In the partially moonlit room, the young prince saw no danger – no evil man, no crowd of enemies.

He rested his head back on his pillow and stared at the wall. He tried to comprehend the complexity of the dream, but to no avail. He did not know any princess. He did not know any man as evil as the one that had chased him. Samuel spent the rest of that night awake in his bed, wondering what destiny was in store for him.

When the sun rose, Samuel dressed and went to the castle kitchen to eat. It was so early that the cook, Belle, had only started breakfast. Nothing was ready. But she liked the boy; so she gave him a slice of yesterday's bread and let him sit near her and watch her work. The warm aroma from the kitchen comforted Samuel after his restless night.

King Salvatore walked into the room.

The king had a great love for his people and his son, but he rarely saw the boy. Whenever Cleric Jeremy brought him to the throne room, King Salvatore saw Queen Kathleen's kind eyes and quick smile, and the sight pained him.

Today, the king had walked the halls in the early morning as he sometimes did after a restless night. As he neared the kitchen, he heard his son's voice and watched him unobserved for awhile. Samuel spoke kindly to the cook; he was not proud or arrogant. He thanked her nicely for the bread, though it was old, and he asked her questions about herself and her family as she worked. Peeking around the corner, King Salvatore saw a look of interest and intelligence that reminded him of himself.

But he felt only grief when he looked at his son.

Entering the kitchen, Samuel looked up at him, startled and afraid. It was the look Kathleen had given him sometimes when he had been too harsh with her. That look on his son's face cut him. He wanted to love the boy, but something inside him had broken.

"You're up early, Samuel. It's good for a king to begin his day in good time, well before his subjects. What are you doing?"

Though King Salvatore's voice was still gruff, Samuel saw that he meant to be kind and answered him with a smile. "Right now, I'm watching Belle make breakfast, your majesty. I start lessons with Cleric Jeremy after breakfast, and then I train with Captain Steven in the afternoon."

"It's a full day," the king approved. "I wonder if I might observe your sword lessons this afternoon."

"Of course, father!" Samuel nearly shouted, hopping off the stool and running around the table.

King Salvatore smiled down at him, his heart still breaking inside him. "We'll see how your training is progressing, young Samuel."

"Yes, your majesty," Samuel answered happily.

When the king left the kitchen, he nearly ran into Jeremy, who had been waiting outside. "Good morning, your majesty. I am glad to see you taking a hand in Samuel's training. He has missed your guidance."

Frowning at Cleric Jeremy, King Salvatore shook his head. "Do not expect too much involvement from me, Cleric. The boy is still more grief to me than anything else."

The king did attend Samuel's lesson with Captain Steven that afternoon, but he said little and went away soon. From that day, though, the king did appear every once in a while when Samuel least expected him, imparting some lesson before shrinking away to his cold throne room and his quiet tears.

The king occasionally trained the boy in the art of war, impressing upon him the importance of nobility and honor. Captain Steven would monitor the lessons instead of teaching during these times. Prince Samuel took to his lessons from his father with pride, and in time he learned a great deal of compassion. The king became impressed with Samuel and how quickly he engaged in swordplay. The prince made his opponents submit with great ease, proving that Samuel was a true master of his weapon.

"Samuel, when engaging the enemy, you must never let your guard down. Always learn to anticipate the next move. Failure to see it will prove fatal. Let your enemy come to you. Draw him in close, and then move in to attack," the king said to Samuel during one lesson.

"Yes, Father – look ahead to the next move, and let the enemy come to you," Samuel repeated.

"Keep your eye on your attacker. If you lose sight, you give him the chance to flaunt your weakness and attack your blind side. Learn to see with your ears and hear with your eyes, my son," the king said sternly.

"But Father, how do you hear with your eyes?" Samuel asked, perplexed.

"You do not have to hear a man screaming in order to tell if he is screaming, do you?" answered the king. "You have to learn to read a man's emotions in the middle of battle to hear with your eyes. This will help you anticipate his next attack."

Samuel pondered this idea for a second, raised his sword, and continued his training. Samuel didn't know that this one piece of advice would someday save his life.

On most days though, Captain Steven returned to his duties of being a full-time mentor in the craft of swordplay. As long hours of instruction on subduing the opponent ensued over the following years, Captain Steven grew pleased with the speed with which the Prince was able to master each skill presented to him.

"Block! Parry! Charge!" Captain Steven would shout as the prince would repeat the steps over and over. After a few hours of instruction on one particular day, the good captain brought the training to a halt.

"Prince Samuel, why don't you go and rest for a few minutes? Get some water to drink. I shall return soon."

At once, the prince brought his sword down to his side, turned, and headed to a shaded area by two giant willow trees. He rested and drank from the jar that had been left to cool in the shade. After a few moments, the prince wiped his sweaty brow and looked up to see Captain Steven leading a magnificent creature into view.

Upon seeing the noble horse, the prince quickly jumped to his feet. He felt an instant bond with this horse, as if he was meeting a long-lost relative. The horse was tall and muscular, and his flowing black mane and brown coat glistened in the afternoon sun. He strutted with his head held high. Beside him, Captain Steven beamed and bowed.

"My Prince, for being the most exceptional student I have ever had the pleasure to train, I wish to present you with this fine creature. It is also a birthday gift from your father in honor of your thirteenth birthday."

The prince could hardly believe that he had been presented with such a gift. The horse, in recognition of the captain's words, bowed his head. He knew at once that this boy would be his friend as well as his master.

After giving the horse to Samuel, Captain Steven told him that in the following days of training, Samuel would learn to use the horse to his advantage in battle. He was as good as his word. Beginning the very next day, Samuel and Captain Steven spent many long hours working on advanced riding techniques, such as perfecting swordsmanship and archery while on horseback. Samuel often spent time grooming and feeding his new companion after hours of training.

One day during a time of relaxation, Samuel suddenly came up with a name for his trusty steed. "I shall call you Earabis," Samuel said, proud of himself for coming up with such a unique and wonderful name for his friend. The horse bent his head and nuzzled Samuel; indicating a personal acceptance of the bestowed name.

The hours Samuel and Earabis spent alone in the evening playing and relaxing created an unbreakable bond of brotherhood and friendship between the two. Earabis showed Samuel the meaning of unconditional love. The horse never cared whether the boy made a mistake in training or if he wanted to give up during the long days. The horse only knew love for the boy; he knew no end to the value of Samuel's life.

Long days of training occupied the years of his boyhood; however, to Samuel the days seemed shorter than ever. He became skilled in mounted combat after only a year of riding Earabis. Samuel could explore more of the Kingdom of St. Mein than he had ever seen before. Samuel eventually rode to the distant green smudge he had seen as a small boy and found woods and wilderness. With Earabis close by, Samuel did not fear anything he found.

The two friends had to learn to speak to each

other and trust each other as they tackled various types of terrain. If the prince thought an obstacle was too dangerous or difficult to cross, Earabis would often prove the prince wrong.

One time, a tree lay across a path the two were hurtling down. The prince thought the log would be too wide for his friend to jump; so he straightened his legs and pulled back on the reins. Earabis, however, just sped up, leapt with great force, and cleared the boulder-thick log with little trouble.

Many times one companion would head into a dangerous situation with nothing more than faith in order to prove this trust, and the other would always prove reliable. On another occasion, the pair was riding in a field when Earabis came to a sudden halt. Samuel knew that when Earabis halted in this manner, trouble was close. Samuel scanned the immediate area and could see nothing, even though Earabis was growing restless.

Again Samuel scanned the area to the front and rear, but he could not see anything. Then on the horizon, he noticed a small figure pacing back and forth, followed quickly by four smaller silhouettes. Several more appeared within an instant.

Wolves, Samuel thought. They were the only danger he knew in this part of the kingdom. Cleric Jeremy had taught him all about them in his natural history lessons. Samuel knew that Earabis was a fast horse, but the numbers of the wolves were growing by the minute. Considering what skillful hunters the wolves were, at some point they would lead him and Earabis into a trap.

Samuel had two options: a stand-up fight for the chance that one of them would make it out alive, or an all-out slaughter. The stand-up fight was the better choice. And thanks to Cleric Jeremy, Samuel knew one thing the wolves would fear, something which was also his only hope for survival. He had to build a fire.

Samuel saw that the wolves were still forming on the ridge; so he had time to get down on the ground and gather brush. He quickly piled sticks and brush together and began to ignite them, striking the flint he always carried against the steel of his dagger hilt above the tinder. The fire quickly started. When Samuel got up, he looked into the distance. The wolves were slowly heading his way.

The fire was catching, but it was still too small. He needed a backup plan.

Samuel counted ten wolves in all at this point; all were quickening their pace while growling in a nerve-piercing way that echoed through the forest and resounded over the field like a wave. Earabis lifted his legs restlessly, looking for an escape route. Samuel walked up next to Earabis, put his hand on the horse's head to calm him, and said, "There were times when I had to trust you with my life. I want you to trust me in return, okay?"

The horse, still shaking, did little more than grunt in response to the prince's request. The prince took his bow from the saddle, grabbed a few arrows, and walked toward the fire, bringing Earabis with him.

The fire at this point had grown to a crackling blaze, and Samuel could see that the wolves were slowing their pace. Samuel took aim and readied his bow. He breathed in slowly and exhaled. He exhaled, drew the arrow back on the bowstring, and as the last of the air in his lungs exited, he paused, closed one eye to focus his sight down the shaft of the arrow, and led his eyes to the intended target. He released his fingers.

The arrow shot swiftly across the field. The wolf in front of the pack was in mid-stride, heading straight for the prince. The arrow struck the beast, forcing it to continue its forward movement in the form of a lifeless ball. The wolf lay motionless while the rest of the pack continued the chase, slowly eliminating ground between predator and prey.

Samuel prepped another arrow, took aim, breathed, and fired. One more wolf lay still. He drew another arrow from its case, took aim, and fired, sending one more predator to its demise. The fire had grown to the height of Earabis at this point, and the wolves were getting closer. He got one more shot off, and he knew that he would not have time to fire another.

Samuel ran up to the fire, pulled out logs from the bottom, and threw them in the direction of the charging pack. This tactic separated the wolves into three groups. One group had three wolves, and another group had two wolves. Off to his right, closer than any of the groups, was a lone wolf. Samuel knew that though the fire was helping to keep his attackers at a distance, he would soon be overrun. Samuel quickly planned his next move, knowing that Earabis trusted him with his life.

Samuel knew that the lone wolf was the leader of the pack. Instead of wasting time trying to fight the rest of the group with a bow and arrow, Samuel unsheathed his dagger from his side and turned quickly, facing the charging alpha male. Raising his arm, he threw the dagger at the wolf with deadly aim, killing it instantly. When the remaining wolves saw their leader dead, they immediately halted in their tracks, turned, and headed back to the horizon from where they had appeared.

Samuel watched as the pack disappeared into the dense forest. He steadied his heavy breathing and walked over to Earabis, who was standing close to the fire. Samuel began to put out the fire, pulling the kindling apart, stamping on it, and kicking dirt over the embers. With his hard hooves, Earabis helped.

"See, my friend - as I have trusted you in some dangerous times, you can now trust me," Samuel said as he repacked his bow and saddled up. Earabis nodded his head and neighed. Samuel could understand him as well as if he had spoken.

The bond of the horse and the Prince now became unbreakable. They had both learned to trust each other not only in the face of danger, but also while facing impending death. Samuel and Earabis rode back toward the castle and into the sun, which melted into the horizon.

They had barely enough light to return safely to the kingdom. Samuel stabled Earabis, and then he trudged up the stairs to his room, where exhaustion introduced him to a deep sleep.

The next morning, Samuel awoke to a loud, thudding knock at his door. He quickly got out of bed and opened it. To his surprise, the king was standing in the hall with his arms crossed, eyes squinted, and mouth pressed into an angry line. "Where in the creator's name were you last night, boy? I had the servants searching the kingdom for you!" he shouted.

"Father, I'm sorry. I was riding with Earabis, and we were surrounded by a pack of wolves. I had to fight them off by building a fire. We are both safe, and Earabis is resting in his stall," the prince explained.

"This is why I tell you never to go riding off on your own, son! The kingdom has dangers you don't understand, and I have no time to keep watch over you. Don't let me hear of anything like this again!" the king scolded.

"But father, we were attacked by wolves, and I managed to make it back safely," the prince retorted.

"Well you should have; you have been given the best training in all the land. Now get dressed. You have a long day of studying to do," barked the king.

The king turned and left the room, slamming the door on his way out. Samuel sat on his bed and felt his soul cry for the warmth of his mother.

He could not understand how his father could be so hard on him while Cleric Jeremy and Captain Steven praised him continually. They respected how well Samuel could learn and train, and even a creature like Earabis could love him as much. He sat on his bed for a few moments and just stared at the floor, letting the depressing emotions that took hold of him color his thoughts.

He was nearing manhood, and he felt strongly that his father should not scold him as if he were a boy. King Salvatore should take pride in how well Samuel had fought and what wisdom he had shown. He should have asked to hear more of the story instead of assuming that Samuel had only wanted to cause trouble and worry.

Samuel, being gifted from birth by the creator with a compassion and understanding for love, did not let his father's anger cloud his judgment for long. One way Samuel dealt with loneliness was to study. Samuel often found himself thirsting for knowledge, a thirst which led him to spend hours in the monastery. Its exterior stone walls made it look like a fortress, but far from keeping anyone out, its majestic spires invited those who would pray for peace. The two towers each held a silver bell that rang three times each morning to remind all those in the area to give thanks to the creator of all life.

On the day after his fight with the wolves, Samuel entered the monastery seeking peace. The main doors to the monastery were colossal. Many times Samuel had used the large iron handles attached to them. Pushing the doors open, he recalled the first time he had set foot in the place; now he noticed how the wooden floors had been warped in some areas by time.

As he continued walking, he took note of the well-trodden paths left by generations of monks walking in procession. The stone walls echoed the sublime chants sung within their confines. Samuel remembered how he would follow the sound of the chants upwards to the high, arching windows that painted pictures of ancient history with their stained glass.

Long ago on the upper floor, Samuel had discovered that the holy men would hold meetings to discuss spiritual issues. Cleric Jeremy told Samuel that he was not old enough to attend such meetings and that he must stay in the lower levels of the monastery while the meetings occurred; Jeremy did not want him to grow confused in his studies.

However, Samuel's thirst for knowledge and pursuit of righteousness did not always keep him obedient. The young prince had often followed the holy men to the meeting chamber, ducking around corners and hiding in small areas to ensure that he would remain undetected. He would wait in silence in the vast hallways outside the meeting rooms until the huge wooden doors would shut.

After the doors were closed, Samuel would remain silent in the halls until he heard the click of a lock from inside the meeting room. This would be his cue to move closer and put his ear to the door and listen to what the holy men were discussing.

One time Samuel had been caught by two of the clerics who were late for a meeting, Clerics Kerwin and Lambert. Clerics Kerwin and Lambert had been men of great influence from the time Samuel was able to walk. The two clerics had known from his early boyhood that Samuel was gifted with great love and compassion.

"Samuel? Come out from that corner. I can see your feet under the curtain, young prince," Cleric Kerwin said softly.

Samuel emerged from the curtain. He moved slowly toward the two clerics, who were looking down at him. The two men stood as tall as statues, immovable objects with eyes that could tell the truth from a lie in an instant.

Embarrassed, Samuel looked at his feet. "I just wanted to see what you were talking about today. I didn't mean to disobey anyone. I just wanted to learn what the elders were doing."

"Samuel, I am afraid you are still too young to understand the nature of these meetings. Perhaps you should go into the garden and pray that the creator will bless you with understanding," Cleric Lambert suggested.

"Or Samuel, maybe Cleric Lambert and I can start meeting with you weekly to answer your questions about the creator or about life in general. You are a gifted young boy, you know," Cleric Kerwin added.

Samuel's white cheeks blushed at the praise, and his eyes shone at the opportunity to hear answers. He nodded in acceptance of the clerics' offer and headed out of the hall and outdoors. In the weeks that followed, the clerics taught Samuel much about how the creator works with men and why love and forgiveness are the two most important gifts a person can give to another person.

Samuel had continued his studies at the monastery and come to feel more at home all the time. The young prince felt a sense of peacefulness and preparation while he studied with the clerics. He did not know what challenges he was preparing to face, only that something was yet to come in his future. This feeling not only stayed with him daily but also grew steadily over time.

Samuel sought knowledge and truth without compromising his morals. The force that guided his feelings became a strong internal compass to guide him through life. He spent hours in the monastery's library. Remembering that time, Samuel now walked down the path toward the library, seeking once again the peace he had found within the quiet walls.

The library was unique in its own way because it was separated from the monastery towers and built into the side of a hill. On the outside, the library looked like only a single room with beautiful stained glass decorated with etchings about the heroes of old.

The building on the inside was an artistic puzzle, a labyrinth of halls and rooms. The older the room, the older and more valuable the books within it; Samuel had his patience tested over many long days and nights before he was granted access to the deeply sacred locations.

Running his hands over the library shelves, Samuel felt that some part of his future was drawing close. Surviving the fight with the wolves meant something. He felt that they had been meant to keep him from some gift, some clue to the purpose of his life. He had won, and in winning, he had opened the door to the next phase of his life. He expected a revelation: some desperate enemy or impossible quest or unmistakable sign at every corner.

As Samuel was leaving the library, he decided to take a different way home through the courtyard of the monastery. The courtyard led past a small waterfall and into a flower garden studded with small pools, stone benches, and whimsical statues. The flower garden contained plants and flowers from the whole realm; among them was none other than the beloved Goji berry plant that Samuel loved so much. This garden was a quiet and peaceful place where the monks would sometimes go to pray or meditate.

On this fateful evening, Samuel spotted a beautiful young woman sitting on a rock bench near a small koi pond in the flower garden. The moment the prince set eyes on this girl, his world stopped. He did not breathe a single breath. The sight of her struck him into a state of peace and amazement.

She was the revelation he had sought.

As he stared at her, he noticed the fine features of her beautiful face and the smile that welcomed the midday sun. Her hair bounced like a flowing wave as she turned her head, following the movement of the fish in the pond. Her clothes were fine, and on her head a tiny crown gleamed: she was a princess.

Kneeling down to pick a flower, the princess stood and lifted it, inhaling the sweet, citrusy scent. Her smile grew radiant, and the prince wished that he could make the princess smile like that one day. She seemed at once familiar and utterly new. She fascinated Samuel.

He watched her silently from a distance behind a small tree until he worked up the nerve to approach her. A branch snapped under his foot as he quietly walked toward her. She looked up, and their eyes met.

Samuel could see in her eyes the kind of rapt fascination and attraction for him that he felt for her. She looked at him as though she had fallen in love with him at first sight. The instant connection gave Samuel courage to walk boldly to her, and she waited until Samuel spoke first.

"Hello," Samuel said. "I didn't mean to scare you."

"I'm not scared," she told him, still staring into

his eyes. "I'm glad you came."

"Who are you?" Samuel asked. "I'm here every day, but I've never seen you before."

The princess smiled. "You must not be in the garden every afternoon, or we would have met before. I'm Princess Kristina of the Kingdom of Ferdinand. My father is King James. I'm studying at the convent nearby for a short time."

"I hope it's not too short a time," Samuel said quickly, and then he blushed at the confession. Kristina laughed - Samuel had found his new favorite sound. He gazed into her eyes and added, "Well, Kristina, I am pleased to make your acquaintance."

Kristina and Samuel felt a strong connection between their young souls that neither one of them could explain. They spent a grand majority of their time together from that moment on. No matter what they did, it was blessed. The happiness and blessing that followed them constantly served as a sign that fate would watch over them all of their days.

As they talked over the next days and weeks, Samuel learned that Princess Kristina was the only daughter of King James and Queen Cynthia. Prince Eric, her brother, was a little older. Prince Eric was intelligent and capable of solving difficult problems for the kingdom when it came to political or economic matters. He worked daily with his father in the kingdom to learn how to govern his people as the future king that he would become.

Kristina was not involved with the political or economic concerns of the kingdom; she wanted to benefit the kingdom by learning how to be a princess. Her role came quite naturally, as she already possessed the beauty to captivate a nation. She had a lot of friends, but she really wanted a sister. She would often seek comfort in the company of her animals; her favorite was her horse, Gunnison.

Samuel and Kristina learned much about each other, such as their mutual thirst for excitement and exploration. Both wanted to visit foreign lands far away from their kingdoms. They both had fathers who were strict. Kristina's father was strict with her for different reasons than Samuel's father had been: Kristina was his only daughter. He made sure that she spent her days learning proper etiquette and useful skills and facts.

Kristina's parents, wanting nothing but the best for their daughter, sent her to a private convent for girls. The school had the reputation for being strict. Despite the difficulty of the complex lessons, the princess was one of the brightest students in her class.

Her parents believed that she should never take success for granted just because she was part of a royal family. They believed in high morals and never belittled anyone. The people of the kingdom respected their king and queen greatly. This way of life instilled the greatest values in the young princess. She was loved much; nevertheless, she did not have the plush life most princesses had.

Kristina felt the need to escape often to her favorite place: the flower garden in St. Mein's monastery. She would ride her horse into St. Mein because she loved the monastery as much as Samuel did. She would sit in the flower garden and enjoy the beauty and serenity the natural wonders provided.

Flowers defying imagination thrived in the garden. There were roses, tulips, and calla lilies, but there were also fantastic specimens neither one could name. Kristina loved to sit on the bench and watch the fish as the waterfall trickled in the background, singing to itself.

The prince and princess continued to see each other after their long days of schooling and training. Some days they would ride their horses together to the vineyard on the hill. Letting Gunnison and Earabis graze in the field, they ran and chased each other through the endless grapevines, heavy with grapes that the monastery clerics made into wine. They took long walks in the woods past the shrines of heroes and saints, stopping and feeding the rabbits that one of the monastery clerics raised. No matter what they did, being together was all that truly mattered to both of them.

People older than Samuel and Kristina might have told them that they were too young to know their own minds and hearts. But none of them could know that the creator himself had chosen Samuel and Kristina for one another and created their entwined destinies himself for them to enjoy. At the moment they had met in the garden, the two of them sensed the bond they were destined to share.

The garden metaphorically served as a place where time and space held no limits, just like the love that the prince and princess shared for each

other. Samuel learned that true love was indefin-
able with no end that existed due to a power greater than him. Love's strength in its purest, deepest
form could only be measured by forever; so, too,
was it as big as the universe.

CHAPTER II

The Wilderness

UNDER the weeping willow tree near a large pond at the bottom of the monastery hill, Samuel and Kristina would often sit discussing their dreams. Samuel told Kristina about the dream that had plagued him since childhood – about the terrible battle and the evil man who chased him. In turn, Kristina told Samuel about a dream that had haunted her.

She was at a dance, dressed in her best and very happy, because she was waiting for the person she loved best in all the world. A door opened, and she turned around, waiting to see the face of the person, but she never got to see his face, because a cruel man walked through instead. He put a hand on her shoulder, and then everything went black.

"I've wondered since I met you if you were the person who was supposed to walk through that door. It makes me wonder if something will ever happen to tear us away from each other," Kristina said sadly.

"Nothing could," Samuel promised, lying on his stomach and looking out to the water as Kristina spoke. "We'll always be together."

"But if it did," Kristina continued, looking fondly at him, "I would do everything I could to come back to you. No matter what I had to face or how long I had to travel, I would find you again."

Samuel's heart glowed. No one had ever loved him so deeply. He didn't know what to say.

"Would you find me?" Kristina asked in a small voice.

"Of course I would!" Samuel promised, turning over and sitting up. He took her hand. "I swear that if we are ever separated, I would find you again. If I knew you were in danger, I wouldn't rest until I knew you were safe."

Neither one of them suspected how soon their promises would be tested.

King James was not happy about all the time his daughter was spending with Samuel. He felt she should be spending her time doing more important things than frolicking with the prince. Knowing he could not keep them apart if they lived so close to one another, he decided that the princess would live with her aunt. If she did this, she could spend all of her time learning to be a respectable woman and perfecting her princess duties.

The princess's mother, Queen Cynthia, disagreed with this decision, but in the end, she bowed to her husband's wishes. They sent a message to their daughter at the convent. It would take three days to arrive.

The day after the message had been sent, the princess brought one of her cherished books from home to share with the prince. It was an old fable book that her mother had read to her at bedtime. The two of them sat under their willow tree, and Kristina flipped through the book to show Samuel her favorite story, the story of the Witch in the Woods. Her mother had never read it aloud for fear of giving the child nightmares, but as Kristina had grown older, she had read it for herself. Today she decided to read it to Samuel.

It was a story of a wicked witch who haunted a forest in search of weary travelers. She preyed on their desperation and offered them temptations that nobody could ever resist. In return, she would steal their souls before they even realized what was going on. Samuel shuddered after Kristina read the story to him.

"If I found myself going on a long journey, I would just avoid going into the forest all together. I would never want to battle an evil crone like that. That sounds too risky for anyone," Samuel said.

The princess teased, "Would you ever fight the witch if it meant coming to save me?"

Without even a moment of hesitation, Samuel said, "My sweet love, to save you I would battle a thousand witches without ever thinking about it. I would fight even the most hopeless battles if it meant having the smallest chance of saving you from danger."

The princess immediately closed his mouth with one small finger. "I shouldn't have asked you; I already knew the answer."

"Even if you did, I'd tell you as often as you asked. I'll always save you," Samuel vowed.

Every day the princess wore a blue-jeweled pendant around her neck. The pendant sparkled in the evening light just as her eyes had a tendency to sparkle in the morning with the radiant sun. She wore the gem as a reminder of her dear grandmother. Samuel loved the way it looked on her.

"Maybe you should wear something to remind you of me," he teased.

She shook her head. "I don't need anything to remind me of you. But that gives me an idea. I have something for you - turn around."

Samuel obeyed, and the princess pulled a medallion out of her pocket. She put her arms around Samuel's neck and latched the chain at the back. When she was done, the prince looked at the medallion. It had a picture of a man with wings who had his arms around a child.

"The man's name is Raphael, and he protects the pure of heart. He represents my love for you. Always wear it, and know that I will always love you, no matter how far away I am. I also have another gift for you: the sunrise. As long as the sun rises, know that my love for you will never fail. So if you ever have doubts, just look to the sun, and you will know that my love for you is faithful."

The prince looked up from the medallion and into the eyes of the princess. Putting his hand on her neck, he combed back her soft, long brown hair. He drew close, struggling to tell her how much the words she had just spoken meant to him. "I have nothing for you," he admitted.

"You're wrong," Kristina said, smiling through her tears. "I have your promise that you will always come for me. That's dearer than any gift in the world."

Smiling, Samuel looked at the medallion around his neck. The chain was hidden under his shirt; only he knew it was there.

One day both Samuel and Kristina were sitting underneath a tree after a long day of schooling. Samuel was playing with the princess' medallion, rolling it between his fingers as it hung around his neck. He looked into Kristina's eyes, and she began to cry.

"What is wrong, sweet princess?" Samuel asked.

"I have to move away," she said.

Explaining her father's decision to the prince, Kristina continued to weep, but Samuel grew in disbelief. He didn't want to hear the words that came out of her mouth; his head became cloudy. He couldn't accept what she was telling him.

"Let's run away together. You have Gunnison; I have Earabis. We'll go away, right now," Samuel proposed.

Still crying quietly, Kristina shook her head. "I can't disobey my parents. That would be wrong. And it would set them against you forever; they would never be able to see the wonderful person that you are. They have to love you if we are going to marry each other someday."

Samuel's head cleared when he heard what she said. She still intended to marry him. He sighed. "You're right. You have to obey your father's orders. But I hate it. I'll hate being away from you."

"I'll hate it, too," Kristina declared. "But it's only for a little while. In a few years, our parents will want to find partners for us. And then, it's only natural that they look close by. I'll keep your name in my mother's ear, and when I'm grown, she'll make sure our fathers agree to match us."

Reassured, Samuel pulled the medallion from beneath his shirt. "And until then, I have this to remember you by."

Samuel and Kristina parted ways, unsure despite their promises if they would ever see each other again. As the princess left, the heart of the prince grew numb and broke.

Trying to alleviate the pain, he sat underneath their tree every night. He tried to do the things they both used to do together, hoping that it would fill the void in his heart, but being apart from his true love left Samuel empty and sad.

One day, Samuel walked into a pond where he and Kristina used to play. As the water rose waist deep, Samuel turned around and floated on his back. Pleasant memories came rushing to his mind, and closing his eyes, he welcomed the thoughts. He remembered how they used to go swimming on the days they didn't have to attend to their studies.

He remembered the days when it was too cold to swim and they would visit the monastery's old theater to watch the monks put on the plays that entertained people in the kingdom. Some days they would explore the underground tunnel that ran under the monastery. Rumor had it that the tunnel led all the way to the Kingdom of Ferdinand, but they never traveled far enough into the tunnel to find out.

As Samuel floated in the pond, another memory rose to comfort him. He and Kristina had sneaked into St. Mein's small chapel while it was dark and empty. The darkness lent them an intimate feeling of privacy and serenity.

While Samuel was exploring the chapel, Kristina walked to the back, where she found a metal candle stand holding several votive candles. She lit a candle and closed her eyes while quietly praying, asking the creator to bless Samuel and protect him all of his days. Kristina was unaware of Samuel's presence during her prayer. Samuel stood unannounced in the corner of the chapel bearing witness to Kristina's deep, heartfelt prayer. In this moment his heart blossomed with the realization of the extent of her love for him.

Samuel, still floating on his back in the water, realized that all of these memories made him miss the princess more than ever. Every place he loved, from the monastery grounds to the castle where he lived, reminded him painfully of his lost love. If he was going to survive the years apart, he needed to clear his mind – not his heart - of Kristina. So he swam to the shore, dried off, and started his walk home towards the castle.

On the way home, he began to consider the loneliness he had endured with the princess being gone. He decided on his walk that he had no other option than to leave the kingdom; too many memories of Kristina were attached to his home. He knew that the only way to ease his pain would be to leave for a time so that he would not be surrounded by painful thoughts of her departure.

He thought about how he could approach his father with his decision when he returned to the castle from his swim. He did not want to anger or hurt his father with his decision, but his mind had been made up. No matter what King Salvatore said, Samuel would leave in the morning for the wilderness.

The next day before breakfast, the king met Samuel by chance in the halls of the castle. The prince was glad that he could finally catch his father alone. Samuel walked with him to the courtyard, sat down next to him, and spoke the words that he had rehearsed over and over.

"Father, I know that you may not agree with me, but I want to leave the kingdom for a time. It is too painful for me to stay here. I feel empty since Kristina left, and I desire to go live in the wild."

"I see that there is nothing that I can do to change your mind," King Salvatore observed.

"No, Father, my decision is final. I need to go and find peace. I leave today."

King Salvatore bowed his head for a moment, and then he looked up at his son. "I ask this not for myself but for the kingdom, Samuel. You must swear to return. The kingdom needs you."

"I will return when Princess Kristina is free to marry me," Samuel promised. "I won't stay away from the kingdom forever."

"Then consult with Cleric Jeremy before you leave, Samuel. There are places in the woods that are not safe. You must ask him where you can go."

Samuel nodded, but he did not promise. He had talked to Cleric Jeremy for years about every inch of the kingdom. Right now, Samuel was so desperate to leave that he didn't want to stop to talk to anyone else. Samuel bowed to his father. His father did not hug him goodbye, but then, Samuel did not expect affection from him, either.

Samuel headed to his room to prepare for his departure. He had an unbearable pain in his heart, a pain so deep it penetrated his soul. The anguish of losing his sweet princess seemed too much to bear. He knew deep down that he should not run away from his problems, but he just had to escape. Prince Samuel knew that he had to leave the Kingdom of St. Mein.

Samuel had already packed lightly the night before his departure. He decided to take only the clothes on his back and a few bare essentials, for he wanted nothing to remind him of the life he was leaving behind. He picked up his knapsack, rolled the coverlet from his bed, and tied it on.

He did not tell a soul he was leaving except for Earabis. Samuel went to the stables and said his goodbyes to his only friend in the world. Samuel did not want to be found; he just wanted to be alone. To some, his departure may have seemed selfish, but it was the only true way he could find himself. After years of training in proper morals, leadership, swordsmanship, and discipline, Prince Samuel had to train his soul to bear loss.

That morning he left the castle and took one last look at the stunning view of the monastery. Samuel took a deep breath and exhaled slowly as he walked into the morning sunrise. He traveled for days until he passed a small town called Bristonia. Another week beyond this town was a river that led to an untouched forest. Samuel entered these woods with the intention of setting up camp.

Three days after the prince departed, King Salvatore sent for Cleric Jeremy. When Jeremy came, the king greeted him with a slow, sad smile. It reminded Jeremy of how the king had looked on the night of the prince's birth.

"I miss him so much, Cleric. I didn't think I would miss someone I have tried so hard to keep at a distance, but I do. I wanted to see you because I knew you must have missed him as much as I have," the king said.

Jeremy looked at him nonplussed. "I'm sorry, Your Majesty, but who am I supposed to miss?"

The king's heart skipped a beat. "Prince Samuel – he left three days ago for the wilderness. I told him to talk to you, to find the places where the woods are safe. I knew that you would guide him away from the wizard's prison."

"No, my king – I never saw him. I didn't expect to see him for a few more days," Jeremy panicked as he realized the enormity of the danger Samuel faced.

King Salvatore looked wild with worry. "I should have taken him to you myself. I should have told him about the wizard! What have I done, Jeremy? I must find him!"

King Salvatore sent messengers through the wilderness in every direction he could think, but they never found Samuel. All returned with the letters they carried unopened. After them, King Salvatore sent the wisest, strongest clerics from the monastery to make sure the wizard's wilderness prison held fast. But they found no trace of the wizard or his prison.

After all efforts had been exhausted, King Salvatore came to see Cleric Jeremy at the monastery. Jeremy welcomed him and sat beside him in silence at the church. The king sat for hours without speaking. Finally he sighed deeply and turned to Jeremy.

"We can do nothing else but leave him in the creator's hands," King Salvatore said sadly.

"It is where he has always been, Your Majesty," Jeremy reminded him.

Though Samuel had intended to spend only a few weeks at his new camp, those weeks turned into months and months. Samuel's first night in the woods was the hardest because he was not used to the rugged lifestyle of building a shelter and hunting his own dinner. In the castle, servants tended to all of his needs. Living roughly may have been difficult, but the prince was determined to make it on his own in the wilderness without the help of anyone. He felt as if he had to prove something to himself.

On his second day, Samuel gathered twigs, river logs, and heavy pieces of brush. He constructed a small lodge for shelter. Over the next few weeks, he became proficient at the art of fishing. He never had to worry about going hungry because of the endless supply of rainbow trout the river had to offer. Samuel carved wooden fishing hooks with his knife and dug in the dirt for worms to use as bait. He found that the best way to catch a rainbow trout was to bounce the worm off the bottom of the river floor as it flowed through the current.

He crafted a bow and made arrows out of hickory wood. With these tools, he hunted small game such as squirrel, rabbit, and pheasant. He found that the best way to hunt his prey was with patience. After firing his shot, Samuel would not move from his position. He would watch the arrow penetrate his target and then slowly lower himself to the ground so that his prey would not spot him as the predator and run away in fear as a last attempt to save itself.

Samuel roasted these small animals over the fire with his handcrafted spit. He took pride in his ability to care for himself in the wilderness. Over the next few months, he mastered his survival technique. Now it was time for him to move onto more important training. This training phase was an essential one, for it brought mind, body, and soul into one clear picture.

He would awake before dawn and hunt. After

dusk, he would check his traps for food. From dawn till dusk on each day, the prince would train himself in the art of the sword. He would practice various movements and techniques to near perfection. He learned to listen to his surroundings, knowing exactly when danger would be approaching and when the forest itself was at rest.

Nighttime always gave the prince a chance to rest from the hard training of the day and to engage in deep thought about his past. The prince favored sitting next to his fire each night and watching the flames leap into the air. He often pulled out the chain around his neck and looked at it, the gold reflecting off the fire. The medallion of the winged man named Raphael was the only thing he held dear to his heart.

The first two years were the toughest for the prince. He had to learn that survival rules changed with the seasons and that he gained discipline only through patience. The winters were harsh, and the summers were hot. However, the prince adapted to all the seasons and the elements that accompanied them. During the third year of the prince's stay in the wilderness, he felt that he finally understood the pattern of living season to season in this sanctuary. He had built a sturdy shelter that resembled a small cottage. He also had a steady source of food from the nearby river and wildlife. Samuel missed his dear princess, and he still held onto the hope that he would see her again once she was old enough to marry.

When the fourth year of his stay approached,

summer time beckoned for him to change. Daily as the prince would gather his food and attend to the camp's duties, he felt a strong need to go home. He did not know why this feeling had begun, but he knew that soon it would be time to move on. He had practiced his swordsmanship for years and become disciplined in his movements. His bow had stood the test of time in this place, and with it he had achieved many kills.

One day when Samuel was down by the river searching for food, he saw something out of the corner of his eye. He turned quickly to see a man in a black cloak walking through his camp. At first instinct, the prince drew his knife; the man's appearance triggered some primal fear in him. But the prince refused to be ruled by fear. He approached the man slowly from behind, saying, "Is there something I can do for you, stranger?"

The cloaked figure turned quickly, startled to hear Samuel's voice. "No need to be alarmed. I mean you no harm. I am just passing through the land, and I was seeking shelter before nightfall arrives," he said sincerely to the prince.

The prince believed the sincerity in his voice and slowly put his knife down. He offered the man a drink of his fresh rainwater. Accepting the offer, the stranger sipped the cool, thirst-quenching refreshment.

"The name is Samuel," the prince offered.

"Delighted to meet you, Samuel," the weary traveler said. "My name is Ablewis. I am a scholar of much wisdom and power, my boy. So what say you? Shall we eat? I am tired and hungry."

Samuel and Ablewis sat beside the fire and anticipated the evening's trophy catch of trout and squirrel. While the animals were roasting over the open flame, Ablewis reached into a small pouch and poured something that looked like black powder on the food. It sparked quickly and then died down.

Soon the food was done, and when Samuel tasted it, he was amazed. "Wow, this is better than anything I have been able to cook out here. What did you use to make it taste so good?" Samuel asked eagerly.

"Oh, that! Well, that is just something that has been passed down for years in my family. It enhances the flavor of the meat in a unique way. Do you like it, Samuel?" Ablewis asked, cracking half a smile.

"Oh yes, very much so," Samuel said with the leg of the squirrel half way in his mouth as he was biting into the juicy morsel. "Can you pass me the bladder of water, please?" Samuel asked.

"I have something much better than water, my dear friend; hold on for a second." The old man reached into a bag and pulled out a bladder. The bladder was red, and Samuel's curiosity immediately sparked once he laid eyes on it. "This, my friend, is Goji berry wine. It is something I like to have for cold nights like this one. Would you like to try some?" Ablewis said as he was already pouring a cup for the prince.

Without hesitation, the prince reached for the glass and took his first sip. Then he took another.

Then the sip turned into a drink, and the cup was nearly back to being empty. Samuel reached out his cup and asked his new friend for more wine. When he did this, a raven above loudly cawed and flew past.

The prince thought nothing of it; so he continued to ask for more wine. Ablewis poured him another glass every time he asked. For the rest of the night, Ablewis and the prince sat around the fire getting to know each other. Samuel was grateful for a companion because he had been alone for so long. Samuel drank the wine through the night and fell into a deep sleep.

The next morning brought Samuel the unfamiliar feeling of an aching head and a dry mouth. "Ugh, did you poison me, old man?" said the prince as he rolled over and held his stomach.

"Hardly, my boy - you indulged yourself quite a bit. On top of that, you started ranting about some princess and a father who is a king. Maybe this Goji berry wine will help you write a good story one day," Ablewis remarked, smirking at the prince.

The prince sensed that he needed to keep his past a secret until he could gain Ablewis' trust; so he just simply agreed with him and rolled over to go back to sleep.

Ablewis got up and kicked the prince. "Come on, boy; we must prep the camp and hunt for the day. Besides, I have some lessons I think you may find useful out here."

"Go away! I'm tired, and I don't want to be bothered right now. We can hunt later. Besides, my stomach feels like it's in some sort of a war," the prince groaned, wincing in pain.

Ablewis walked over to his bag, pulled out some white powder, and put it into a glass of water for Samuel. "Here, drink this, boy. I swear by the powers that be that you will be feeling better in a moment's time."

Samuel sat up slowly, took a look at the cup, and began to drink the water. No sooner had the prince finished the elixir than he was on his feet, feeling back to his normal self. "I can never thank you enough for that! You really do have a lot of things you can teach me," Samuel said with a smile on his face. Handing the cup back and shaking the old man's hand, Samuel agreed to go into the woods to hunt and to learn whatever his friend could teach him.

As the days passed by, the prince spent his time with Ablewis learning about various plants that would heal as well as those that were poisonous. For the first time since Captain Steven, the prince actually began to admire someone for the wisdom he possessed and was willing to share.

Samuel and Ablewis were walking deep in the woods one day when Ablewis noticed a plant that he thought he could use to his advantage for a later purpose. "Do you see this plant, Samuel? If you extract the seeds from this plant and crush them up, they will release a slimy chemical that can be used to coat the tips of your arrows or your sword. The chemical will produce something close to paralysis for just a few minutes only," Ablewis said.

The plant was a bright red color and had black lines running down the inside of the petals. The flower emitted a scent that pleased the prince. As the prince smelled the flower more, he began to draw closer.

"Careful, Samuel, if you touch the flower with your eyes, nose, or any open part of your body, it will produce the same effect as piercing your skin," Ablewis said as he slowly pulled Samuel away from the flower. "This flower, Samuel, is found only in two places in the whole realm. It is found here in the forest of Bristonia, and again in the highest mountains of the Brana Province. Should you ever find yourself in a dangerous situation facing an enemy, take some of this flower and use it against your foes."

Samuel stared at the flower, trying to remember the plant in exact detail. The old man beckoned Samuel to follow him more, but Samuel just kept staring at the plant. Something was telling him he would need to remember this plant in the future. After a moment, Samuel shook his head and followed Ablewis.

He led the prince to the river where Samuel always caught fish. They fished, and the catch was bigger than normal. Samuel began to wonder how much power this mysterious companion really possessed.

Samuel had fished in this river for the past few years and never caught more than a few fish at a time. Today, with Ablewis by his side, he caught more fish than the two of them could carry back to camp. Samuel was grateful for the feast that lay ahead; however, something did not sit quite right with him.

Once Samuel had his hands full of fish, he turned to head back to his camp. Suddenly a large raven swooped down and cawed really loudly. "Caw! Caw!" the raven alerted as he flew nearly to ground level between Samuel and the scholar. The raven weaved its way through the two while both just stared at it. The raven then gained altitude and flew off above the trees and toward the horizon.

"Something does not sit well, Ablewis. Do you feel the same thing?" Samuel asked curiously.

"Why, no, my boy - that is just a pesky bird trying to cut in on our meal; there is nothing to worry about, I assure you," said Ablewis as he picked up his things and walked past Samuel.

Samuel could not explain the growing feeling that something was wrong. Either way, there was not a lot he could do; so he followed Ablewis back to camp.

Once they were back at camp, the sun was nearly below the horizon, and the fire was roaring. Ablewis and Samuel began feasting on the fish. As Samuel was eating, he was about to drink water from his bladder when Ablewis suddenly interrupted. "Now wait, my boy, how about some of that Goji berry wine? It will go really well with today's catch, you know," Ablewis suggested cheerfully.

"I think I have had enough wine for one year. Thank you, though, friend," said the prince.

"Just one cup, to celebrate the day's catch, perhaps?" Ablewis insisted.

"I suppose just one glass couldn't hurt, but no more, mind you," chuckled Samuel. Before Samuel could even finish his sentence, the scholar had already started pouring a cup of the tastefully sweet Goji berry wine. Samuel took the cup and raised it, saying, "To a fine catch."

Ablewis in turn raised his cup and put it to his lips; however, he was sure not to drink any of the liquid. He pretended to drink from his cup as he kept a sharp eye on Samuel, ensuring he consumed all its contents.

Putting his cup down, Samuel began to eat his fish. Suddenly he noticed that his lips were numb. He thought nothing of it at first, but then Ablewis spoke.

"How is the wine, my boy? Do you notice anything different about it? Hmm? You may be noticing some slight effects from the drink you just tasted," Ablewis said slyly.

"What, what did you put in my drink, old man? What is happening to me?" Samuel slurred.

The wizard stood up, brushed himself off, smiled, and said, "Oh, just something to help you sleep. I have a confession to make. I didn't just wander into these woods, and I am no humble old man. Oh no - it was no mistake that I found you. See, I have been looking for you for a long time. My name is Ablewis, and I used to be the Grand Wizard in your father's kingdom until he grew too greedy for power and cast me out to the distant parts of this realm," the wizard said to Samuel as he was packing up his things.

Samuel attempted to stand up and draw his sword, but he couldn't. He was too weak. He was too numb from the effects of the drugged wine. Samuel fell to the ground on his side and could not move. However, he could hear the wizard speak clearly. He could also see everything around him.

"The potion is working just as planned," the wizard exulted as he stepped closer and kneeled next to the prince. "You see, Samuel, I have been plotting my revenge for a long time, and that revenge starts with you. I will leave you here, where you will slumber. If you wake up, your father will be dead. I say if, because you are not just going to dream; no, my boy, that would be too easy. You are going someplace much worse than a dream. Oh, and don't worry about your dear Princess Kristina. I have plans for her as well. If your father had only told you about me, maybe you would have been more prepared," taunted the wizard as he picked up his sack, staring in satisfaction at the paralyzed prince.

Samuel tried with all his might to move. He focused on his legs and demanded that they move, but no movement came. He focused on his hands. If only he could grip his sword, he might somehow get close enough to the wizard to pierce his heart. But his hands would not listen, either. Samuel tried to roll over on his back, for maybe he could call for help. But he could neither roll nor speak. Samuel lay in anger and frustration at himself for drinking the wine and falling for such a trap. His thoughtlessness would most surely be his and his family's downfall.

Samuel turned his head toward the wizard, and as he stared at him, the wizard waved his hand and transformed into a much younger man wearing clothes like the servants of King Salvatore wore. Samuel didn't have to be told what the rest of the wizard's plan was, for his transformation gave it all away.

The wizard would sneak into the castle as a servant. He would kill the king and capture the princess. Samuel immediately felt hopelessness and failure consume him as he stared at the wizard, for he could do nothing else. He was beginning to feel weak and tired indeed. In only a matter of moments, Samuel would be carried away into an unknown darkness.

As the wizard finished transforming, he took one look at Samuel and then walked into the darkness. Samuel felt a tear fall from the corner of his eye, and then his eyes shut.

···

Back in the Kingdom of St. Mein, King Salvatore's court began preparations for a huge birthday party in honor of his fiftieth birthday. Time was running short; the party would be held in two weeks in the castle's ballroom. Citizens from all of the surrounding kingdoms would be attending this grand celebration. The guest list also included King James, Queen Cynthia, Prince Eric, and Princess Kristina.

Princess Kristina had spent three years with her Aunt Jayne, who lived in the small town of St. Anthony, which was far away from St. Mein. Kristina had returned home from her aunt's two years earlier.

At Aunt Jayne's, Kristina would spend long hours in the evening going over the day's lessons and doing homework. When they weren't busy with schooling, they would relax under the shade tree outside the cottage. Aunt Jayne would tell her stories about when she and King James were growing up. Kristina was deeply saddened when the time came for her to return home. She knew that she would miss her dear aunt greatly, as they had formed such a wonderful bond during her stay.

Although she was saddened by her departure from her aunt, she was in sheer bliss knowing that she was about to return home to the prince that she had missed so dearly. When she returned home, Kristina was completely devastated to learn that the prince was not there, for she longed to see him again. She had always pictured that he, too, would be waiting anxiously for her return. That thought had gotten her through the lonely times when she was away. She almost felt betrayed when she heard that he had left the kingdom and was nowhere to be found.

Kristina longed for answers as to where Samuel was and why he had departed from the kingdom. She questioned the maidservants at the castle of St. Mein and all of the townsfolk near the castle looking for these answers. The storekeeper informed the princess that there had been a possible falling out between the king and the prince years ago, and no one had seen the prince since then.

The storekeeper had heard from one of the maid-servants from the castle that the two had been arguing, and the next day the prince had bruises on his face. The prince had disappeared within the next few days. The maidservant told the store-keeper that she wouldn't be surprised if the prince returned home one day to get revenge on the king. Kristina asked several more people throughout the kingdom. All she heard everywhere was the same sordid story; that gossip had spread like wildfire. This rumor was the only answer she could get.

Nevertheless, she searched for Samuel faithfully from the moment of her return home. She never stopped asking questions. She rode Gunnison over every bit of the kingdom. She refused to believe the gossip that Samuel had left in a fit of spite.

The princess knew in her heart that Samuel was not capable of revenge. She hoped that one part of the story was true: that Samuel was coming home. She still planned to attend the king's party in two weeks only because she had a glimmer of hope that her prince would return home for his father's birthday.

Ablewis also knew of this party; he had known of it before he set out to find Samuel. He knew as well that Samuel's sweet Princess Kristina would be attending. This piece of knowledge was vital in his evil plot to avenge himself on the king. He sought out the prince and earned his trust, only to destroy him in the end.

Ablewis could not wait to tell King Salvatore that his son was as good as dead. Only when the king was in the depths of misery would Ablewis conde-scend to snuff out his life.

CHAPTER III

The Dream

SAMUEL was thrown into a tunnel of light, unable to move. He felt paralyzed, as if he were under the control of an unseen force. Samuel did not focus so much on trying to move his arms or legs as he did on noticing that he was moving through a tunnel of light at an accelerated rate.

The light vanished, and Samuel stood upright, becoming aware of his new surroundings. He found himself standing on a road in the middle of a large village where turmoil reigned supreme. People were moving about mostly in the buildings with just a few on the road, but none of them paid attention to the prince. As his focus returned, he noticed that every nook and cranny of every building and person emitted an eerie, rusty-red glow.

The prince looked at his clothes; he shared the same depressing color as all the other inhabitants and buildings. Trying to dust himself off, he found that the red tinge could not be wiped or brushed away. But the color was not the worst part of this place. Samuel felt such intense fear and hopelessness that his soul screamed, countered by restraint. The prince had rarely felt true fear in his life; at this moment, however, he was becoming close friends with the emotion.

Samuel decided to inquire of the nearest person he could find about the nature of this realm. After a short time, the prince approached an old man wearing a dark cloak and standing against a wall on the corner of the first building to his right. The prince mentioned two familiar places so that he could get some kind of a bearing.

"Excuse me, sir, can you tell me where I am? Do you know where the Kingdom of Ferdinand or the Kingdom of St. Mein are?"

"Kingdom? Ha! Boy, do not bother me with such fairy tales. You will find no kingdoms here," the man scoffed.

"But sir, can you tell me where I am?" the prince persisted.

"Leave me alone, boy; I have work to do. I am busy!" the old man shouted back.

Samuel was so desperate that he couldn't take no for an answer. "Can you at least point me in the right direction of someone who can help?"

The old man quickly raised a dagger from his cloak, grabbed the prince, and pushed the sharpened edge against the prince's throat. "If I have to tell you one more time to leave me alone, it will be the last thing you ever hear."

The prince stepped back and moved his right hand to his hip where his sword normally hung, but he found nothing. He looked up at the man, apologized, and backed away slowly. After keeping an eye on the man for a few paces, he turned and headed down the road.

As the prince traveled farther down the street, he noticed tall buildings that were three times the size of normal cottages. These buildings stood in rows that lined the street. The red dust persisted constantly wherever Samuel looked. Depression and anger, feelings that radiated toward him like a silent scream, ruled this dismal place.

No one stopped to talk or make conversation, but in some of the top rooms of the buildings, the prince could see people shouting down to the streets. He could not tell what the random shouting meant, or whom the screams were meant for. The prince understood more by the minute how much hatred, despair, and confusion plagued this unfamiliar land.

Making his way cautiously down the road and seeing more of the same cottages but fewer travelers, he realized that the cottages began decaying. The buildings looked remorseful, with collapsed roofs, caved-in walls, and busted doors. Shouts continued to come from the buildings, but upon examining the rooms above, Samuel could find no people there.

The scenery continued to change. To his left and ahead of him rose mountains of great size, while to his right through the maze of cottages, the prince glimpsed a massive lake.

Samuel walked for what felt like hours. As he walked, he realized that although he never lost his strength, the walking was consuming him internally with exhaustion. His body was able to move, even though his soul was weary and wanted rest. Samuel also noticed that no matter how far he traveled down the street, the scenery remained constant. The lake was always to his right; the mountains were always to his left and front.

Desperate, the prince cried aloud, "Where am I?" No sooner did the prince beg the question than he noticed a man sitting outside a brightly lit cottage ahead of him. The man was short, round, and bald. Samuel had walked so much in the dismal scenery that hope began leaving his soul; this time, he prepared to fight to get some kind of answer.

But he didn't have to fight. As Samuel drew close, the portly gentleman stood straight up and started to advertise to an empty street as if Samuel were part of a crowd. "Come one! Come all! Get your fair share of your heart's desire in wealth. We have gold! We have jewels! We have everything that can buy anything!" he blustered.

"Sir, what is this place? What is it you have to offer here?" questioned the prince.

"Ah! A new customer! Come. Come inside, and I will show you how to acquire great riches, enough riches to buy your way out of this wretched place!"

The prince nodded in acceptance and entered the building. As he entered, he noticed that the walls were lined with shelves. Each held the most beautiful and precious stones the prince had ever laid eyes on and some he had never before seen.

Just glancing at a few of the illustrious gems brought the prince minor relief from this place of torment. Here was something different to see; here, everything was not red and decrepit. The prince walked slowly around the room, drinking in the beauty of the priceless treasures. The prince moved toward one of the nearby shelves and started to pick up one of the gems.

"No – I'm sorry, my friend, but you must be deemed worthy before you can so much as touch my precious trophies," the man said, sharpening his gaze.

With every beat of his heart the prince felt a growing urge to hold one of the gems. "What must I do to attain such riches? I must have one gem. What must I do to possess such a thing, sir?" the prince asked in a trance-like voice.

The man took note of the lust in Samuel's eyes, smiled, and commenced with the same routine he had done for thousands of years to countless victims. "Ah, now we can get down to business! Here, my boy. Just sign this paper. All I need from you is a sworn testimony, nothing more. It's just a minor detail, really."

Samuel could not tear his gaze away from the jewels. He barely listened to the bald shop owner.

Chuckling in a satisfied way, the bald man pulled up a table and put an ancient document on it. "And did I mention that these riches will buy your way out of this realm? Oh, they most definitely will. All you have to do is sign the paper here. Go ahead!

Make your mark, and be free of this place. Then you'll live just as richly as these trophies do! You will have all that your heart desires! You will be as glorious as my trophies!" the bald man exclaimed, hardly able to contain his enthusiasm.

But his gloating shook Samuel out of his trance, and the prince really looked at the document for the first time. "Sign this paper? What does it say? And why do I need to sign anything?" he said, confused.

Suddenly, the medallion of the winged man around his neck glowed warm. I already have a very fine necklace, he thought, looking down at it. Through his state of torment and depression, the prince felt yet another emotion, a sense of caution that told him to walk away. He felt he was destined for trouble and needed to leave immediately.

The bald shop owner seemed to sense that his sale was slipping away. "What! Never mind the questions! Just sign the paper, and you will be rich beyond your wildest dreams. You'll have enough to buy your way out of this place and live a happy life for the rest of your days. The paper merely states that you will take these riches, which I will give to you, and in return, you will be made to shine like the riches themselves. It is my way of saying that all who come to me to get rich will indeed have what their heart wants! It's all about desire, my boy!" the bald man said happily. He could not hold his excitement much longer, as he wanted more with every second for the prince to seal his fate.

The prince's feelings about walking away grew at

an alarming rate. He did not know why he was in this place, but he reasoned that signing the paper would not be a good idea. The moment he made his decision, the medallion cooled. "Well, sir, you do have some nice things, but I am going to pass on the offer. I will have to find another way out of here, I suppose." The prince started to step back from the man.

"What!" the bald man exclaimed, pounding his fist on the counter through the paper. The man's eyes glowed a dark red color, darker than the red embedded in this place. The old man lifted his fist, stood up, and pointed to the door.

"Fine then, have it your way. You can find your own way out," sneered the man.

The prince left the room at once. Upon stepping out, he felt a burden he had not realized that he carried lifting from deep within his chest. The prince shook the feeling off and moved further down the street. For a time, he pondered the fate he would have created for himself should he have signed that paper. However, he also could not rid the feeling that he had given up his chance to leave this place.

Suddenly, a sickening feeling grasped Samuel, drying his mouth and turning his hands numb. A powerful sense of urgency broke through his confusion. As he walked, he thought harder still about it. He could not remember where he had come from. Samuel had no estimate of time, nor any understanding of why he felt the need to be someplace else.

At a loss for what to do, Samuel decided to continue his journey down the same road from which he'd come. After walking for a time, the prince could hear off in the distance the clashing of swords. He hurried his footsteps in that direction. He recognized the sound on instinct as swordplay, but try as he might, he was unable to connect the sound with his memories. His confusion grew, yet he knew without a doubt that the sound was something he had known most of his life.

As the prince drew near, he saw a field to his right in front of the lake. This was the second change in scenery that the prince was able to notice since he had arrived. But how long have I been here? the prince wondered.

While the thought gnawed at him, his focus shifted back to the swordplay. In the distance, a large crowd caught his eye. People cheered for their choice of victor. Two men stood in the middle of a circle, engaged in armed combat. The men swung at each other, fighting for their lives.

CLINK!

CLANG!

CLINK!

CLANG!

The sound of metal echoed through the air. With each sword strike, the crowd cheered. Samuel joined the crowd and watched the fight curiously. When a blow injured a man, the crowd erupted in delight.

Over the loud cheering, the prince shouted to the man next to him, "What is happening here? What quarrel sent these men into such a rage against each other?"

"A prize," the man answered, slightly turning his head. "If one slays the other out of anger or self-ishness, he wins. The prize is not only to be grant-ed the power to be ten times stronger in sword-play, but he gets to leave this place." As he spoke, the man's eyes never left the fight.

The two swordsmen battled fiercely in the ring. The fight ended with one man letting out a loud cry as he brought his blade down swiftly on the oth-er. The defeated man's body fell lifelessly to the ground. The victor raised his sword, and the crowd cheered.

A man dressed in all black stepped forward to the center of the ring and raised the victor's hand. "This man has shown no mercy to his enemy! I de-clare him the winner!"

As the man in black spoke, the victor swelled with power. He glowed a darker red for a few seconds and then left the stage, pushing his way through the crowd. "I will now go and use my power to en-force my will!" the victorious man exclaimed.

The cheering crowd parted for the winning man. As the winner left, the circle of patrons closed, turning their ears toward the announcer. "Now, for this next fight, we will bring out a former champi-on! He has won this match many times and has had his power increase tenfold with each victory. I give you Chadorian!"

The crowd cheered wildly as Chadorian stepped into the middle of the ring. He emanated a red glow of intense power and carried a large, double-bladed sword that bore the reflection of the nearby burning lake. He breathed deeply, raising his giant chest for the crowd to see. Hatred and anger burned in his eyes. The rage in this man's soul was so powerful that Samuel was able to feel it pierce through the crowd.

"We have one issue with this particular match. We are missing a challenger. Is there anyone brave enough to stand up against this man? Your reward for defeating him will be an increase in your sword skill tenfold. Anyone? I beckon anyone to step forward and take a chance at fate. You will also have the choice to leave this realm, if you so desire," the announcer called. As he did so, the crowd looked around at one another, waiting for someone to answer the announcer's call.

The prince felt a strong sense of confidence burst from within, which was fueled by the indirect rage of Chadorian. A distant feeling came to life that held vivid images of swordplay. He could not quite recall where these images were from; however, he felt a strong passion to use the sword.

Regardless of his missing memory, Samuel made his way through a roaring crowd of spectators. He wanted to use a sword and do damage to something; that was all he knew. Samuel stepped to the front of the crowd and spoke loudly, confidently, to the announcer, keeping eye contact with the current champion. "I'll take your offer."

A hush came over the crowd, and the announcer turned his attention to the prince.

"Very well! Come up here, boy." Turning to the crowd, the announcer shouted, "We have a competitor! What is your name, boy?"

"Samuel."

"Ah, Samuel! Our competitor's name is Samuel!" the announcer shouted to the crowd. The crowd did nothing but boo and hiss at the prince. Smiling widely, the announcer promised, "We shall begin momentarily!"

The announcer moved in close to the prince, put his hand on the prince's shoulder, and spoke quietly into his ear. "You do know the rules, don't you? There are no rules! And should you kill this beast of a man in armed combat, your skill will increase tenfold, and you will be granted passage out of this place," the announcer smiled deviously at the prince.

"I understand the rules; now give me a sword," the prince demanded.

At once, a sword appeared in the prince's hand. It was a thin blade, sharp on one side and dull on the other. In the back of his mind, he knew he was at a disadvantage, because the weapon did not balance the odds. But his confidence and desire to fight grew as he twirled the sword in his hand, taking note of the small details of his opponent's body language.

The prince smirked and laughed to himself as he took up a stance and prepared to fight. Visions of himself using a sword came to mind, increasing his confidence. The prince shook off the vision and waited for the competition to begin.

"All right, fighters, you know the rules and rewards. The punishment for losing is death. So without further speech, let the fight commence!" the announcer yelled as he stepped out of the circle.

Wasting no time, Chadorian raised his large sword above his head and struck down, aiming to cut the prince in half. The prince reacted by bringing his sword across his own head in a defensive posture.

The two swords connected. The weight of Chadorian's strike was heavy enough to bring the prince down to one knee. The prince parried the attack, swinging his sword from right to left across his attacker's body. He meant to slice open the stomach of the attacker, but Samuel's sword was too short.

Samuel recovered from his kneeling position after his first strike, and he raised his sword over his head to strike downward on his opponent. Chadorian's sword blocked his. Chadorian swiftly kicked the prince in the chest, where he was vulnerable. The prince landed painfully on his back, out of breath.

With his sword raised, Chadorian ran toward the prince, who was lying on the ground, and with all his might he thrust the sword to the ground. The prince, noticing the attack at the last moment, rolled to his right and out of the way of what would have been a fatal blow.

The prince regained his ground, and the two opponents were quickly toe-to-toe. They evaded and blocked each other's attacks. The crowd was full of shouts and cheers; some were chanting Samuel's name while others were still cheering on the current victor.

Both parties continued swinging, missing, blocking, and kicking. The crowd grew as the fight raged on. Chadorian moved in and swung his sword across the prince's chest, cutting him right below his collarbone. Another strike came from Chadorian's backhand and cut the outside of the prince's sword arm.

Feeling weak from the skirmish, Samuel dropped his sword. The competitor continued the match with great ferocity. Chadorian charged toward the prince, lunging his sword toward Samuel's stomach for a final blow. The prince immediately spun in a half circle, throwing off the attack. Chadorian's movement carried him a few steps past the prince as he stumbled to the ground.

The prince retrieved his sword and turned to see his attacker off balance, allowing for the opportunity to strike. The prince's blade drew down forcefully as Chadorian turned, leaving no time to block. Samuel's sword gashed deep into the muscle of Chadorian's shoulder, rendering his once-powerful arm useless. He roared with agonizing fury.

Chadorian started swinging aimlessly in all directions to inflict maximum damage on the prince. The attacker was in a fit of rage, his concentration blinded by anger. Wave after wave of unsuccessful attacks made Chadorian begin to understand the great skill of his opponent, and for the first time in his life, he felt the fear of failure. Chadorian had never known failure, and his arrogance on this day would become his demise. Chadorian, however, would give up his life before letting defeat mark him and sully his reputation with failure.

He drew upon his final strength within and swung at the prince. Deflecting the potentially deadly blow, the prince brought his sword down in a half circle motion that sliced the attacker's sword hand. Chadorian's sword fell to the ground, rattled, and became silent. The prince turned and cut the fearsome warrior on his thigh. Accepting his fate, Chadorian fell to the ground, kneeling before Samuel in defeat.

Stepping back, Samuel took stance to finish off this beast-like man. As the opponent held a firm kneeling position, the prince drew close to slice off his head. Samuel looked upon his foe one last time as he raised his sword overhead. With every ounce of hatred inside, he brought the sharp edge of the sword down, cutting the air swiftly and aiming straight for Chadorian's neck, only to stop within inches of his target.

The medallion around Samuel's neck grew warm, almost hot. Samuel came to himself and saw the fear and sorrow deep within the eyes of the attacker. Pity froze the prince mid-strike.

Samuel blinked, holding the sword firmly against Chadorian's neck; his eyes widened and pulse slowed as his soul spoke, questioning his actions. What were the true crimes of this man? His eyes tell another story, and I am not the one to end his life.

The crowd was cheering the prince to end Chadorian's life. The prince, feeling compassion for his attacker, could not commit such an act. The prince lowered his sword, displaying mercy the crowd had never seen.

He thought once again about how he arrived in a place that thrived off such chaos. His thoughts returned to him no answer, leaving him with the question of how he had learned to fight in the manner that fed the hungry crowd. He knew that it was not his authority to take a life for his own personal gain. Samuel was born with better morals, and the decision of mercy confirmed his inner feelings.

As the prince lowered his sword, he felt yet another burden lift from his chest, but the angry crowd hated his choice of mercy. The prince stood in the center of the circle, looking at his attacker, whose eyes begged for life. The prince offered a hand and helped the defeated opponent to his feet; the crowd fell to a hushed silence.

The announcer quickly came to the center of the circle. "You must finish your opponent if you want to gain the rewards from the fight. Besides, there is a crowd that is waiting for you to appease them. I would not let mercy deny you the power of a god. Great power is something you already possess, but much more awaits you."

"Something does not feel right; this place does not feel right. I understand what the rules are, and since there are none, I am going to let this man leave here with his life," the prince replied, looking the announcer in the eye.

The crowd roared with boos and scornful remarks toward the prince.

Scowling, the announcer spat, "Fine! Have it your way! Be gone from this ring, and leave your sword. You are a disappointment to many here today." With these words the announcer turned toward Chadorian and waved his hand. Chadorian fell prostrate on the ground. His body twitched, and then the movement ceased.

The prince looked at the announcer with eyes of anger and raised his sword to attack the man. "Ah-ah! I would not do that," said the announcer while pointing to the angry crowd. "Only one snap of my fingers, and this crowd will tear you to small pieces. Go. Be on your way, Samuel. Samuel, ha! What a name for a prince!"

The crowd parted, and Samuel hurried out of the field and back onto the road from which he'd come. As Samuel regained his composure and continued walking down the road, he pondered why the man had called him a prince. Memories slowly came back in short flashes about another time in his life. He remembered a girl and a horse, but the visions were blurry. The confusion of memories still clouded his feelings.

Samuel kept pace on the road, still noticing the unchanging scenery as he walked for a time with his mind deeply buried in thought. Suddenly, from the alley at the corner of a nearby building, the prince noticed a bright light. Expecting to be fearful, he instead felt comfort and was drawn to the light.

Samuel approached as the light diminished, revealing a man in an olive-colored cloak with gold lacings. The man looked at Samuel with welcoming eyes and motioned for him to come closer. As Samuel walked up to the man, the man leaned in close and spoke.

"Samuel, you do not belong here. You are under the power of an evil wizard. His spell has brought you to this realm. This is the place of judgment for those who have used their lives for their own benefit and then died. As you can see and feel, there is no hope here. Anger and lust rule this dominion, and once you reach this realm after you die, you are imprisoned to wander out your existence here."

As the man spoke, a wave of clarity hitting the shores of illusion snapped the prince out of his daze. Eyes growing bigger in the recognition of reality, he spoke with astonishment. "I remember now! But I still don't understand why I am here. Was all this just to keep me from foiling the wizard's plan to kill my father and hurt the princess?"

"That is one reason. The other is that you are supposed to do many great things in your life. I only have a short time, and I cannot explain about things that will come to pass. However, I will say that you should keep faith with regards to your inner judgment. It will be of great aid in the future, just as it has aided you here today.

"Let me explain. When you first got here, you came across a shopkeeper who offered to make you rich. You felt the lust that went with giving into riches, and it almost swallowed you. I watched you on my journey here, and I feared all was lost. Then, I noticed how you conquered your emotions and found relief."

Samuel touched the chain around his neck. "The medallion of Raphael that Kristina gave me grew warm. It brought me to myself and gave me the chance to resist temptation."

The man in the olive cloak nodded. "Then Kristina has been a good friend to you. The man in the shop was no man at all. He is a purely evil spirit. His goal was to take all of the souls that are brought here and promise them one gift: to make the strongest desire of the heart a reality."

"He does this by turning the souls that accept his offer into one of his precious rocks that lay on his shelf. For all time, you would have been worth some value only to the shopkeeper himself. All of the gems that were on the shelves were men who gave in to their own greed. Now those men will stay for all of eternity, with no hope of escape," the man said sadly.

Samuel shivered. "I was nearly one of them."

The man in the olive cloak nodded. "And the shopkeeper was not the only danger you faced. Had you given in to rage during the fight you encountered, the price would have been to serve as a slave to the announcer. That was why your opponent disappeared when you did not kill him. His fate has long been sealed, and he is a slave of the announcer. Your fate has yet to be decided.

"Treasure the medallion as you treasure the woman who gave it to you. She has done you more good than you or she could have expected. Fortunately, your judgment and use of good morals allowed me enough time to work with the creator to break you free of the wizard's spell. You have been in this realm for one week's time in your world. Now, close your eyes."

As the prince shut his eyes, the man waved a hand in front of his face. Feeling tired, Samuel drifted in dreams for an unknown amount of time. He felt at peace. The red color and haze of anger, lust, and despair faded around him.

Moments later, the prince sat up. He was covered in leaves, and the morning sun's rays burst through the treetops. Wasting no time, the prince grabbed his things and headed for his kingdom. Samuel was finally going home to St. Mein.

CHAPTER IV

A Prophecy Foretold.

THE prince sped quickly through the woods, weaving between the trees. Keeping a keen eye out for the quickest path to the river, the prince accelerated his pace. Samuel's lungs felt as if they'd erupted in flames as he pushed harder through the woods. The prince ran for what seemed like hours through a maze of trees.

Finally, hearing sounds of rushing water, he felt a mingled sense of relief and unease as he processed in his mind the obstacle he was about to undertake. The prince rushed to the edge of the bank that cradled the raging waters. He looked around at the trees, broke off some branches, and began to form a raft.

The prince wove limbs to form a base for his raft and coated the inside of the structure with branches. The branches possessed thickly coated pine needles. The needles themselves seemed to fight for every inch of space allowed by the branch that harbored them, creating a somewhat waterproof coating for his raft. Holding the raft, the prince set it in the water. The raft stayed afloat, and so the prince climbed into the raft and began to ride along the rushing waves, down the stream, and toward his long missed homeland.

The waves tossed the prince like a rag doll. His body jerked with the motion of the waters, humbling the prince and making him realize he was at the mercy of the water. The raft held together and kept him safe as he journeyed down the river.

The rushing waters increased in speed and carried the prince down the path the water followed. A series of memories from his childhood began to flood Samuel's mind as the waters flooded the river he was now traveling. He thought deeply about the times he'd spent with the princess and wondered if she would even recognize him after all the time that had passed. He recalled his final words to his father and the thoughts that he'd entertained about him. Samuel also thought of the friend that he'd left behind, Earabis.

Samuel was a man now. His early mornings of disciplined training had brought him to a state of maturity that he never before knew existed. His body was hardened from the unforgiving wilderness that had provided shelter for him during lonely years. Samuel would have to use all his instincts and training to save his father. These thoughts kept Samuel company, along with the constant sound of the flowing water during his ride down the river.

Day turned to night, and night turned to day. The two periods of time rotated in alternating sequence as Samuel urged them to hurry. The water began to slow around the end of the second day. The prince stared into the night sky and wondered how soon he would be back home. Three days on the river passed before the prince was able to recognize familiar territory. He saw a pair of cliffs overshadowing the riverbed, nearly touching each other; they formed a bridge that had yet to be completed.

These cliffs told Samuel that he was entering the outer edges of St. Mein and could not travel downstream much longer for fear of alerting the wizard that he'd escaped the trap. It would take Samuel another three days to reach the kingdom. Samuel soon found a place he could disembark from the river and began paddling his way to land. The river was shallow and slow, showing no signs of danger. Samuel floated next to the shore and got out of his raft, disposing of his vessel at once. He broke apart his raft and set the pieces afloat with the stream's current.

Back on land, Samuel gained his bearings and started traveling immediately toward his father's kingdom. It was late afternoon, leaving the prince with only a few hours of daylight. Fear gripped him as he began to move on his plotted course. The fear shouted that he may already be too late, and it urged him to hurry. In acknowledging this emotion, Samuel began to run as fast as he could until he reached sight of the castle he used to call home: the castle of St. Mein.

The prince headed straight toward the castle, not even taking a moment to catch his breath. As he ran, he could see the ballroom lit up in the distance. There must be a celebration this evening, he thought to himself. He had lost track of time in the wilderness and was unaware that it was his father's birthday.

As he approached the castle, he slowed his pace while still gazing into the ballroom window. He caught a glimpse of Kristina, dancing a slow waltz with her father, King James. Seeing Kristina for the first time in years, Samuel stood motionless, mesmerized at the sight of his princess. He found it impossible to focus on anything but her beauty.

To Samuel, it felt like an eternity had passed since he'd last laid eyes on her. As he watched her rhythmically glide across the floor in her long, flowing coral dress, the old feelings of love, hope, and childhood innocence came rushing back into his mind and inundated the depths of his soul. Once again, Kristina made time stop for Prince Samuel, bringing every fiber of his being and every moment of his existence to a standstill.

Staring at the princess, his heart pounded, sending blood racing through his body. The beat of his heart echoed through his veins. The pulsing blood filled the vessels, flowing all the way through his neck and into his head. Weakness gripped him, causing his legs to buckle. His lungs took in their fill of air, only to force it out, beckoning for repetition. His mouth grew dry instantly, as if the prince were inhaling the desert itself.

His feelings erupted as he thought about their last night together before she had left the kingdom and how losing her had left him heartbroken. He remembered how he had gently wiped the tears from her cheeks as she looked deeply into his eyes before they parted ways.

"Princess," he whispered, lacking breath to speak aloud.

Suddenly, the hoot of an owl in a tree towering overhead snapped Samuel back to reality. Shaking his head hastily as if to expunge the pleasant memories, he focused on the reason why he had returned home. Looking through the window again, he searched for a glimpse of his father.

Though Samuel didn't see the king, he noticed a banner that ran between two statuesque pillars in the back of the ballroom. "Happy 50th Birthday, King Salvatore," he read. Could it really be my father's fiftieth birthday?

Peering around the room again, he saw no sign of his father. Where could he be? Samuel thought. Samuel ran around the castle to the front, up to the outer gatehouse, which was surrounded by guards. After seeing what the wizard was capable of doing, knowing the castle was well protected gave Samuel a sense of comfort.

But that protection also presented a quagmire. Samuel had not been seen in the kingdom for five years. During that time he had changed and grown into a man. And right now, he looked and smelled like a hermit from the wild. No one would recognize him, and their challenges and questions would take too much time. He had to get inside without their interference.

He waited patiently around the corner until there were only two guards at the gate. The rest of the men had headed to the ballroom to keep watch. Samuel walked along the wall toward the gate, keeping his eyes on the guards at all times. The two men turned to each other and began conversing about something that Samuel could not hear. He took this opportunity to slide through the opening of the gate, right past the guards. Then he gripped the wall with his back and heels.

At that point, both guards turned around just in time to see a man walk into the inner gatehouse.

"Halt! All visitors must be announced!" yelled the husky guardsman as he and his partner raced toward the prince. Samuel turned and faced the two men. Both of their jaws dropped simultaneously at the sight of the prince. They bowed reverently, still in astonishment that the prince had returned.

Stunned at their recognition, Samuel stepped forward boldly. "It is I, Prince Samuel. I am here to see my father," Samuel said. Samuel proceeded through the gates, running past the curtain wall to the iron gate that led directly into the castle.

Behind him, he heard the guards calling forward to other guards ahead, "The prince returns! Prince Samuel returns!" Every other guard bowed in respect as Samuel passed.

Once he was through the gate, Samuel wasted no time in heading straight for the king's bedroom. He quickly climbed the long, narrow, spiral staircase that led to the king's private tower. He could hear voices as he steadily climbed the passage that seemed never to end. All he could hear were mumblings that grew louder.

Finally, one voice rose above the rest. "Who's there?" the king shouted.

Out of breath, Samuel didn't answer.

Upstairs in his chamber, the king continued dressing himself in his finest silk garments. He turned to give himself one last look in his full-length mirror before heading to the ballroom. All of a sudden, behind him in the reflection was none other than the wizard.

"My, my, you didn't have to dress up on my account," the evil wizard smirked.

"How did you get past the guards?" asked the king, whirling around.

"I have my ways," retorted the wizard.

Before the king could even shout for help, the wizard snatched him by the throat and squeezed with an iron grip. The king struggled and gasped as he fought for air. The wizard just squeezed tighter and tighter with a grimace of pleasure on his face. The king could feel the life drain out of his body.

Samuel climbed the stairs faster, skipping steps as he tried to hurry his way to the top. He finally reached the long corridor that headed down to the king's chamber.

The prince bolted down the hall, trying to tread lightly on the red carpet so as not to make any noise. He reached the end of the hall where the arched mahogany door stood that led into the king's room. Samuel put his ear to the door and heard the faint sound of a struggle and a gurgling wheeze. Wasting no time, he kicked in the door to find the wizard standing over Salvatore.

The wizard, startled by the prince's arrival, pulled out a dagger. At once he thrust it into the chest of the king. He then leapt to his feet, releasing Salvatore from his grasp and withdrawing the dagger. Salvatore fell to the ground, motionless.

"NO!" Samuel's loud cry echoed throughout the halls of the castle. The prince charged at the wizard.

But the wizard was too quick for Samuel. He dodged his charge, causing Samuel to fall to the floor. Samuel quickly jumped back up. It was too late; the wizard had already fled the scene.

The prince's first instinct was to run after the wizard. However, he heard a painful moan from his father and rushed to his side instead. Samuel knelt down, lifted his head, and laid it in his lap.

The king, slipping in and out of consciousness, gazed up at his son.

"Father, I am here. Everything is going to be okay," Samuel said.

With noticeable effort, the king finally gathered enough strength to speak. "My son," he said between struggling breaths. "Please forgive me for all I have done to you. I had my reasons for being so stern. I had to protect you. And I – I was weak, and sad."

"Don't speak, Father; you need to stay still. I

forgive you," Samuel said, tears streaming down his face.

Hearing forgiveness, King Salvatore smiled and took his last breath.

Samuel kissed his father on the forehead and laid his head gently down on the soft carpet. He found a purple silk blanket lying on the king's bed and draped it over his father's body. The prince was infuriated. He wiped the tears of grief and anger from his face, took a deep breath, and stood up. Samuel's only thought now was to find the wizard and bring justice upon him. Hearing commotion, the guards rushed in to see Samuel covering his father's body. "The wizard just killed my father. Search the castle for him as quickly as possible!" Samuel said as he left in a hurry.

Samuel strode down the corridor, descended the stairwell, and ran towards the ballroom. He could hear violins echoing in the hall as he sped towards the entryway. All at once, the soothing sound of violins was replaced by the sound of piercing screams.

The prince darted to the doorway of the ballroom, but it had been bolted shut. He ran back outside to the window he had looked through when he arrived at the castle just moments earlier.

When he reached the window, he saw the wizard on the main stage with Kristina. The wizard had Kristina's hands restrained behind her back by one of his long, cloaked arms. In his other hand he had a black wand that he waved over her head in a threatening manner, cautioning everyone to stay away from her.

Prince Samuel felt rage course through him, igniting his blood. Crashing through the window, he sent shattered glass skittering across the ballroom floor. Everyone ducked and protected their faces as Samuel entered the room.

Samuel ran directly toward the stage without pausing to brush the glass off him. He lunged at the wizard with every ounce of hate and strength he could conjure. The wizard's wand was pointed straight at him, and Samuel could see his lips moving. Light shot at Samuel.

The medallion of Raphael grew warm and sent out a shield of light that blocked the evil spell. Samuel locked eyes with Kristina. Her eyes were happy to see him but her fear of the situation clouded any other emotion she could display with a single look.

In an instant, a cloud of black smoke filled the stage, bringing with it an indescribable smell of evil that caused the crowd to gasp in revulsion. The prince leapt through the cloud of smoke and used every ounce of strength to grab the princess before she could disappear with the wizard.

"Samuel!" Kristina called, struggling to break the wizard's hold on her. "I love....!"

But with his hands empty, Samuel came to a halt, Kristina's final cry echoing in his head. As quickly as the smoke had appeared, the stage was empty. The wizard, the princess, and the smoke were gone.

Samuel froze and numbly dropped to his knees, oblivious to the commotion around him. Fearing another attack by the wizard, the guests hastily ran out of the castle. Samuel was left alone in a ball-room filled with broken glass and the stench of evil.

Eventually, he slowly arose and walked dazed across the floor as broken glass crunched under his feet with each step. His mind unable to grasp what had happened, Samuel felt powerless. He had lost his father to death and the princess to the wizard.

Worry for Princess Kristina filled his mind, blocking all other emotions. He could not rest knowing that she was out there somewhere, in the power of the wizard. One thing he did know was at this very moment, time was working against him. He had to move quickly, grab Earabis and ride out -but where?

To Samuel, it did not matter where; he just need to leave and find a way to pick up the wizard's trail. He turned his sorrow and worry into determination; he was a warrior set on a mission. Samuel gazed straight ahead at the ballroom doors, and then he headed straight for the stables, intent on grabbing Earabis and departing.

Samuel heard a familiar voice upon exiting the ballroom. "Samuel! Stop!"

Freezing in his tracks, Samuel immediately recognized the old cleric's voice. "Jeremy?" Samuel said, turning around.

It was Cleric Jeremy, his old friend. Samuel walked over to him, looked at him with joy, and hugged him. "It's good to see you. I cannot tell you what I have been through in the past few days, but I really must get going."

"And where exactly are you going to, Samuel?"

Jeremy asked patiently.

"To find Princess Kristina and kill the wizard."

Cleric Jeremy nodded; he had expected nothing less. "My dear boy, I know you must find her, and the time may come when you will have to decide the wizard's fate. However, please do your father the honor of burying him, and after that, I will use as little time as possible to prepare you for your journey. There is a reason this terrible fate has befallen us, despite all our efforts to prevent it, and I promise to disclose everything to you. First, let's lay the dead to rest with a proper blessing."

"You are right," Samuel realized. "Let us bury my father, and I will hear what you have to say. By dawn, regardless of what I know or do not know, I am riding out of here."

"Agreed. I am sorry that this is a bad homecoming for you. I do hope that whatever you searched to find these past years is now yours."

"It is, and so much more," Samuel answered.

Privately, Cleric Jeremy thought that if Samuel had sought a king's appearance and demeanor, he had indeed found it. The boy he had tutored was gone, replaced by a man and a king.

The two climbed upstairs to the king's quarters, where Jeremy instructed the servants to prepare the king's body for a burial immediately. He urged Samuel to bathe and dress in royal clothes as a sign of respect for the dead. Samuel agreed, though he rushed through his grooming, eager to leave on his journey.

King Salvatore was laid to rest in the courtyard

of the castle around midnight. Cleric Jeremy performed the funeral ceremony. It was a small, quiet
ritual, which only Samuel, Captain Steven, and King
James attended. After the events that had taken
place at the castle hours earlier, the kingdom folk
were leery to leave their homes.

When the funeral was over, King James pulled
Samuel aside and said, "Should the moment during
your journey ever arise that you need the aid of
the Kingdom of Ferdinand, we will respond to your
call, bearing full arms immediately. From this moment until you return, I shall prepare my army for
battle. My daughter is the most important thing
in the world to me. Please bring her back safely,
Samuel."

"I swear on my life that I will bring her back. I
shall place Captain Steven as Steward of the Kingdom of St. Mein until I return," Samuel said, turning
toward Captain Steven.

"The honor and duty of protecting the kingdom
has always been my sworn oath. I will prepare our
army as well. Both armies will stand ready to aid
you, King Samuel," Captain Steven said, bowing.

"Not yet," Samuel said gently. "I must avenge
my father and win my queen before I can claim my
kingdom and my crown. Then I will be King Samuel.
I urge you - do not let the townspeople know that
I have left on this journey. Tell them I took my father to the countryside to bury him and will return
shortly. This way, you will not have a panic on your
hands in my absence."

"A wise decision, Prince Samuel," Captain Steven

bowed.

Cleric Jeremy stepped forward. "And now, Captain Steven and King James, I must speak with the prince privately. Come, Samuel – we must go to the monastery."

Captain Steven and King James left the graveyard in one direction, while Cleric Jeremy and the prince climbed the hill to the monastery. Approaching the ivory steps that led to the main entrance of the cathedral, the two walked down the long corridor to the chapter room.

Samuel had never been allowed in this place before, because this was a room reserved for men of the holy order. Cleric Jeremy did not hesitate; he opened the doors wide and beckoned Samuel inside. Upon entering the double doors, Samuel gasped at the detail and artistry of the room.

He first noticed the ceiling. It was painted with scenes from the life of one of the great monks who had lived long ago. The doors closed behind Samuel, and when he turned, he noticed the tall, slender carvings of two wooden monks beside each door. It looked as if the statues were guarding the entryway. Chairs made of polished pinewood lined the walls. The front of the room had a throne-like chair reserved for the supreme cleric of the kingdom. In the middle of the room stood a podium for the speaker of the meetings to use as he addressed the assembly.

"Please have a seat," said Cleric Jeremy. Samuel did as he was told and sat down in awe of the room's magnificence.

"What is it you need to tell me?" asked Samuel.

Jeremy took out a black leather-bound book that was hidden in a secret compartment built into the floor, right below the throne-like chair. He sat down next to Samuel, resting the book on his lap. The cover was brittle and almost completely worn. Jeremy carefully opened it, turning to the middle of the book.

"What is that?" Samuel asked with great wonder in his voice.

"It is a book of prophecy passed down from generation to generation of monks in the monastery. This book shows what is to come and what destinies must be fulfilled. Samuel, your destiny is in this book, as well as what is to come if you do not fulfill it. Let me explain," Jeremy said, leaning closer. Samuel gazed at the book as Jeremy spoke.

"It is written that Princess Kristina would be taken by a powerful wizard. Your fate is to go on a mission to save her. If you fail to carry out this quest successfully, the wizard will gain enough power to take over the world. The wizard gains his power from the souls of the purest maidens in the land. Possession of Kristina's soul will bring him one step closer to completing his mission to destroy the world.

"The wizard also seeks two young girls upon whom the creator has bestowed a blessing at a young age. The blessing makes them invisible to evil. Should anyone of the holy order ever seek them out, their location would be made known instantly, for the wizard watches every move the clerics make. Not only must you save Kristina, but you must also defeat the wizard before he finds the girls. Should you fail, evil and destruction will reign throughout the land."

The prince listened intently while Jeremy continued to tell Samuel more details of the prophecy, as well as the measures his parents had taken to protect and prepare him.

Jeremy then walked up to a large bookshelf and pulled out a rugged, age-old map that looked like it had been rolled and unrolled a hundred times. He pointed out the long, treacherous road ahead that the prince must take. There was plenty of rough terrain to cover, but Earabis would be by his side for most of the journey.

"You must travel far beyond any territory you have ever known. Darniem is the area on the map where you must go, for it is the stronghold of the wizard. You will find that it is well guarded, and his men are well trained."

When the cleric finished speaking, he walked back to where he retrieved the map and took out a large, jagged key that looked to be made of glass. He inserted the key into the back panel of the bookshelf, and a small compartment opened.

"Regardless of how well-trained his men are, you should find this gift useful in your trials."

The cleric pushed his arm halfway into the compartment and withdrew it, holding a brightly polished, razor-sharp, silver sword.

The prince stood up slowly and walked to Cleric Jeremy, who said a blessing over the weapon. After blessing the sword, Jeremy presented it to the prince. "Use this sword for protection on your journey, Samuel. It is blessed by the creator above and will serve you well while you do his will."

Samuel bowed his head and graciously accepted the sword, sheathing it slowly. Picking up the map, he said his farewell and thanked his old friend for all the help.

Walking out, he shut the cathedral doors and turned to find Captain Steven at the bottom of the ivory steps holding the reins of his childhood friend, Earabis. Samuel rushed to greet his long-lost friend.

Earabis nuzzled the prince's face as if to say hello. Captain Steven said, "Now that you two have been reunited, Earabis can join you on your quest to save the princess. He will provide you with company and transportation; you will need both."

"Thank you, Captain," Samuel said as he patted the horse on the side. "You've gained a little weight, Earabis, but we shall take care of that. We have a long road ahead of us."

Once again, Samuel was headed on a journey away from home, but this time he would not wander alone.

Captain Steven wished Samuel a good journey with his trusted friend. Cleric Jeremy laid hands on man and horse and prayed the creator's blessing on them.

Dawn spread across the sky as Samuel rode away. He did not know that the prophecy had begun to unfold long before he departed for his quest. The wizard, who had fled to Darniem when he escaped his woodland prison years before, had assembled an army to watch the Kingdom of St. Mein and the surrounding area for the two girls in the prophecy.

The wizard sought mostly paupers and people of failing mental capacity to accept his offering of evil. These people were easily persuaded, not reserving their violence and ruthlessness for a specific purpose. They formed a band that terrorized the countryside, raiding kingdoms and searching for the two girls.

The two little girls that the wizard sought were named Darby and Gabriela. Their parents lived in constant fear of these evil terrorists. They were forced to keep their precious daughters hidden, confiding in no one that their children were the girls the wizard's thugs sought. Not even the girls knew that they had a special destiny; they only knew that the wizard was dangerous to them.

Darby was a sweet and naive child. Her mother made her believe that the attic in which she lived was a magical place where all her wishes would come true. She enjoyed spending time in her enchanted little room where she could wish everyone's cares away. She had a deep, unconditional love for everyone around her, the kind of love that only someone innocent and pure could have.

Darby's older sister was named Gabriela, which means "the creator is my strength." Gabriela definitely lived up to the meaning of her name.

She kept her family strong during the time of battle in the kingdom. She was only thirteen, but she was wise beyond her years. She was a living reminder to her family that no mere mortal alone could preserve and defend them.

When Gabriela was eight years old, she contracted a form of tuberculosis by drinking contaminated cow's milk. The village doctor was called to look in on her every day. She was getting worse as the days went by. Finally, one evening the doctor told Gabriela's parents that she would not make it through the night.

When the doctor departed, the parents shut the door to Gabriela's room so that she could get more rest. The parents could do nothing; they were losing hope at this point and could only pray for a miracle.

Darby, being only four years old at the time, had an uncanny ability to comprehend grave matters. She awoke to hear the doctor telling her parents that Gabby did not have much time to live. Hearing this, Darby felt a pain in her heart that she had never known before. She left the attic, went into Gabby's room, and kissed Gabriela on the forehead.

A tear streamed down Darby's face as she wept over the pain her sister was enduring. She cried with her eyes shut, hugging her dear sister. Gabriela sat up at once. Her skin color immediately returned to normal. She looked well. Darby looked at Gabriela and stepped back for a moment; all she could do was joyfully laugh and embraced her sister again.

When the parents heard the laughing from Gabriela's room, they looked at each other, perplexed, and hurried in the direction of the laughter. When the mother opened the door, to her surprise, she saw Gabriela sitting on her bed and smiling while she hugged Darby. The parents ran to Gabriela and hugged her as well; they felt her face and noticed somehow that she had been cured. The parents requested the presence of the doctor to examine Gabriela. He concluded that she had indeed been miraculously cured from her illness.

Gabriela was young when Darby was born, but she took her under her wing. She had a great motherly instinct. She knew that she and Darby were special, and she knew that they would both need strong protection when they got older, although she wasn't sure why.

Darby's love for others and Gabriela's faith in the creator were so strong that they nearly drove the wizard mad as he searched for them to no avail. His only aim in life became to harness their love and faith and turn them into hate and despair, so he could enslave the entire world. He hadn't counted on the power of love and faith extending from Darby and Gabriela all the way to the prince and princess. He couldn't understand that Samuel, Kristina, Gabriela, and Darby were all bound by fate and the creator's hand in some way.

But he didn't have to understand the power of the creator in order to work against him.

The girls' parents were going to the village market one fateful evening, when a group of thieves wanting nothing more than the food they carried attacked the couple. Though the thieves were some of the wizard's hirelings, they did not know how near the wizard's marks they had come. They were only evil, careless men doing what evil, careless men did.

Little did the thieves know that murdering the parents sealed the creator's blessing over the girls. The little house in the woods became invisible. The deaths of their parents left Darby and Gabby to fend for themselves.

Darby and Gabriela cared for their chickens and a little cow and tended a garden. Though they missed their parents terribly, they were safe and well fed. As scared as Gabriela was, she told Darby that the creator would watch over them and send them help. They only had to wait.

Darby spent her days loving her sister and the creatures on the farm. Gabby spent her days praying to the creator that someone would come and rescue them before the wizard's army found them. Love and faith kept the girls and wove its way into Samuel's prophecy.

And now that Samuel had left for his quest, the wizard searched the kingdom and beyond and offered great promises to anyone who would capture the prince and bring him to Darniem dead or alive - it did not matter. The wizard knew after seeing Samuel that he was not a force to be taken lightly.

Anthony Farina

CHAPTER V
The Lost Forest

SPEEDING through the countryside, Samuel and Earabis traveled for eight days. Through hills and tree-laden forest, they traversed the lands outside the reaches of St. Mein and Ferdinand. The sun rose to its peak on the ninth day as Samuel rode through a field, coming into view of a large, thick forest. He noticed the massive tree line as he drew closer and began to see how thick the trees grew together. It looked from the outside as though little sunlight, even though it was midday, could penetrate the thick treetops.

He was still in the middle of the field and a considerable distance away from the forest when he took in this sight. Halting Earabis, he scanned the territory to the left and right. The dense tree line ran as far as his vision could reach. There was no telling how long it would take to go around the forest. As he sat atop Earabis, he pondered his options and found there were few. Samuel reached into one of his leather-bound saddlebags and pulled out the map given to him by Cleric Jeremy.

"Well, ole boy, we have come farther than I expected. Everything from St. Mein to this point on the map shows nothing but hills and small groves of trees. If this map is correct, then the only way to get around this tree line would be either traveling one hundred miles to the north, where there are mountains, or going two hundred miles south, where there is an ocean. After these woods is a desert; our best bet is to go straight through." Samuel put away his map and squared his shoulders. Kristina was waiting for him.

Earabis' hooves treaded lightly on the darkened ground as he and the prince made their way into the forest. It was impossible to tell where the forest ended; so Samuel's only hope of finding and saving the princess was through the maze of darkness that lay ahead of him. He could feel an evil presence in the dim confusion. I have to find a way, and if finding a way means facing that darkness, then so be it, he thought to himself.

On the path ahead was a tangled mess of weeds, vines, and trees thick with a mossy covering. Only small rays of sunlight glistened through the canopy overhead. The suffocating smell of nature in its raw form overwhelmed his senses.

It is impossible to perceive any sense of direction in this place. However will I make it through? the prince thought to himself, desperate for an answer from anyone or anything. He even looked to Earabis for some type of answer, but the horse remained silent.

Earabis awaited his master's command. As he waited hesitantly for guidance, he shied at the continual silence of such a desolate yet crowded place. His thoughts seem to filter to Samuel.

Just how many ages has it been since this wood has last seen a man? the prince wondered in bewilderment.

With no more than his current thought to occupy his mind, the prince dismounted his steed, unsheathed his sword, and began to cut his way through the forest, looking for any trail or sign of a direction that could lead him onwards. After hours of cutting through thick forest, the prince came to a small opening in the woods. What lay ahead of the prince was a series of trails that led in every direction imaginable.

An angled trail went before him and crested on a nearby hill, making it impossible to see where it would turn next. The path directly to his front was clear for the length of a field, for the woods ahead would swallow the path entirely as soon as the path entered it. The paths to his left and right appeared to circle back in the general direction from where he came. The one on the left led to a rocky area, and the one on the right just faded into the distance.

The only advantage the prince could see at this point was that the clearing showed signs that the sun was still high in the sky. From that he could tell he had only been traveling for a few hours, which in the woods seemed to feel like days.

Not knowing that within a few moments he was about to face the greatest test of temperance a man could possibly endure, the prince continued on the path that was directly in front of him. Paying no attention to the paths on his left or his right, he concluded that the best route would be to stay in the general direction that he had been going.

As the prince set off down the path, he took one look back. Then, with a deep breath, he began his journey forward. Stepping onto his chosen path, the prince began to feel something eat away at him; it was the uncomfortable feeling that he used to get as a child, telling him he was alone in the world. Earabis was right by his side, but loneliness still gripped the prince.

Once the path became more overgrown, thick brush lay ahead; so the prince began the laborious task of cutting down the foliage blocking the path. Hack! Chop! Hack! Hack! Hours went by before the brush finally gave way to an open path.

On the path before him, the prince saw trees and rolling hills; the path itself seemed to be clear of any debris. The forest was peaceful for once, and as the prince walked on the path, he was able to mount Earabis and move fast to gain ground and make up for the time lost from cutting away all the foliage.

Prince Samuel and Earabis traveled the path together as the sun slid below the tree-lined horizon. He did not know how far into the woods he had traveled, for the sun was his only timepiece. The prince could see, as cool air welcomed the night, a small glow off in the distance.

A fire perhaps? Who else could be out in a place such as this? thought the prince, though he welcomed the possibility of some sort of human contact, something to reassure him he was not alone on his travels. As soon as the prince noticed the light, however, Earabis stopped in his tracks and slowly backed up.

"Earabis, what are you doing, boy? Come on, let's go see what company lies ahead at the fire," Samuel urged.

Earabis, reluctant to obey his master's orders, kept backing up. The prince dismounted the horse, and once he was on the ground, he patted his friend on his neck to keep him calm. Samuel could tell that something was not quite right in the air, and Earabis was a guaranteed alarm for the situation.

Samuel longed for light and warmth and companionship. But that longing was not the only force drawing him onwards. He felt that he must get to that fire, that nothing could stop him – that getting to the fire was the only thing in the world that mattered. He could not explain the feeling or act contrary to it; it was controlling him.

The prince took the reins and began to pull Earabis forward while walking toward the fire. Earabis, persistent in the fear that plagued him, dug his hooves in the ground and would not budge.

"Okay, Earabis, have it your way. But the smell of roasted pheasant is driving my hunger wild; so I know something good is waiting over there. You stay here, and I will be back momentarily," said the prince as he tied Earabis' reins to a tree next to the path.

When the prince finished lashing the straps to the tree, he began to walk along the path. Earabis, not satisfied with the prince's choice, reared up on his hind legs and cycled his front legs in the air, as if practically screaming that Samuel should not venture down that path. The prince, regardless, headed towards the fire and the unknown.

As the prince headed down his path, the light in the distance began to grow. Before long, he could see the makings of a small shelter and smell the pleasing scent of roasted pheasant and potatoes.

The prince's pace increased along with his pulse as his hunger lowered his guard and set him to discover exactly what was in store for him at this fire. At the tiny encampment, a pheasant roasted on a spit, the scent painting an accurate picture in his head of the environment. Outside a small shelter, Samuel saw a bed made of animal fur, and on it rested a woman with flowing golden hair, her slender figure lovely in a red and blue dress. The prince could not help but to marvel at her beauty.

She wore a stunning pendant around her neck that caught Samuel's eye instantly. It was a purple stone encased in ivy leaves. The stone reflected the hypnotic dancing fire. And it seemed to erase any fear or caution Samuel had felt since he entered the forest. Void of all protective instincts at this point, he walked up to the camp as if he were a welcomed guest invited to join a feast.

"Come, weary traveler - rest and eat. I know you must be hungry from such a long journey, for there is no one else in this area for miles." The woman's calm, soothing voice nearly took control of the prince's mind, as if he were under some type of spell that told him to obey her every command.

Samuel smiled. "Thank you, madam. I have not seen a soul in these woods, nor do I hear any sounds of people anywhere. Can you tell me where I am, exactly?"

"Do not trouble yourself with such questions, my dear. Here, eat and regain your strength. Drink your fill, and be satisfied. Rest, and be comforted." She walked to the fire and came back with a plate of cooked pheasant and potatoes and a cup of wine. "Drink and eat to your heart's content. There is no cause for worry here."

At those words, Prince Samuel took a bite of the pheasant; the succulent meat was roasted to perfection. Juices filled his mouth from the single bite, and his hunger became enraged. The wine he drank burst with the flavor of the long-missed Goji berries that grew in his homeland. At this moment, that faraway land was becoming a distant memory.

As he ate, his eyes shifted to the pendant once more. The luminous purple appealed to the prince. He noticed the ivy leaves held together by a single piece in more detail.

"What is the meaning behind the necklace you wear, madam?" inquired the prince.

"This jewel was a gift given to me long ago. It has been with me for most of my life, and it holds great power."

As the woman spoke, Samuel began to feel different. Something is happening to me. My senses are numb. My memory is fading. Coming to this realization, the prince slowly put the plate of food aside, along with the glass of wine.

As he did, his hunger became insatiable, while his thirst almost drove him to madness. He wanted nothing more at this point than to devour the entire bird that was still roasting. He gazed upon the roasting pheasant, its golden skin popping and crackling in the heat of the fire. He turned his attention to the barrel of wine and noticed that the Goji berries' juice was seeping out of the cracks in the barrel, making it a treat almost impossible to resist.

Still, the prince set his cup and plate down, stood to regain his posture, and fought with an inner strength that he had not known he possessed. He sensed that he must resist the temptation to take just one more bite of pheasant or drink of wine. His hunger continued to grow; however, something was not right about the situation. He wondered how many had come before him and fallen into whatever traps this woman had planned.

How is it that she came to be in this place, with all this food and wine?

No sooner did he finish this thought than the woman came next to him. She was clothed enough to cover herself decently, but she moved toward him in a provocative motion, beckoning him to be comforted. As she neared the prince, he focused on the woman. She was beautiful beyond words. Her beauty had increased with his desire for her in the short time of his stay. Her lips were red and juicier than the wine.

She drew in close, her breath an intoxicating scent. She ran her fingers through his hair, relaxing him and instantly taking his mind off the food and drink. "Come, take off that heavy sword and your armor. Rest awhile with me, and I will take your troubles away."

Samuel shook his head. "I can't, I have a job to do."

"But your journey is long, and the road ahead of you is nearly impossible. You need rest, food, and comfort," the woman invited.

In this moment, the gold medallion around Samuel's neck glowed, and he heard Kristina's sweet voice as she put it around his neck to protect him. Immediately his senses cleared, exposing the trap he had walked into. How long had his mind been wandering? If he had continued to accept the food or wine or the witch's caresses, he would have lost his way.

"I cannot give in to my lusts, to do so would sacrifice all hope for saving the princess," the prince whispered to himself. No matter what small happiness this woman was able to provide the prince at this one moment, it would never equal the reward the prince would receive for remaining true to his soul, the princess, and the path of righteousness.

In realizing this one true fact, Samuel noticed something about all the trees in the area that he had not observed before. The trees appeared to have the faces of men. They were well concealed; the wine and food made their camouflage as deceptive as the world's finest predator in the night.

But in an instant, the trap made sense. This woman was the witch from the old fable book Kristina had read to him. He remembered Jeremy's warnings during his boyhood lessons that he must never go in the lost forest alone, for the temptations of this place were too great for any man to stand. The woman had been here for a time longer than the prince could imagine.

She preyed on tired, weary travelers. The woman would feed them and give them wine to drink, which would magnify the hidden lusts inside them. This lust would distort a person's judgment, and then the woman would seduce her weakened prey, transforming them into one of her trophies.

Then, something else came to mind. With his training, he remembered the morals that Jeremy had taught him. Marrying the princess was the morally correct decision, not indulging in the food or wine or the woman next to him. The prince had to think quickly, lest he become another of this woman's victims.

A jolt went through Prince Samuel's mind, and he was brought back to clarity. He felt as if the creator was rewarding him for passing a test and proving that he could remain true to himself and his morals. The prince reacted by pushing the woman away, lessening her seductive grip. Her beauty quickly faded as his senses returned.

He reached down for the wine, and in doing so he noticed the woman smiling at him with razor-sharp teeth. The teeth did not belong to any human or other creature he had ever seen. They were pointy, close together, and jagged all at the same time.

After noting this one small detail, the prince quickly grasped the goblet of wine and threw it on the fire, causing the fire to rise in fury. The prince then stepped back, drawing his sword in defense of whatever evil would come at him next. Thanks to gifts from Kristina and Jeremy and the creator, the woman's spell on the prince had been broken.

With a terrifying scream, the woman stepped back and gained distance from the prince. She hunched over, and out of her back sprouted wings. Her hair changed to a grey mop that grew down to her feet. Her face became wrinkly; her hands grew long, sharp fingernails. Samuel could see clearly now that this was no woman; this was a witch!

As soon as the witch transformed into her true, gruesome shape, she screeched so loudly that she seemed to have made time come to a halt. In the distance, the prince could hear Earabis making noises and trying to break free while neighing as loud as he could.

The witch bent her knees and looked up to the sky as if preparing for flight. The prince charged toward her. As soon as he was close enough, he swung his sword at the beast, aiming for her wings so that she could not fly.

WHACK! The sword connected with one of the wings and tore a hole in it. The witch screamed in pain and quickly shot a hateful gaze at the prince. She then took her good winged arm, her claws fully extended, and aimed straight for the head of the prince. As her arm came slashing, the prince raised his sword and hopped back. The distance was not enough, though; the claws of the beast missed the prince's head but scratched his exposed chest as he held the sword high above his head.

"ARGHHH!" The prince roared in pain as he stumbled back and fell partly to the ground on his right leg. Quickly realizing the amount of damage that this creature could inflict with a single blow, the prince ignored the pain and got back on his feet. He charged toward the wounded beast and began slashing at her. She in return struck back, each blow drawing blood from the hero, but not enough to wound him mortally.

The prince parried and blocked the beast as her arms swung left and then right, trying to tear the prince to small pieces. Next, the prince spun around in a small circle and ducked to his knees while swinging his sword downward.

SLICE! He cut one leg off the beast. SLICE! Again, the prince connected his sword with the other leg of the beast, and at once she was forced to bow in front of the prince. With little life left in her, the beast still tried to claw at the prince. The prince stepped back and prepared to deal a final blow. As his sword swung from right to left across his chest, he brought it to within inches of the witch's throat and came to an abrupt halt.

The prince wanted nothing more than to end the

miserable, evil existence of the witch's life. However, something spoke from deep within. The inner voice calmed his anger and told Samuel to show mercy to his adversary. He could not explain the feeling that was washing away his anger like a tidal wave that washes away sand on a beach.

"Why did you try to trick me?" the prince demanded. "Is it true that all of these trees are men that you lured to your camp in the past so that you could make slaves of them?"

"Yes, it is all true, Prince. I am the witch you have read about in your storybooks. I am the one that haunted these woods in search of weary travelers for almost a thousand years," the witch said in a raspy voice, barely able to speak.

"I shall spare your life, but you must release the men you have bound and live the rest of your life in peace." As the prince finished speaking, the witch began to glow brighter and brighter, until there was an explosion.

BOOM!

The prince was flung from the blast, and he landed on his back. When the smoke cleared from the explosion, the witch stood before him in her original, beautiful form, healed of all injuries from the fight. So was Samuel. The witch's purple pendant glowed brightly on her chest, its color growing ever more luminescent. The glow died down, returning the stone to its original color.

Prince Samuel not only felt a weight lifted from his chest, as if killing this woman would have been a grave mistake, but he also noticed that something else was different. It was the trees. The faces were gone. The witch had fulfilled Samuel's request.

The witch stood before him in a clean, white gown. She walked to the prince and smiled. When she spoke, her voice was kind. "Through your compassion, I am now free. I have been a prisoner for a time longer than I can remember. Here, take this."

She handed Samuel the pendant she wore. "I do not need it anymore. When you find true love, give the pendant to her. She will use it to defeat the evil you seek to destroy. This pendant has been with me longer than I can remember. It was given to me by my father, who once tried to battle the wizard but met his end. The pendant keeps hope alive when there is none; so, take it, Samuel, both as a gift for freeing me and as a reward for not falling victim to me. The wizard has controlled me for a thousand years. The only reason I am not dead is because of this pendant."

As she handed the prince the pendant, she kissed him on the cheek. But before the prince could respond, the woman faded until she was gone.

Samuel stood alone with more questions but few answers. What powers did the pendant possess? Did the woman mean for him to give it to Kristina? He did not want Kristina to be engaged in any type of fighting with the wizard at all. Yet Kristina was his true love.

Shaking off the thoughts and questions for now, the prince dusted himself off. He knew the rest of his answers would come in time. He made his way back to Earabis, who was still struggling to break free of his reins.

Untying the reins from the tree, Samuel apologized to his friend. "I'm sorry, old friend. Next time I will listen with my head instead of my stomach – although I suppose that a lot of what I felt was the witch's enchantment. I thought I was done for. Can you ever forgive me, buddy?" Earabis just nodded as the prince mounted the saddle. They continued down the dark path past the battle-ridden encampment.

Soon they found a small clearing where they could rest for the night, as both were in need of a good night's sleep. His battle with the witch had showed Samuel how much further the wizard was willing to go to keep him from his quest than Samuel had imagined. The battle also reminded the prince that he should trust his friend Earabis, who would without question give his life for the prince.

The next day Earabis and the prince continued their journey through the forest. During the long hours of the day, the prince thought about all he had learned and contemplated the future he would have made for himself should he have continued to drink from the cup. After the spell the wizard had put on him, forcing him to pass a series of tests or perish in an unknown realm, Samuel wondered about the future. If this is only the wizard's first line of defenses, then what other trials lie ahead?

The prince's determination grew. He knew that if he was to save the princess from a horrible fate of captivity and abuse by the wizard, he must remain vigilant, no matter the cost.

The sun began to slip below the tree-lined horizon, and as the prince and Earabis rode over a final hill in the forest, they began to see the trees grow thin. A vast expanse quickly opened before the two.

Desert lay ahead of them, hot and dry and forbidding, and the prince knew it. He halted Earabis by one of the few remaining groves of trees to make camp for the night. He gathered necessary materials for a shelter and built a small fire. After finding a pheasant, the prince made a meal of it while Earabis gnawed away at one of few lush trees remaining in the sparsely vegetated area.

After the meal, the prince lay next to the fire, drifting away to sleep and thinking about the princess. He remembered how his heart stopped along with his world the first time he set eyes upon her. Even now, just a small thought of her seemed to stop all time and space around him. Nothing mattered on the desolate forest floor except for the one thought he held of the princess.

He held it tightly on this night. It was the promise from her to him, and it kept him warm with hope. In a way, he dreaded what lay on his path ahead, but he also felt joy at the fact that some of the harsh trials of his journey were behind him, bringing him closer to the woman who would one day become his queen. Already, she was his queen in his heart, and his heart would be the one thing to guide him in his journey to save her. The rescue of the princess ultimately meant saving himself, for the prince was nothing without his queen.

CHAPTER VI

The Desert

SADDLING Earabis, Samuel watched for a moment as the sun broke through the darkness and toward the distant sands he had to cross. Thoughts of Kristina kept him company, provoking passion for her freedom and directing him on his path. The thought of her served as a moral compass. His longing to be with the princess and to see her face grew stronger with every hoof beat.

Riding for hours in the hot desert through blasts of hot air that felt like the breath of a furnace in the underworld, the prince and the horse could feel their strength evaporating quickly. Samuel and Earabis needed water, and Earabis needed rest.

Kristina, however, needed to be rescued, and in order to free her, Samuel had to focus on something else other than his pain. It would require great endurance to complete just this task ahead of him now. He knew that others had attempted to cross the desert before him and given all they had, but it was not enough. Samuel would have to press himself farther through the sweltering sun and blistering air than he had ever thought possible.

He rode for hours more until the sun began to fade into the horizon and night air slowly offered cool winds and a bright, starlit sky. It's finally time to rest for the day, he thought to himself. I need to find wood, shelter, water, and if possible, some food.

The night brought feelings of loneliness and peace at the same time. The prince found a small snake under a nearby rock bed, built a fire, roasted the meager meal, and sat next to his fire to finish it. The embers from the fire sparked and reminded him of his childhood, when there was no wizard to be fought or any desert to be crossed.

As the fire danced with the cool evening desert wind, his thoughts carried him to sleep. When the prince awoke, the sun was barely cresting the desolate horizon, but the air already stale with heat served as a warning to him that the day would be hotter still.

Breaking camp, Samuel extinguished the fire and erased any signs that would show he had stopped in the area, just in case anyone or anything tried to pick up his trail. After saddling his horse, he rode into the already hot morning sun, gaining ground between him and the princess he must save. Saving her ultimately meant saving himself, because he could not live without her.

With each hoof beat that struck the ground, his body rose briefly and then fell back down onto the saddle of the horse. Womph! Womph! Womph! Earabis' hooves went as he sped quickly across the rugged desert. What seemed like days actually turned out to be just another full day of riding that led into another night of little rest in the wilderness.

When they stopped, it was so dark that Samuel couldn't see anything around him. He removed the horse's saddle and bridle and spoke gently to him. "Earabis, lay down, boy. You need to keep your head down so that you won't get beat up by the desert sand when the wind picks up."

Earabis moved over to his friend and slowly became one with the ground. His reclining bulk offered the prince some protection from the elements as well. As Prince Samuel drifted into a troubled sleep, he found comfort in his only friend.

Another morning roused the prince, this time with a covering of frost and an air that made his breath visible every time he exhaled. "All right, Earabis - where did all that heat from yesterday go, my friend?"

Earabis just stood up and grunted a little as his way of saying that he did not know, but he could understand the discomfort that went with experiencing the bitter cold first thing in the morning. The prince caught a small rodent to eat and found some thorny foliage for Earabis. Their breakfast was a small one, but the meal would provide valuable energy for the day ahead.

The prince and Earabis gained ground across the

desert, but as the sun rose, the temperature did, too. There was still much flatland to cross with nothing more to entertain either of them than the crest of the horizon. So they rode together on a quest that would take not one, but many miracles from the creator of all things to fulfill. Impossible scenarios raced through Samuel's thoughts just as Earabis raced through the desert.

After a time, the noble steed's pace went from a full gallop to a trot and then to a slow walk. As the horse slowed, the prince slouched. The two travelers were growing weary as the sun grew hotter. How much longer till the day ends? thought the prince, while his eyes searched the area for some sign of cover and hopefully some water.

Earabis, as strong as he was, showed signs of weakness on this day. The pair had been traveling for nearly a week with little in the way of comfort or supply. The lack of sleep through each night along with limited amounts of food and water had finally taken its toll. Prince Samuel and Earabis found themselves moving more slowly with each beat of Earabis' hooves.

The prince knew that his friend needed just as much rest as he did; the only thing he could think of doing was to dismount Earabis and walk next to him. When he began, the prince could see that Earabis disagreed with the action. As a friend and companion on the same quest, Earabis knew that the prince's life meant more than his, and if giving his life meant that the prince could take one more step towards defeating the wizard and bringing peace to the land, then Earabis would freely give his life.

But Earabis couldn't make the prince ride, could he?

As Prince Samuel slowly walked next to Earabis, his feet dragged deeper into the sand. Samuel felt like trees had been tied to his legs, making moving just a few feet seem that much more impossible. "My good friend, I am afraid that if we do not find water soon, we surely will not survive this place."

Earabis could sense the danger rising with each step the prince took in the thick sand. He knew without a doubt that something had to be done, and done quickly. If someone did not save them soon, all hope would be lost.

So Earabis moved behind the prince, bowed, and pushed his long nose into Samuel's back as if forcing him to take more steps. Samuel assumed that Earabis meant to let him know that as long as his heart beat in his chest, the noble steed would not desert his friend.

The horse thought of a plan, and he knew he had one shot at it because the prince was losing consciousness. Soon Samuel would fall, and he would not get back to his feet again. If the prince fell to the ground, this plan would fail, because Earabis needed him on his feet in order for his trick to work.

After another subtle nudge from Earabis, the prince beckoned the horse to leave him be. Then another nudge, and the prince still asked to be left alone. Then another and another, until finally Earabis took a few steps back, aimed, and charged for his friend.

He trotted as fast as he could to ensure that the momentum was just enough to lift the prince into the air and land him on his back so that he could carry him the rest of the way. He charged and kept his gaze fixed upon his target, knowing that this move had to be timed just right with the prince's awkward footsteps.

Closing the distance between himself and his friend, Earabis ducked his head between the legs of the prince and lifted him up in the air, just enough to clear the horse's mane. The prince let out a loud "UMPHH" and passed out as he landed on Earabis's back.

Earabis cantered into the sun with a passion that he, as a horse, had never before felt for any living thing. He was tired and broken from the journey, and he could feel his body giving out with every beat of his hooves. But his pain did not matter. Getting the prince to safety was what mattered.

So he rode straight into the hot sun as if provoking the sun to radiate more heat and to give the desert everything it had, because the horse would defeat the sun. For the rest of the day, Earabis charged toward the sun, determined that the next time he would stop was when he had brought the prince to safety.

Later, Samuel opened his eyes, and they adjusted to the dim light of the evening sky. As he awoke, he found Earabis making a dinner of a small bush. The horse tugged and pulled viciously at the branches, taking bite after bite. Sitting up, the prince felt a soreness he had not felt in ages. The last time he had felt this sore was when he spent his first few weeks alone in the wilderness. Now he longed for his father, the kingdom, and a warm bed.

Thoughts like those could not do him any good, and within an instant of realizing so, he was up on his feet. He walked over to Earabis and ran his hand down the long, black mane of the strong, brown horse, appreciating the fine muscles in his neck. "You are one true friend; you know that, Earabis?" said the prince.

Earabis stopped wrestling with the bush for a moment, turned his head, and nodded toward the prince as if saying it was he who was honored to be the prince's friend.

Patting the steed once more, the prince looked

around the immediate area in search of water.

Sparse brush littered the landscape, along with a few trees and some tall, weed-like grass. The prince could not tell the fine details of the area due to nightfall; however, he was able to tell that they were out of the worst of the desert. One problem still existed though; there was no water to be found.

So the prince broke a sturdy branch off one of the trees and began to dig. He knew that even though Earabis could survive and regain his strength on green brush, they both needed water. As Samuel began to dig, he felt the stiffness of his muscles give a little bit, and he was grateful for the laborious task.

Not more than a few feet into the ground next to a tree, the sand gave way, and a hole opened. The hole was no more than a few feet deep by a few feet wide, and in this hole was a large supply of clear water. The walls of the hole were lined with stiff clay.

The prince at once got down on his knees and started to drink the water as if it was the first time he had ever tasted such a substance. Seeing this from the corner of his eye, Earabis joined his companion in drinking the fine, clear water. After the two had drunk their fill, the prince stood for a moment in silence, thinking.

"Boy, you really did it this time, Earabis. Do you see this?" said the prince excitedly as he picked up some of the clay that surrounded the pool of water. "Do you know where you brought us to, old friend? This clay means we are close to the mountain! We are one step closer to completing this journey!"

The horse, unable to speak, lifted his front right leg in a gesture that shared the prince's happiness at his discovery.

"Okay, my friend, I'm going to find some food that will go down a little smoother than leaves off a bush," grinned the prince.

Earabis sputtered at his friend as if to tell him there was nothing wrong with a good bit of green Evan brush, and went back to feasting on his plant.

"Oh, don't walk away mad! After I get some food, I will make a fire, and we can settle in for a good night's rest," said the prince.

Earabis, already heading back to his meal, just flicked his tail in the prince's direction and set to eating the rest of his dinner.

The prince had his fill of water and rest, but now he needed some food to regain his energy. Unsheathing his knife, he walked away from the small camp and stalked his evening prey.

In the past, hunting was easier. When he was young and lived in the kingdom under his father, he could go on the grounds as he pleased and hunt away at the game that was preserved for the king and his royal family. When he lived in the woods on his own, he was secluded and only hunted when he needed. The animals were plentiful, because he was the main predator.

Now, the prince was in the desert. Though the area contained more foliage and signs of life, it was still the desert. Everything fought to survive in this desolate place. Nothing in the desert submitted for free; everything here, including the hole of water that the prince had had to dig, fought for survival in some way. So here the prince had to fight for his survival.

After walking some distance from the area, the prince found a prime spot with enough cover to conceal himself, and he waited patiently. Soon, a lizard the size of the prince's arm crawled into view. Slowly it moved, being careful to attract no attention to itself, for it was seeking an evening meal, too.

As the prince looked at the lizard, his heart began to beat and his stomach growl. This would be an excellent meal, he thought to himself. The lizard did not take notice of the prince; he crept closer to the prince, never looking directly at him but to his left and right. In this game of stalker and stalked, the prince thought about his current situation and was able to relate to the lizard. The more the lizard took his eyes off the danger, the closer he was to danger itself.

Even closer now, the lizard came to the prince's concealed position. The prince could feel his mouth watering. His plans to roast the creature to a crisp golden brown were becoming more of a reality with each step the lizard took toward the prince.

Within moments, the lizard was so close that the prince could almost feel the tongue of the animal flickering on his nose. The lizard used his tongue not only to see but to smell for danger in the area.

His tongue failed him on this night.

No sooner did the lizard come within inches of the prince, than the prince brought forward his knife, raised it in the air at an angle, and slammed the sharp tip of the weapon into the lizard's side. The lizard jerked, squealed, and froze. Then the lizard's heart stopped, for it was a quick death.

The prince never saw the point in torturing an animal to its death when ultimately it was a gift from the creator, one that would nourish him in his journey. "Sorry, fella, you're going to make a good meal tonight, and I promise to do good in the world with the energy you give me," said the prince gratefully.

Samuel picked up the carcass and moved back to the camp, only to find Earabis finishing up the last of the bush he'd started earlier. The prince started gathering the necessary supplies to build a fire for the night to cook his trophy dinner and keep him and his companion warm and protected from the night's cold air. Once the fire was built, he had to skin his dinner.

The lizard's skin was tough, almost too tough to cut. The lizard obviously developed this trait after living a life in the realm's harshest conditions. After the prince was able to break through the first layer of thick leather, there was yet another and then finally the prized meat. Samuel saw that his knife had entered a small, softer spot that he had been lucky to hit.

Samuel dug a hole and disposed of the bones and head of the animal. He did keep the skin, however, knowing that it could serve as an excellent pair of gloves for future endeavors. Any material that gave his knife trouble was sure to prove its worth in other valuable ways. He knew he would have to climb a mountain soon, and he could not afford to pass up this kind of protection for his hands.

As the prince roasted his meal, Earabis came over near him and sat on the ground behind the prince, affording Samuel the opportunity to use him as a pillow. Samuel sat back against his friend and finished cooking his dinner. After he was done, the prince watched the fire dance him into a deep, welcome slumber.

His slumber did not stay peaceful long – a dream found him.

He was running toward the small cottage, searching frantically for an entrance as panic threatened to overcome his mind. Pushing against various parts of the outside of the cottage, he felt a section of board give way, and pushing inward, he stepped through the entrance. Entering the house, he found that he was actually stepping through a tall grandfather clock.

As soon as the prince was completely through the clock and inside the house, the clock's door slammed shut, and both hands on the face reset to twelve and did not move. The prince took one look at the clock and began to search the house frantically, as if his life and the lives of others depended on it. He did not know why, but for some reason, time seemed to be rushing him to hurry on his journey.

The prince looked around the downstairs of the cottage, searching all the rooms for signs of life, but he found none. He searched the closets and even the cupboards in the kitchen, yet to no avail. While in the kitchen, the prince noticed a tall door, and upon opening it, he found a staircase that led to the second story. This puzzled the prince, because from the outside, he could see the cottage as only a single floor.

The urge to search grew tremendously strong as the prince eyed the huge staircase that led to the unknown. So the prince ascended to the top floor of the cottage. Being careful not to alert any enemy that may be waiting for him, the prince treaded lightly on the sides of each stair to decrease the noise he made while moving upward. As he emerged in the center of the top floor's hallway and the top floor came into view, the prince noticed that there were four rooms.

There were two rooms to his immediate left and right, and two rooms to the left and right behind him. Beside the rooms behind him, there was yet another staircase that seemed to disappear into the ceiling. The prince began to search the rooms at once, finding nothing in the room to his immediate right. The rooms to his back left and right turned up empty as well. It was the room to his front left that bugged him as he entered the hall from the staircase. He saved this room for last, because he was afraid of what it may reveal. Slowly, the prince approached the door and turned the handle.

As he stepped into the room, he found it empty. Out the windows facing the east, however, he could see the twin towers of the monastery. The view was like that of his old room in the castle. He was caught up in a series of memories at this point, smelling the fresh grass, hearing the bells ring, and feeling the sun rise on his face in the early mornings. Wherever he had been brought, he did not want to leave.

Then, snapping him out of his memories, he heard a loud scream coming from above. "Ah! Hurry, Prince, hurry!" came the sound of a young girl's voice. The only place the prince had left to search was the staircase that led to the ceiling; so he headed directly for it. Ascending to the top of this staircase, he pushed on the ceiling, and it opened to the final floor of the cottage.

There in the corner of the room were two girls who waved him away from where they sat. The prince paid no attention and at once drew close to the girls to save them from whatever danger they faced. As he stepped onto the rug the girls were on, the prince heard a loud click, followed by the chiming of the grandfather clock. "Hurry, Prince, we only have sixty seconds to get out of here before the clock's door seals us in the house for good."

The prince grabbed both of the young girls in his arms and literally jumped down the first flight of stairs. Time was not on his side. He had yet another staircase and more rooms to cross before he reached the clock itself.

Fleeing even faster, the prince hurried down the second flight of stairs and through the kitchen.

Twenty seconds now remained before the clock would shut its doors permanently. From the kitchen, the prince made his way through the main room and down the hall to the clock itself. Once at the clock, the prince noticed two problems. The opening itself was shrinking, and it would take just a few seconds for each person to get through. The clock showed only ten seconds remaining.

The prince picked up the smaller of the two girls and pushed her through immediately. Eight seconds remaining. Then the prince began to push the older of the two girls through, but she hesitated. All of the sudden, time stopped.

The older sister turned back to look at the prince, her eyes glowing a fiery blue. Grabbing the prince's wrist, she said, "Follow the mountain to the abyss, for the abyss will lead you to the castle. The castle will lead you to the princess, and the princess will lead you to us."

As her hand gripped Samuel's wrist, it started to produce a white light. The prince felt a burning on his hand. Time all of the sudden resumed, and with only seconds left, the prince picked up the oldest girl and pushed her through. Once she was through, the door slammed shut, and all went dark.

He was trapped.

The prince awoke, yelling, "No!" He sat up, shaking in a cold sweat.

He was loud enough that Earabis woke from sleep as well, lifting his head. He looked at the prince and lay back down.

The prince felt something burning on his hand; he looked down and noticed that there was a mark composed of a straight line with small dots. The prince had not the slightest clue as to what the meaning of this mark was. He gazed at the glowing embers of the fire trying to figure out exactly what the dream meant and why he felt such raw emotion. After a few hours, the sun crested the horizon, welcoming Samuel to a new day.

Chapter VII

The Mountain

WITH the great sandy plains of the scorching desert to his back, the prince felt that a harder task lay ahead. In the midst of the sky rose a mountain of astronomical size. It shot straight up through the clouds until it disappeared into the heavens.

How am I ever going to get over it? he thought to himself in disbelief. The mountains were intimidating, shouting to the prince that he should turn back if he didn't want to meet his demise. The prince shook off the feeling of despair and moved forward, approaching the base of the mountain.

This was not a well-traveled area. Getting his horse through the rough terrain that lay ahead would be a problem. Deciding that climbing this mountain would be a sure death for his valiant companion, he began to untie Earabis's reins.

As Samuel unloaded the equipment, Earabis could sense that something was wrong; so he drew close to the prince. Not being able to speak, the horse bowed his head in respect and nudged the prince.

"Oh, come on, boy, you know that you can't make it over the mountain. It's far too steep! Besides, they do not have the Goji berries that you love so much, and you tend to become nice and grumpy when you don't get your fill of those," Samuel teased.

The horse stomped his lead foot on the ground, pursing his lips and sputtering some air at the prince to tell him that even though he had to go, he could still be stubborn. Once more the horse nudged the prince, beckoning him not to go on the path without him.

"Okay, Earabis, you can follow me up the trail until we hit the first cliff. There we will stay the night, and after that, you must go on your way. Head back to Captain Steven, and let him know I made it to the mountains."

With those words, Earabis neighed loudly in approval. Prince Samuel packed his things back on his strong friend, and they both began the journey up the mountain together.

The path was wide with thick trees on both sides. The prince could hear all kinds of small forest animals in the distance, and their presence comforted him, as he knew that they would have fled any evil in the immediate area.

For most of his mission, his thoughts had focused on the princess and how he would save her. He focused now on how he would overcome all the obstacles that lay ahead. And on this day, a new obstacle arose.

It was not a physical obstacle per se. It was an obstacle of loss, one that he knew he would have to face in the morning when he and his noble friend and companion Earabis would have to part ways. He would have to face the rest of his journey alone. Prince Samuel had not accounted for this loss earli-

er. He'd figured he would have Earabis with him the whole time; so the thought of being alone dampened his spirits.

As the two continued up the path, Earabis stopped, and then suddenly he started to buck forcefully, almost to the point where Prince Samuel lost his grip on the reins. "What is it, boy? Easy, easy," the prince said in a calming tone.

Then out of the bushes, the biggest snake the prince had ever seen slithered his way out from the cover. Raring up until the snake reached the height of the horse, he stopped and looked at the two heroes with anger and disgust.

Suddenly the prince drew his sword with a speed and fierceness that he had not known before. Stepping in front of his friend Earabis, he prepared to engage in a fight to the death. Earabis bucked harder in an attempt to beat the snake with his hooves.

"HALT!" the snake rasped. "I am not here to cause you harm or fight you. I am nothing more than a messenger sent by the wizard." As the snake said this, he lowered himself to the height of the prince and moved in closer.

"Then speak quickly before I have your head, serpent, for no messenger of the wizard is a friend of truth or justice," the prince said with a steely gaze, his eyes fixed upon his target in case this was some sort of a trap. Earabis remained ever vigilant.

"This is a warning," whispered the snake. "Turn back now, or you will surely die. All that you know will be wiped off the face of this realm. Your kingdom will suffer much pain, and the princess you long so desperately to see will remain a prisoner for the rest of her days if you continue in your attempt to rescue her. All will be lost, princccccce," said the serpent with a loud hiss on his last word.

"And what makes you think I will listen to such a claim from the likes of you, one sent by the wizard?" the prince said angrily.

"The wizard has offered a truce," the snake informed him calmly. "If you turn back now, he will grant you power over the people in your land. You will have riches unimaginable, and there will be no man who can stand against you. Refuse this deal, and you will face your doom, princccccce." This time the serpent put even more emphasis on the last word of his sentence.

The prince could tell that this hiss was the sign of an arising anger in the serpent; so he remained vigilant. "Let me ask you something, serpent. How is it that you intend to relay my answer to the wizard? How will you get back to tell him what I am doing when I know that the great abyss lies through this mountain pass? You cannot cross alone."

"My master is aware of everything I do, for my thoughts are connected with his. Within no more than an instant, I can see what he is thinking, and he can see what I am thinking. We are one force that is too great to conquer, princcccccccce," the snake boasted.

"Then be on your way and out of mine; our business is done here," said the prince.

"Prince Samuel, I must advise you that even though I came here with no intent to harm you, I must not let you proceed on this journey." With those words, the snake reared up once again and arched back, intending to strike.

The prince stood his ground and readied his stance. But Earabis charged straight for the snake, knocking the prince out of the way. He stomped on the ground close to the serpent and smashed his huge tail. The serpent loudly squealed and hissed.

The serpent's mouth grew wide, and he darted straight for Earabis, who was stomping on the snake even harder out of anger as well as to protect Prince Samuel. Out of the corner of his eye, Earabis noticed the snake aiming for his stomach and realized that he would not be able to move out of the way quickly enough. Afraid, Earabis sensed his impending doom.

And then the prince's sword came down lightning fast, and he cut off the head of the serpent. "Send that answer back to the wizard, you vile creature!" spat the prince in disgust.

"Earabis, are you okay, boy? Let me check you out," the prince said as he searched Earabis for any sign of a bite from the foul serpent. The prince could find no mark, and for a moment, he just stared at the dead carcass of his attacker, wondering just how many more traps lay ahead until he could finally do battle with the wizard himself.

After the prince was satisfied that Earabis was not injured, he mounted the horse and directed him to keep walking. Earabis carried the prince through miles of a winding trail that was the size of a normal road. To the left, a steep wall shot straight up; to the right, a cliff shot straight down. So the only thing left to do was to follow the tree-lined trail until it became impassable for Earabis.

The two traveled throughout the day, and the day grew colder with each hour. As the sun began to fade, the prince halted Earabis. Traveling at night on a path that kept getting steeper and narrower could only lead to disaster.

The prince built a small shelter and a fire for the pair to keep warm. "Well, my friend, we are going to have to rest here. In the morning I am going to have to continue alone. Go back to my father's kingdom and deliver this note to Captain Steven. It will explain what has happened and prepare the kingdom for war should I not return." Samuel stuffed the note in a pouch on the saddle and latched it shut.

Being a horse, Earabis could not speak, but he could show emotion in his movements. His gestures told the prince that he did not want to part. He'd just reunited with his dear friend mere weeks ago, and now he was being told to go back home. Earabis didn't know if he would ever see his friend again. The horse's heart felt grief. Earabis walked over to Samuel, sat down behind him, and turned his head as if he were trying to hug the prince. The prince patted his friend in return, and they both sat next to the warm fire and drifted into a deep sleep.

As the sun rose above the horizon, the prince woke to see that the fire from the night prior was now smoldering. It produced little heat, but it was just alive enough for the prince to revive it so that he and Earabis could enjoy the warmth one last time together before they parted. The prince gathered some food and made a meal while Earabis found some leaves to eat. Breakfast ended, and it was now time for the two heroes to part ways once again.

"Earabis, you are the best friend I could have ever

asked for. Thank you for being there during all my times of trouble. I am sure there are many times in the future where I will need your assistance, but I must go alone on this road ahead. Make sure Captain Steven gets my note, okay? And make sure you ride as fast as you can to get back home. Take the path back down the mountain, and then head straight south for three days. Then I want you to cut east. When you see green lands, you will know you are almost back home. This shortcut will save you from crossing the desert and the deadly forest. You will have to spend most of your time at the base of the mountain, but the dangers of our journey will be nowhere in sight, my friend," the prince explained as he unpacked his belongings.

As the prince was finishing, he began to move just a little slower than normal. He knew he had to journey alone, but he just did not want to. He knew great danger lay ahead, and for the first time in months, perhaps years, he was afraid. He knew this distinct type of fear, because it was the same fear he'd felt during his first few nights alone in the woods.

Uncertainty, danger, and an uncharted path ate at the prince's heart. With Earabis, he was able to draw strength in times of need. Now he would have to rely on himself and whatever blessings the creator would bestow on him.

"Okay, my friend, you are free. Go safely," the prince said as he drew close and looked Earabis in the eyes. The horse knew it was time to go; so he took one last look at the prince, arched back on his

hind legs, and let out a loud neigh. The horse landed on his front two legs, rubbed his nose against
the prince, and then trotted back down the mountain path.

The prince turned to look back at his friend, and
as Earabis was descending the path, he could see
the steed picking up speed. As Earabis faded out
of sight, the prince took a deep breath and picked
up his belongings. "Okay, it's just me and my feet
now. Let's go, feet," said the prince as he began to
head up the mountain and into the unknown.

As the prince ascended the mountain, the terrain grew much steeper than he was used to, and
he often found himself having to stop. The rapid
increase in elevation was making it hard for the
prince to breathe. The trail he traveled became totally unpredictable, for at times it would grow very
wide, while at other times it would become narrow.

Often, the prince found himself having to think
ahead lest he put his foot on ground that would
give way. As the prince continued on his journey,
he kept finding himself skirting the side of the
mountain at a very slow pace. The thin air and un-
even terrain were not the only problems, for as he
became more exposed to the elements, the wind
pushed and pulled the prince around. The prince
balanced with his hands and locked his position in
with his legs and feet as he moved along the steep
trails up the mountainside.

After a time, the steep trail started to widen a
little bit, and the prince found himself with more
room on both sides of his trail. Though he was

steadier now, he was much colder. The wind chilled the prince as he traveled higher onto the mountain, and he found the sun dipping below the mountain's crest. The temperature followed suit and dipped to near freezing. The prince knew at this point that he needed to find shelter and prepare for a very long and cold night ahead.

The prince stopped at the sight of a small cave ahead. He quickly rushed to it, took a look inside, and found it had been abandoned for some time. Samuel set his belongings down and headed back outside the cave to search for materials to build a shelter and a fire. After an hour, Samuel had constructed a nice blockade that would deny the wind access to the cave. This one structure alone helped to preserve the temperature and keep it from dropping to deathly levels. After constructing the covering for the cave, the prince built a fire and quickly fell asleep.

The prince exited the cave when morning came and left no trace of his night's stay. The landscape began to spread out as he traveled deeper into the mountain, and looked more like a forest with endless rolling hills. He knew he was high on the mountain at this point, but he began to fear that he was losing his sense of direction.

The mountain was vast; little sunlight shone during the day save a faded glow through the snowy clouds that clustered above in the sky. The snow began to fall with rushing winds and a freezing temperature. The prince traveled up and down hills on the mountain only to find yet another.

Is there any way out of this endless terrain? the prince wondered.

The prince continued his movement as the ground turned into a white, formless blanket that mimicked the features of the mountain. The trees were thick and laden with snow that covered the green pine needles. The prince knew he could never climb one of the trees to find his way, as he once had when he was a child. In this part of the mountain, branches grew only toward the tops of the massive, hundred-foot trees. He had no way of getting to the top and finding a route out of this forsaken place.

The prince's journey during the following days was long and agonizing. He found little food, for few things lived at such a high elevation. Snow soaked the wood from the trees, making a fire almost impossible to bring to life. The prince had little hope during the cold nights except to dig a deep enough hole to crawl into so that he could block the wind.

After a week of moving through the mountain in this manner, the harsh conditions had taken a toll on the prince's hope. He never knew what it felt like to give up, and spiritually, he was far from it, however, he was at an end physically.

The wind was blowing harder than ever, making the snow a thick, white wall. The prince could only see in front of him about as far as he could step, and as he took each step, he slowly sank up to his knees. He was using all his might to gather strength for one more step.

Samuel began ascending a hill. The hill was steep, but at least the snow was not deep on the incline.

Still, the prince required more strength than usual to make each step.

As the prince reached the top of the hill, he was out of breath, drained of all his strength, and barely able to move one more foot. A flat part of the hill overlooked a frozen lake. As Samuel stared at the lake, he remembered the pond back home in the kingdom where he used to sit and read with Kristina.

Suddenly the medallion around his neck glowed, and the princess appeared. She was the last thought that he could muster as he dropped to the ground and passed out.

He was asleep, but another part of him was not. That part of him was walking with his mother in a field. She strode ahead, and he followed her straight, slim back and curly brown hair. He grew tired, and so he went to lie down next to a tree. His eyes closed. She came over to him and told him to get up.

"Get up, Samuel. Get up. You must get up, Samuel," a voice urged him.

Samuel was coming out of a dream-like, hazy state as he felt the cold ground pressed against the right side of his face. His lips were moving, and the taste of the snow on the ground brought him back to the world of the conscious.

The voice was still speaking. "Get up, Samuel, get up. Your time has not come yet."

As Samuel became more aware of his surroundings, he realized that the voice was his own. Samuel snapped out of his state of sleep at once, and his eyes shot open. His mother's voice was echoing in his head as he was waking up.

When he awoke, he did not find the woman with curly brown hair and a calming voice. He found only himself echoing her words in the wilderness. With no choice but to arise, Samuel picked himself up and began to stumble around in the dark. He could see the moonlight's reflection off the lake ahead; however, that was barely enough illumination for him to move any great distance. He was still very tired and weak, almost to the point of freezing to death.

The prince looked around, trying to concoct a plan to keep alive, but none came to mind. As he looked to his right, he could see a figure not ten feet from where he stood. The figure was glowing, with a hint of blue to its aura, and its features told him that the glowing being was a woman.

Samuel stared, paralyzed, as the woman walked toward him. She seemed familiar, too familiar, though he knew he had never before seen her face. As she approached, he saw that she had two floating yellow orbs with her. The orbs seems to be chasing each other in circles, and for a moment the prince thought he could hear one of the orbs laughing. It was a high-pitched, fast-paced laugh, one that made him feel calm and almost ready to laugh himself.

Samuel began to step back; as the being slowly came closer toward him, he was still unable to speak. "Who, who are you? What are you?" Samuel said, intrigued.

"Samuel, do not be afraid," the woman said softly. He suddenly recognized her voice; it was the voice from his dream. As he spoke, the figure came into clear view; her glow lit the area all around her. He could see her face and her hair. It was curly and brown.

He had never met this woman before, but he knew in an instant who she was. "Mother!" Samuel said, running toward her. She opened her arms and embraced her son, and the two hugged each other. He stepped back and could see that his mother was laughing joyfully.

"Samuel, it is good to see you! The creator has given me permission to help you for a short time on your journey. Ablewis is very powerful, and the creator sent me to your aid," Samuel's mother said as she held her son's face in the palm of her hand.

Samuel felt the touch of his mother and was comforted. He had never met his mother; he had only heard stories from Cleric Jeremy about what a great woman she had been.

"First, I know you are cold, tired, and hungry. I have brought guardians to attend to your needs, my dear son," smiled Queen Kathleen. "Summer, Laci, come and help Samuel. We need to make a fire and a shelter and prepare some food for him to eat." The two orbs of bright yellow light sped toward Samuel, flying in figure eights. The smaller of the two balls of light kept breaking into a high-pitched giggle. Samuel started to laugh as well.

"Hey, Laci, check this out. Kathleen taught me a new trick!" Summer giggled. Summer, with her white wings and jaw-length, short brown hair, was a happy spirit who brought Kathleen much joy.

Summer arched back her hand above her head, and in one swift motion she threw her arm toward the ground, pointing at a spot. WahBOOM! There was a bright flash of light, and a hurdle of blue sparks landed on the ground. The smoke cleared in an instant to reveal a furry little creature.

"Um, oops!" Summer giggled. "Well, Samuel, maybe this bunny will keep you warm!" Summer said as she giggled away and petted the little creature.

"Summer, let me show you how to do this. How many times do I have to tell you? You have to concentrate on the object you want to appear," Laci said to her sister. Laci had deep blue eyes and longer brown hair that went down to her waist.

Laci chose a spot on the ground and pointed her finger. WahBOOM! Another bright flash appeared with yellow sparks, and there was a roaring fire on the ground. "See, you just have to concentrate on what you want, Summer, and it will appear," Laci instructed.

"Now to make the shelter." Laci found an open area to the left of the fire. She pointed her finger at the empty space and focused. WahBOOM! On the ground appeared a life-size gingerbread house. "Well, Samuel, not only can you sleep in it, but you can eat as much as you like!" Laci said, mildly embarrassed at her handiwork.

Samuel could do nothing but laugh. His two gracious hosts had genuinely entertained him, and the fire was already warming him up from the long days of suffering the cold in the wilderness.

"Okay, Laci, watch how it's done," Summer said as she floated in front of her sister. She aimed at the gingerbread house and pointed her finger. She concentrated really hard and all of the sudden: WahBOOM! A three-sided shelter appeared in place of the candy house. The inside of the shelter was lined with animal fur. The walls were tightly sealed with mud, and the frame was made of hardened oak. The top of the shelter had three feet of pine needles to ensure that the structure was water-proof.

"Mother, your friends here are really talented. I see I can have anything from a bunny to a ginger-bread house! Where did you find these two charac-ters?" asked Samuel.

"Well, Mr. Samuel, that is for us to know and you to find out!" Summer said as she floated up to Sam-uel and tapped him on the nose with her finger. She floated away giggling.

"Oh, Summer - be nice. Samuel, we have known your mother ever since she joined us in the cre-ator's realm some time ago. We have watched you grow up over the years, and when we heard that Kathleen, or should I say Grandma Kathy, was com-ing to help you, we begged and pleaded until she said it was okay for us to join," Laci explained.

"Ah, I see, and from the looks of it, it didn't take much convincing," Samuel said as he pointed to Summer, who was busy playing with the bunny on the ground.

"No, hardly any at all, Son. These two have been

a great comfort to me. I have missed you, and I am very proud of the man you have grown up to become," Kathleen said, putting her hand on Samuel's shoulder.

"I have missed you, too, Mother. I always wondered what you looked like. I was walking some time ago, and the last thing I remember was falling to the ground and seeing the lake in the distance. I had an odd dream, and you were in it. I awoke hearing your voice in a distance, but found

that I was the one speaking, but you were really in my dream! Was I really meeting my end, Mother?" Samuel asked.

"Yes, Samuel, I was in your dream, and yes, you were at your end. But the creator has decided it was not time for you to come home yet. He sent me with my two little guardians. They are here to help you for a time, Samuel. For now, my son, I want you to rest and regain your strength. Come and sit by the fire, and my two little helpers will make you something good to eat," Kathleen said.

Samuel sat down next to the shelter and warmed himself by the fire. As he waited, Laci and Summer prepared him a feast involving all kinds of foods the prince liked. They conjured up bowls of Goji berries, cheeses from the entire realm, meat from the finest animals in the land, and baked loaves of bread. The prince ate his fill while the two sisters played with the bunny that Summer had mistakenly conjured up.

Just watching the two little fairies and her son enjoying the evening made Kathleen content and filled her heart with joy. She was happy to come to her son's aid for once in his life. She knew he was a blessing and would have much greatness to fulfill. She prayed a silent prayer to the creator, as her son was eating, giving him thanks for the opportunity she had.

"I am very grateful for the help of the pixies, but I must turn in," Samuel said.

"Fairies," Summer said quietly.

"You have wings, and you glow. You shoot stuff out of your finger. You're a pixie. Sorry, I call it as I see it," Samuel grinned.

"Okay, bear. Yeah, you're a bear because you're as grouchy as one. Did a bear eat you at some time in your life, Samuel?" Summer giggled.

"Watch it, pixie, before I hang you by your feet and use you as a night-light," Samuel yawned as he covered himself up.

"Okay, you two! Just go to sleep!" Kathleen laughed. She could not help but find humor in the two arguing.

"All right, fine. I'll see you guys in the morning. Good night, Mother. Good night, pixies!" Samuel teased.

"Fairies!" both girls shouted back.

"All right, good night!" the prince exclaimed.

In the background, Samuel could hear Summer giggling and Laci yawning. Kathleen just sat next to the fire and stood watch over the camp as her son rested.

The next day, the prince awoke, and Kathleen was still sitting by the fire. The two girls were busy fixing the prince a breakfast fit for a king. The prince awoke refreshed. He felt better than he had in weeks. Uncovering himself, standing up, and exiting the shelter, the prince walked to his mother and sat down by the fire.

"I feared last night was a dream. I am very happy to see you, Mother," Samuel said as he hugged his mother.

"It is good to see you too, Son. Watching you from a distance, I have been able to observe your trials and struggles. After we have breakfast, I will reveal to you events that took place prior to your birth. First, though, let the girls make you breakfast. Laci! Summer! Let the bunny have some freedom for a moment, and come make Samuel breakfast," Kathleen said to the fairies.

"Gee, Samuel, all you have done since we met

you is eat and sleep. You're supposed to be saving the princess. What are you going to do, eat your way through the mountain and then just go to sleep and dream her up?" Summer said sarcastically as she floated away from the bunny.

"Summer, you should be nice to the prince. I am sure he has gone through a lot to this point, and he needs our help. Would you have been any match for the giant snake or the witch in the woods? No, I don't think so," Laci said as she floated next to the prince. She smiled at him and then looked at Summer, cocked her head, and smirked, suggesting she was going to get on the good side of the prince early in the day.

"Yeah, Summer, listen to your wiser sister here. You might learn something before I come through on that promise of making you into a night-light, you little pixie. Oh, and sorry, Laci, I meant fairy!" the prince said, laughing uncontrollably.

Smirking, Summer floated up to the prince's face and said, "Look, Prince, if you're not careful, I'll turn you into something worse than a bunny. I'll turn you into a... a..."

"You'll turn me into what? A prince! Sorry, Summer, got you beat on that one!" the prince smiled as he started to laugh again.

"A toad! Yeah, I'll turn you into a toad, with ugly warts on your face. And then you will have to wait until a princess comes along and kisses you!" Summer laughed and floated in circles.

"Okay! That is enough, you two. Laci, get breakfast started. Samuel, leave the poor fairy alone,"

Kathleen demanded.

Kathleen had longed to see her son grown to this point, and to her, this was a happy reunion. She could just enjoy being with Samuel while the fairies provided for him. They made a hearty breakfast of eggs, Goji berry pancakes, juice, and fruits of all kind. Some foods Laci conjured up as a treat that were not even known to anyone in the prince's realm.

The prince delighted in his breakfast and the comfort of good company. He was in desperate need of rest and nourishment, for the mountain had almost taken his life.

After breakfast, the fairies began playing with their newfound friend the bunny while Kathleen and Samuel went on a walk. Kathleen was happy just to listen to her son talk about the princess and his journey thus far.

He told his mother about the fears and dangers he had encountered. She knew already everything he had done and suffered, for she had watched him every step of the way.

She delighted in hearing the story from his point of view. She learned what gave him faith and kept him strong.

Samuel insisted that he felt the creator was somehow involved in his journey, even to the gift Kristina had given him. He also talked about his love for the princess and how his absence from her made his love even stronger. He confided in his mother that though he had never before kissed the princess, when the time came, it would be magical.

As mother and son walked through the serene mountain, winds mildly blowing the flexible branches to and fro, Samuel's story grew sad. The prince began to tell of his father's early neglect and later sternness. He told of how, after the fight with the wolves, he questioned his love for his father.

Then the prince spoke sadly about the deception of the wizard and the passing of King Salvatore. "I know that I made amends with my father prior to his passing, but I just cannot get rid of the pain I carry about the years of distance that led up to our falling out," Samuel said sorrowfully as he searched the ground for more to say.

"Samuel," Kathleen said as she stopped the prince from walking and put a hand on his shoulder. "Your father was a great man. He loved me with everything he had. He did many great things prior to your birth and many great things for his kingdom after you were born.

"I know it is hard for you to understand now, but when you return to the kingdom, you will see the greatness that your father worked so hard to achieve. The people loved him. After my passing, I could see in your father's heart the loss he felt. He loved you more than anything, but he felt such grief over losing me that he had a hard time showing you love," Kathleen said softly.

"You see, in his younger years, your father suffered very much as you did. Salvatore's father, a great king as well, was very strict. He accepted nothing but the best from his son. I believe that after your father endured my loss, he had no idea how to be a father; so he relied on his memories childhood. Unfortunately, my dear son, he made you suffer his anger and sadness. That is why you have had to suffer so much in your time," Kathleen said as tears streamed down Samuel's face.

"Thank you, Mother. You have taken a great burden from my heart today. I feel renewed and refreshed, as though I can continue my mission with a new goal in mind. That goal is to honor my father's death by restoring the kingdom to what you and he had built. To do that I must rescue the princess and defeat Ablewis," the prince said confidently.

The prince continued chatting with his mother as the two made their way back to camp. After being gone for hours, they returned to find that Laci and Summer had prepared food for a midday meal beside a roaring fire.

"Mother, how long will I be able to stay in the peace and solitude of this place with you?" Samuel asked.

"I am afraid that you have not long at all, Samuel. I can stay here long enough to see that you have regained your strength, and then I must return. Laci and Summer will be with you for a while to guide you through the mountain pass and show you the way to the castle," Kathleen said.

"Well, their company will be most welcome. These mountains, though beautiful, can be very desolate and lonely. If I get lonely, I will at least have Summer for some interesting conversation," Samuel joked.

"Yes, Summer is a character all her own. Laci is

pretty responsible, as you can see, and she knows the direction to the castle. I have given it some thought, and even though I did not originally intend to bring them with me, they will be able to serve a great purpose," Kathleen said.

"I am sure my purpose will be great wherever I go," Summer said as she floated next to Kathleen.

"Oh, Summer, I am sure you will make all the torches in the land really proud one day seeing how bright you can glow with that confidence of yours!" Samuel laughed.

"What's wrong, Mr. Samuel? Jealous because you can't float around and bring light to everything like I can? Yeah, I thought so," Summer said as she floated around Kathleen in a circle.

"Jealous? Hardly. I tell you what - why don't you come over here while I tie you down to an arrow? I'll show you how I can make an area light up," Samuel smirked.

"Okay, you two! Samuel, be nice to Summer. Summer, let's all just sit down and enjoy something to eat," Kathleen said, stopping the teasing.

"Here, Grandma Kathy, we made a soup tonight. The creator gave us some special herbs to use for an occasion like this, seeing that it will be your last meal with your son," Laci said as she passed out bowls to everyone around the fire.

"Oh, we are so blessed by the small things the creator does for us. This will be a delightful meal indeed," Kathleen smiled.

The small group sat around the fire talking and laughing about all sorts of subjects ranging from

Samuel's younger days to what it was like in the realm of the creator. The roaring fire warmed them all, as the light darkened. Samuel grew tired, and he kissed his mother, settled down to sleep, and drifted into a state of peace.

Morning came, and Samuel awoke to find that breakfast was set. He noticed that his mother looked sad. He rose from his shelter and walked over to her. He knew why she was sad because he felt the same. Such a short time together didn't seem to be enough after the life together they had missed.

Samuel knew there was really nothing he could say that would make time move slower and extend his visit with his mother. Samuel chose to think only of how much he had enjoyed meeting his mother and spending time with her. He was the recipient of a great blessing; he had not known anyone who ever got the chance to visit with a loved one that had crossed into the realm of the creator.

Samuel ate breakfast; then he packed his things and watched the fairies break camp. The two used magic to erase any signs of their camp. Samuel had requested that no trace be left behind should an enemy be trying to spot their trail, and the fairies did an excellent job shielding him.

The time for Samuel to say good-bye to his mother finally came. It was a sad moment that neither chose to prolong. Kathleen bade farewell to the fairies, urging them to listen to Samuel, and she gave Laci strict guidance on watching over Summer and playing the role of mother hen.

Kathleen asked Samuel for his sword. Surprised, Samuel handed it over. Kathleen held it carefully, concentrating before she spoke.

"Samuel, you will face much more danger in your time ahead. Sometimes you will be outnumbered, and you will need the strength of a hundred men. I am going to bless your sword. It will remain a normal sword while you carry it, but only in your hands when you are in grave danger of your life will this sword display a furious power. You will be able to cut through any object made by man, and magic will have no power against you."

Kathleen laid the sword across both hands, raised it above her head, and closed her eyes. The sword glowed luminescent green, and fire etched it with holy words and symbols. The glow lit the surrounding area so brightly that Samuel could hardly see. He raised one arm and partially covered his face while the sword was being blessed.

When the light faded, Kathleen brought the sword down and handed it to Samuel. When Samuel took the sword, he could feel new strength flowing through him, burning away any fear in his soul and making him feel as if he could take on the whole world.

Samuel raised the sword into the air swiftly, thanking the creator for such a wonderful blessing, and then he pointed the sword in the direction of the castle. "Ablewis! I am coming!" he shouted.

Lowering his sword, he gently sheathed it and faced his mother. He hugged her and thanked her once more for the time they had shared.

"Don't forget everything I told you, Samuel. When your life is threatened and in grave danger, only then will the sword display its true power. This sword will protect you from much evil." As Kathleen spoke, waving goodbye to her son and to the fairies, she began to fade. Laci and Summer both flew close to Kathleen as she was disappearing and kissed her on her cheek. Samuel could hear a quiet laughter echo out of existence, as she faded completely.

"All right, Samuel, we need to get moving. The path through the mountain is still going to take us a good day of walking," Laci said.

"Let's get going then. Oh, and Summer, if your little wings get tired, you can sit on my shoulder, and I'll give you a piggy back ride, but if I happen to run into a branch on the way and you get smacked, then I can't help you," Samuel teased.

"Oh, it's okay, Samuel; my wings never get tired. As a matter of fact, if you start to stumble again, you can jump on my back. You have to be careful, I won't be able to avoid any falling rocks from the mountain that might happen to smack you in the head on your way," Summer giggled.

"Okay, you two, the mountain is going to be enough to tackle. Can you guys just try to get along a little bit so that we can get this part of the journey over with?" Laci could not help but laugh and shake her head as she scolded them. Summer and Samuel were going to need some kind of a mother hen, and her instincts would serve the journey well.

Anthony Farina

CHAPTER VIII

The Great Abyss

AS the trio began to travel down the mountain to the abyss, the girls filled Samuel's mind with stories of the creator's realm and how they had met Samuel's mother. To keep Summer from getting complacent and floating off the mountain, Samuel made sure that she stayed on the inside of the path as the three traversed the steep parts. Even though he loved to tease the little fairy, he still protected those who served the same cause.

Through the trip that day, the three bonded in friendship, and Samuel saw clearly that these two companions were dependable. Samuel's fear of loneliness and being lost subsided through the day, as Laci randomly kept pointing the direction they were traveling and telling Samuel how far they had left to go.

Closer to the abyss as the friends descended the mountain, Samuel began to notice a peculiar flower sprouting. At first he could not place the flower, but then like a shock, he remembered vividly what it was. This flower was the exact one the wizard had told him would paralyze his enemies should he ever be in danger. Thinking that he could use it at a later time, Samuel wanted to take the flower with him. But he also remembered the wizard saying that he could not so much as touch it.

"Laci, can you help me, please? I want to take this flower for the journey, but I cannot so much as touch it without suffering its effects. Can you pick it up while I find something to wrap it in?"

"Sure thing, Samuel, I would be glad to help." Laci floated over to the flower and pulled it out of the ground with ease. She held it in the air as Samuel tore a piece of his shirt to use as a wrapping. Samuel wrapped the flower up and tucked it inside his trouser pocket, patting it once to make sure it was secure.

Samuel and the fairies continued on the journey until dusk. They finally gained their footing, after descending the rugged terrain for hours, to flat land.

As the sun dimmed, they entered a small clearing, taking note of the obstacle that lay before them: a gap in the mountains, cutting deep into the unknown, with no way of telling how far the bottom sank into the belly of the earth.

The three decided that the best option was to make a small camp with no fire, should trouble be lurking in the immediate area. Early the following day, the three would assess the obstacle in further detail and make a plan to conquer it.

The night was very long and cold for the trio; the two fairies found comfort in the prince's shirt pocket. The prince found comfort in the feeling that he was very close to the castle. And being close to the castle meant being close to the princess, his future queen.

While Samuel drifted into dreams of the princess, far away two small girls woke from their dreams.

"Gabby, Gabby? Are you awake, Gabby?" Darby said as she shook her older sister, who was lying silently in a peaceful sleep. After another shake, Gabby's eyes fluttered and then opened to see Darby standing over her.

"Darby, are you okay? What's wrong, sweetie?" Gabriela asked, concerned.

"I had a bad dream; it was about Mom and Dad. These men came to take them, and I was so scared. But later there was this man, and he was so brave! He fought off all of the bad men, and I was not scared anymore," Darby said, relief evident on her adorable face.

Gabriela immediately reassured Darby. "It's just a dream, Darby. Yes, Mom and Dad are gone, but everything will be okay. Before Mom and Dad left, they put a protection blessing on the house so that no one will be able to find us if they want to do us harm. Only people who are friendly will ever see this place, okay?"

Mere months had passed since wicked men had taken Gabriela and Darby's parents' lives. Before the murderers could subdue them completely, the girls' parents had put a spell on the place, making sure the girls could never be found by anyone or thing with hostile intent, should anything happen to them. Only whole hearts and sound minds would be able to see the hidden cottage. The children's parents knew of the special gifts they both possessed and had been determined to protect them.

Gabriela had the gift of compassion and understanding. There was nothing in the world that Gabriela saw as bad, just things misunderstood. She always had a keen sense to set apart good from evil. The point when misunderstanding turned into hatred and became pride equaled evil in Gabriela's eyes. Gabriela knew that the men who took her parents were full of the evils of pride and anger. What Gabriela lacked in brute strength, she more than made up in her quick wit and intelligence, and keeping these forces from ever getting hold of Darby was Gabriela's personal life mission.

Darby had the gift of ultimate love. Her capacity for love was immeasurable, and therefore it was immeasurably powerful. The creator had blessed Darby with this gift so that one day she might carry out a prophecy that would set the world straight.

Just as he had blessed Darby with this gift, the creator chose Gabriela as her protector. What better protector could a young girl have against the world than her older sister? A divine plan had been set in motion.

Should the wizard succeed in his plot, all hope would be lost for future generations. There was hope that he would not succeed. The fates of the two girls would soon entwine with the fates of Samuel and Kristina, and the prophecy would unfold and bring peace to the land.

Away in the foothills of the great mountains, the sun began to crest in the morning sky. Samuel could not see it because of the mountains that rose high into the atmosphere, attempting to touch the sky and whatever lay beyond. It was cold, very cold indeed, and the prince could feel the rapid vibration of two little fairies shivering in his shirt pocket.

Even though the sun was not visible, the prince had enough light to make out his immediate surroundings. A large cliff rose behind him, and a trail led back the way he had come. To his left and right grew more of the flowers that carried the paralyzing toxin. Before him lay the great abyss.

The abyss spanned roughly twenty feet in width. The length, however, seemed to stretch forever from left to right, disappearing into the distance. There was no telling how far he must travel in either direction to make his way around the abyss without crossing it.

As the prince noted the details of his surroundings, Laci and Summer exited his shirt pocket, only to find themselves back in the pocket after a short moment, seeking the warmth it held. The two fairies poked their heads up over the brim of the pocket so that they could take in the surroundings as well.

The prince walked toward the edge of the abyss, looked down into it, and noticed a large metal stake protruding from the wall of the cliff. The stake pinned a large metal chain to the cliff. It was hanging straight down; however, from the looks of it, the chain had to be easily twice as wide as a man.

When Summer noticed this, she drew in a deep breath and let out a loud cry: "HELLO!" The word echoed downward and did not fade for a few long moments.

"Summer! What are you doing? We don't know what is down there. It could be some goblin or troll, and you know trolls like fairies for breakfast," Laci worried.

"Oh, don't worry, trolls are all so dumb. We can convince a hungry troll to eat Samuel. I mean, you did survive getting eaten by a bear before, didn't you, Samuel?" Summer laughed.

"Yeah, and you know what? Once I come back from the troll's stomach, I will be sure to recommend you for dessert, Summer! Don't Goji berries go great with fairies - especially little ones who like to cause trouble?" Samuel smirked.

"SHHH! The chain is starting to move! Good job, Summer!" Laci exclaimed.

The huge chain began to rattle, sending a vibration through the mountain.

Rattle, clank, rattle, clank - the chain swayed to the left and right for a few moments, shaking and then suddenly tightening as it reached its limit, then suddenly it stopped. The prince slowly peered over the edge and stared into silence and darkness. Laci and Summer gazed with wide eyes as they both held their breath, waiting for the darkness to release the horror it held tightly.

"HWRAWK! HWRAWK! HWRAWK!" came a nerve-piercing sound from the darkness. Following the blood-curdling sound came a paralyzing anticipation of the abomination that was capable of producing it.

Quickly, the prince stepped back and drew his sword. He then grabbed the two fairies and set them safely behind a nearby rock to conceal them should the prince meet his fate with the creature. Then the prince headed to the cliff to face the creature. No sooner had he stepped away from the rock hiding the fairies than the creature burst into life from the deathly prison of the abyss.

The beast was winged, and it shot straight to the sky, mimicking the mountains reaching for the heavens. It rose so high that the prince could see in great detail the enemy he was about to face.

The creature resembled a dragon, pale in green color with faded black scales. Its blade-shaped head cried in anger, while its arrow-like tail struggled against the chain connected to it. The belly of the beast was covered in the same scales as well, all except for one small, pale-blue, oval spot, right below the neck.

Samuel immediately noted this spot as the only vulnerable place on the creature; the creature, however, still strained at the sky. Suddenly the chain grew taut, stopping the creature from its ascent and forcing it to glide back down to the mountain. Gliding, the creature descended to the surface at a sharp angle in half-circular movements.

Only moments passed before the beast spotted the one who was responsible for waking it from deep slumber. Darting for the prince, the creature gained speed, meaning to dispose of him in one swoop. Straightening his legs and extending his sharp talons, the beast dove for the kill.

The prince stood his ground and did not move until the time was right. If there was one thing he knew, it was that winged creatures were experts at killing moving prey. Timing the swing just right, the prince's blade contacted the talons as they came within inches of his head. He had for the moment deflected the first attack.

The creature ascended and then quickly descended again, attacking the prince in the same manner for a second time. Again, the prince stood his ground and deflected the attack.

The prince knew that he had to thrust his sword into the blue-skinned, oval spot below the beast's neck. In both attacks, his sword had connected with the beast, only to be deflected by the scales that seemed to have the toughness of armor. Only at the blue spot did he have a chance to use his sword.

Quickly, the prince ran toward the mountain and found a small ledge that would give him a height advantage. The creature would have to come in close, exposing himself to the prince just long enough for Samuel's sword to penetrate the lone soft tissue.

As the creature was finishing his third ascent, the prince planted his feet steadily on the ledge he'd chosen. His right arm drew back as he brought his weapon to his waist. He pointed the blade of his sword to his front so that when the creature provided the opportunity, the prince would strike a deathly blow, defeating his attacker.

The creature descended quickly, drawing close to the ground directly below the ledge where the prince was standing. The creature then looked up and slowly and powerfully thrust his wings up and down to become eye-level with the prince. When the creature came into view, he met the prince's gaze and for a second stared him down. The creature's eyes sharpened, and the prince in return sharpened his gaze to show the creature he had no fear.

The prince somehow in these moments of life and death thought only of saving the princess. His thoughts of protecting the woman he loved turned his fear into rage. The prince could feel his blood heating up, and his mouth opened, exposing grinning teeth to the beast that he was confronting.

The beast in turn huffed strong, foul breaths of hatred and anger at the prince, showing him as well that he feared neither his sword nor his might. In an instant, the beast drew his neck back, keeping his gaze locked on the prince. The prince knew that the creature was about to dart forward in an attempt to swallow Samuel whole.

The prince thrust his blade in the straightest, most accurate attack he had ever executed on any living thing. He thrust it straight into the pale-blue, soft tissue under the neck of the dragon. Extracting his blade, he stood for a second, watching to see what the creature would do.

The beast screamed, loud and boisterous: "SHREEEK!!!!" Flying backward and shaking, the beast retreated to the sky to gain time to recover. The prince stood shocked in amazement that the beast had not fallen from the injury it had just sustained.

Suddenly below him the prince heard Laci shouting. He looked down to see her floating up to him.

"Samuel, I know of this creature. It is not from this realm. You cannot defeat it. However, you can use the serum from the flower to paralyze it. Here, quickly, set your blade out straight, and I will rub the flower on it. When the beast comes back, strike him in the same place," Laci instructed.

Samuel held the sword out straight while Laci retrieved the flower from Samuel's pocket, unwrapped it from the cloth, and rubbed it on both sides of the sword. She then floated back down to the rock where Summer was. By this time, the creature was descending to face the prince once more. Just before it came down from the sky, Samuel glimpsed the spot where he had inflicted the wound. The wound was totally healed.

This time the prince moved to the crest of the ledge. He drew the hilt of the sword up to chest level and held the sword upright. He would swing the sword across his chest as soon as the opportune moment arrived.

The beast stayed on course, swooping down to the ground below the ledge where the prince stood and then slowly moving upward until it met the prince with a sharp, red gaze. The prince knew what this gaze meant; should he fail in his task this time, it would surely be the end of him.

The creature huffed rapidly. Its breath grew so fiery red that the prince could feel the heat coming off its mouth. The prince needed to act quickly before he was consumed by fire.

The creature arched back, fire building inside its mouth, waiting to torch the prince. The prince, without thinking and filled with more anger than before, swung at the creature, connecting his sword with his intended spot. The blade sliced through the skin of the creature with great ease.

However, the creature still had time to lurch partially forward and spit out a giant fireball. The prince did not have time to get to cover, and should he jump from his current spot, he would meet death far below. He was certainly doomed, for the fire was closing in on him. The prince could feel the heat singeing the hair on his hands. The metal from the sword grew very hot, and he was forced to drop it. The fire closed in to envelop him entirely.

The medallion the prince wore shone bright then. The golden light seemed cool, so cool that the fire couldn't penetrate it. The prince was thrown backward, knocking him unconscious. A few moments later, the prince sat up. His vision was blurred, but he sustained no physical injuries.

He saw the fairies hovering anxiously above his face and asked them, "What happened?"

Summer wrung her hands anxiously. "We don't know, Samuel. We saw a powerful force field around you just when the fire was going to hit, and that force field threw the fire back with ten times the force at the beast. And since you paralyzed him at just the right time, he turned stiff as a board. The force threw the beast to the other side of the abyss and stretched him out solid on the ground. If you look, you can see that the chain that was on his tail is now a bridge that we can cross. I don't think you will be waking him for a while. So now not only do we have a way to cross, but we no longer have a beast to worry about," Summer told the prince.

Samuel reached his hand to his neck and gratefully felt the medallion there. He hoped the princess knew that he was safe and coming for her.

Samuel got up and dusted himself off. "Wow, guys. I wish I had seen that! The creator is watching over me for sure."

The three slowly made their way from the side of the mountain, across the giant chain, and past the sleeping creature from the abyss. They moved through a small pass in the mountain, and as the sun was beginning to set, they stopped to make camp for the night. At this point, they were miles away from the creature; so they knew they were all safe from danger should the beast awaken.

Just when the prince sat back to rest for the night, he noticed small lights coming to life in the twilight a few miles ahead of his position. When the sun set a little more, those lights distinctly illuminated the unique shape of a castle. It was the wizard's castle at last, and he had finally arrived in the dark realm of Darniem.

CHAPTER IX

The Castle Gate

DAWN broke. The prince and the fairies covered their tracks at the makeshift camp they had set up for the night. Samuel could see the castle in the clear, cloudless day. It appeared to him that in leaving the mountains, he had also left a part of the world that was lost and dreary. With the sunlight shining and warming his face, he was momentarily absorbed by a distant memory.

He began reminiscing about sitting under a tree near the monastery of St. Mein with the princess. She had placed the medallion around his neck and told him always to look to the sun and remember that her love for him was real. Samuel took a moment and let the sun drench his face, almost cleansing him of worry and despair.

The moment was soon over, and he opened his eyes and viewed the castle once more. Even from a few miles away, the structure advertised its might through the sheer enormousness of its being. It warned all who dared approach that doom awaited. It was a castle like no other. Golden onion spirals topped the dark rock of the main body.

Samuel felt reluctant to move from the camp he had made to the trail ahead of him. He knew he couldn't march down the trail, straight to the castle gates, and kick down the door. That would alert all of Ablewis' guards and ensure him an unknown yet certain death. He needed a plan.

"Laci, Summer, I need you two to scout ahead for me. I only need you ahead by fifty paces. Go through the woods and see if you can find any traps or guards roaming the area. I am going to stay off the main trail. We need to be quiet but quick. When you enter the woods, keep the trail to your left. At the first sign of danger, stop where you are and immediately come back and let me know what you have found. If we have to, we will take all day so as to not be detected. I need to get as close to the castle as possible without being caught."

Laci immediately nodded and darted into the woods, keeping the trail to the left just as Samuel had instructed. Summer followed Laci, and the two began scouting the area. Samuel waited for a minute and then began to walk slowly into the woods, remaining on guard. He had to cross roughly three miles of woods before he would be close enough to the castle to assess how he should enter.

The three moved through the woods in the form of a triangle. Laci and Summer, separated by about thirty paces, formed the base of the triangle. Samuel, hanging back to the rear of the group at the fifty paces he recommended, was the tip of the triangle. This type of movement gave them an advantage: should one of them be captured, the whole group would not perish.

Creeping through the woods for hours and finding no signs of danger, Samuel signaled to the fairies to re-group and stop for a few moments' rest. After a quick break, the three continued toward the castle. About an hour had passed when Laci approached a thick group of bushes. She backed up and noticed that Summer, entangled in the brush, was bobbing up and down in the air like a marionette. She was caught on something and could not get free.

"Samuel! Come quick," Laci called quietly. "Summer is stuck in the bushes!"

Samuel came trotting through the tree line to aid in Summer's rescue while Laci stood watch. After snapping a few sturdy branches and clearing some thick vines, Samuel freed Summer.

"Shew! Thank you, Samuel. I could hardly move in that mess. I was floating along, and before I knew it, my foot was tangled in the bushes," Summer said, breathing deeply.

"No problem, Summer. I'll help you out anytime. It's not like I would leave you there to get eaten by a bear," Samuel laughed. As his laugh grew louder, Summer smirked at him.

But Laci, sensing danger, immediately flew to the prince's mouth and silenced him. "Shh! Samuel, look to the left, through this small clearing. Do you see it?" Laci said in excitement.

Samuel ceased his laughing and turned his attention to an object that stood not a hundred paces from them. It was a wall, protruding hundreds of feet into the air.

As he emerged from the woods, Samuel gazed upon the castle that held not only the princess, but also the one man he would have to defeat in order to bring peace back to the land that he loved so much.

The three friends snuck up to the castle wall and crouched against it as they proceeded to move left toward a giant ivory staircase. Taking care not to be seen while moving, they kept a low profile. Once Samuel had a clear view of the staircase, he was able to spot a large, spiked metal gate. There was no lock; however, armored guards stood vigilant, keeping a watchful eye for any signs of an intruder.

Each guard wore a black cape attached to a shiny red breastplate and carried a sword, sheathed on the left side when not in use. A highly polished gold helmet covered each guard's head and neck, only leaving small openings for the eyes, mouths, and noses. They stood within one pace of each other, making a half circle around the gate. Defeating the guards was indeed the key to getting inside the castle.

Samuel stepped a few paces back and found a small spot to conceal himself while he beckoned Laci and Summer to come close so he could whisper to them. "This is where we have to part. Is there any way you two can make your way back to St. Mein?"

"Yes, the creator has given us permission to channel ourselves to any monastery in this realm. We are the only fairies who can do this, and we have to travel only in your aid. What do you need us to do, Samuel?" Laci asked.

"I need you to find Cleric Jeremy; he lives at the monastery of St. Mein. Tell him what has happened so far, and then tell him to send Earabis to me. I will need some way to escape from the castle once I free Kristina. Tell Earabis that I will wait, concealed someplace, and I will find him when he gets here. Then the princess and I will ride him all the way back to St. Mein."

Laci and Summer both nodded and kissed Samuel on the cheek. They did not make any noise when they faded out of sight; they just slowly disappeared while waving good-bye. Just before they vanished, Samuel could hear Summer telling him to be careful.

Samuel knew he was outnumbered. He was an excellent swordsman who could take out two or three of the guards, but not all seven at once. Samuel thought for a time, but he could discover no way to make the guards part without giving up his hiding place. Samuel just took a deep breath and said a short prayer, for he felt fear. He did not want to die in Darniem and leave Kristina a prisoner. He prayed to the creator, asking him for strength to defeat the enemies that outnumbered him.

While he was praying, his sword vibrated and began to change. Its edges sharpened, and the blade turned ivory but glossy as a mirror. As he held onto the sword, it extended by a few inches, giving him more reach. Samuel at this point remembered what his mother had told him, that when his life was truly threatened, the sword would come through for him. The sword finished its transformation and glowed dull blue. Samuel began to feel confidence, courage, and anger all at once swelling within him.

Samuel stood up, exposing himself from hiding, and walked to the bottom of the steps. He stared at all the guards, breathing slow and deep, not wavering in his stance. The guards did not know what to make of this intruder who stood so boldly before them. The guard closest to the center pointed to the guard at his right hand and then pointed to Samuel. The guard followed the order and headed down the steps to engage Samuel.

The guard moved quickly, coming at Samuel with a thrust aimed directly for his head. Deflecting the blow, Samuel spun around in a circle and brought his sword down on the guard's back, bringing the guard quickly to his knees, where Samuel then thrust his sword through the guard's chest; after this, Samuel proceeded halfway up the steps.

While he was approaching the halfway point of the ivory staircase, the head guard pointed to two guards, one on his left and one on his right. He instructed them to stop Samuel. The first guard that got to Samuel came at him swinging, knocking Samuel off balance briefly.

As Samuel was stumbling, the second guard brought his sword down to slice Samuel in half. Samuel dodged the attacker's fatal blow but was cut on his left arm. Samuel grew angrier and fought on with the two attackers, exchanging blow for blow and cut for cut. The fight demanded full use of his skills, and he was getting winded.

The two guards cornered Samuel at a turn in the staircase. The one to his left raised his sword overhead, preparing to bring it down and cut through Samuel with brute force. The guard on the right took a stance and reared back to swing. At the exact moment that both guards exposed their chests, Samuel took the opportunity to gain an advantage. As the guard to his right brought the sword across his own chest to strike, Samuel deflected the blow and simultaneously kicked the guard in the chest.

Samuel turned his attention to the guard to his left, striking him on the helmet with the butt of his sword and throwing him off balance. He then moved in and thrust the sword through the red breastplate. Samuel noticed the guard to his right was moving again to attack him. Samuel deflected the high-angle blow and stabbed this guard as well.

Taking in short, suffocating breaths, Samuel had taken out three well-armed guards in mere moments, boosting his confidence in the fight and faith within himself. Regaining his composure, the prince resumed climbing the stairs. He stopped every few steps and took long, deep breaths so that he would not enter the next round of fighting so winded. He stumbled up a few more steps, stood taller, and breathed easier. He was quickly regaining his strength, thanks to his righteous anger and his will to save the one true love waiting beyond the doors of the castle. Finally, Samuel came ten steps away from the top of the staircase, where the rest of the guards stood.

No sooner had Samuel gained the top than the chief guard ordered the last three guards in his command to attack Samuel at once. Samuel rushed to meet the attackers at the top of the large, ivory steps. Immediately he sliced at the attacker closest to him, slitting his throat.

The second man attacked Samuel from his left, swinging low, attempting to take out the prince's

legs. Samuel was only partially able to deflect the blow, causing him to cry out in agonizing pain when the guard's blade sliced his leg at mid-thigh. Samuel went to a knee and raised his sword above his head just in time to block the next attack. The same guard then kicked Samuel in the chest, causing him to fall backward and roll down the stairs.

Samuel's body tumbled down the ivory staircase, feeling each sharp angle of every step as he descended to the ground - rolling, rolling, rolling. His head beat against the hard stairs, and every blow to his back wrung from him a painful sigh, while his wounded arm and leg suffered over again as they beat against the cruel ivory. Somehow his sword stayed in his grip without piercing him.

After what seemed like an eternity, Samuel finally came to rest at the bottom of the stairs. His vision was blurry; so he used his hands to help him see. Stumbling, trying to get up, Samuel put one hand on the bottom ivory step and the other on the rocky ground. When he managed to stand, he saw two blurry figures coming down the steps toward him. Taking a few steps back and inhaling deeply, Samuel brought his sword up to his chest and parallel to his body.

The two guards quickly attacked Samuel, striking at him with deathly blows. Samuel swung with all his might, deflecting each blow from left to right. As he swung, his sword began to shine with a bright light, and he felt power surge through his body, blocking all fatigue and pain.

Time slowed down for Samuel. His focus was unlike anything he had ever experienced before. Looking left, he could clearly see his attacker swinging a sword that was meant to go through Samuel's chest. Samuel steadied himself and swung with lightning speed to deflect the attacker's blow. He seemed to be moving full speed while the attacker seemed to be moving very slowly, almost halting altogether.

As Samuel's sword met the guard's, it grew brighter with light, and then the sword the guard was using shattered into a thousand pieces.

Samuel, in absolute awe of what had just happened, maintained his focus and turned his attention to the other guard, who was also moving slowly. This guard was swinging from the ground up, aiming for Samuel's head. Samuel took a moment to notice the fine details of the guard's movement. He could see the attacker's body slowly twisting, yet somehow Samuel could still move at full speed. He did not question his ability; he just continued to use it to his advantage.

Noticing that the guard had only moved maybe a half an inch toward him, Samuel spun around in a circle to gain momentum, and as he finished spinning, he briefly locked eyes with the attacker. Time stood still for a brief moment as Samuel glared with anger at the guard. Samuel then brought his sword down from the air and on top of the attacker's sword, shattering it as well into a thousand pieces.

When the second guard's sword had shattered, time resumed normal speed for all. Full of anger and rage, Samuel stood to finish off the two at-tackers. He raised his sword above the neck of the guard whose sword he had just shattered. But he stopped.

The man had no weapon to fight anymore. Even through the rage, anger, hatred, and all of the oth-er emotions he felt at that time, Samuel knew that to kill an unarmed man would make him no better than a cold-blooded murderer. He could not do it; he could not kill an unarmed man.

So he stopped and just stared at the men. They looked at him in return, hesitating to see what fate the prince would grant them. The prince lowered his sword and then spoke.

"Go away from this place, and serve evil no more. Let freedom and justice be your masters. If you vow at this very moment to follow my words, I will spare your lives. But you must leave this place," Samuel said as he lifted his sword and pointed to-ward the woods.

Without hesitation, the two guards fled into the woods. Within moments they were both out of sight, and then Samuel turned his full attention to the final guard standing at the top of the staircase. Samuel took one look at the man and began to climb the stairs. The man stood his ground firmly, refusing to move.

Bloody, bruised, and broken, yet somehow feeling the energy of his youth, Samuel climbed the stairs to fight the final guard. As he climbed the steps, he took deep breaths, and with these breaths, thoughts of the princess came to mind. She was his focus, his reason for succeeding. He had not failed her so far, and this man would not stand in his way.

As Samuel ascended the staircase, he watched the chief guard draw his sword from its sheath. Samuel increased his pace, closing the distance between himself the final guard. The chief guard grabbed his sword with both hands, inverted it, and drew it above his head so that the tip of the blade pointed to the ground. Samuel anticipated that the guard wanted to use the elevated position and strike a deadly blow straight down on him.

Knowing this, he climbed faster, putting only a few steps between himself and the attacker. Samuel drew mere feet from the guard. The guard took a deep breath, arching his chest back, and brought his sword down. Samuel moved in for an attack.

Samuel drew his blade back as if to cut the final guard in two, keeping him from doing any harm. Swinging with all his might, Samuel suddenly connected his sword with the guard's sword. The two swords did not move. The guard's sword had impaled the ivory of the staircase. He held it there tightly, knowing that Samuel would strike it and trusting the building more than his own arm to stop Samuel.

Samuel held his sword steady against the guard's, neither flinching nor moving, just staring at the guard as the guard returned the prince's steely gaze. A few moments passed while the two warriors stood, swords crossed, maintaining the stalemate. After a few more moments, Samuel finally relaxed his grip on his sword, pulled it back from the guard's sword, and stepped back.

The guard maintained his posture for a few minutes, and then he relaxed his stance, too. Slowly, deeply, the chief guard spoke.

"I know who you are, Samuel; we have been waiting for you for a long time. Our orders were to destroy you at first sight. We were told that you were coming here to tear down this castle and bring harsh rule to the land. For many years, I and my brothers, some of whom have just perished at your feet, have been waiting for this day. My first instinct was to send all of them at you simultaneously. However, I wanted to make this moment last.

"You proved your worth in swordsmanship as well as something else, something that changed my life completely; it was compassion. You have great compassion and honor for those you fight. I could tell this by your movements, your stance, and of course your mercy. I shall flee this place, too, and find my brothers, who left just moments ago. We will live lives of justice and honor. I submit because, despite being told that you were going to destroy us, I have always heard rumors of the opposite.

"I have heard rumors of a man, a true prince who will bring peace to this land one day. Peace is what we all want. I have known for some time that this place is dark with evil, but I did not want to believe it. Today, in showing my brothers great compassion, you have shown me the truth, and that truth lies in you, the true prince who brings peace."

Samuel stood, shocked. He could barely comprehend his adversary's words. He thought: Are compassion and forgiveness really this powerful? All

Samuel could do was stand and listen to the guard and take in the brief moment of victory and peace.

But the guard was not finished. "I am going to lend you aid, prince. Here, take my armor and cloak. Hide your sword, and carry mine, for the handle of the sword bears the mark of the wizard's kingdom. Go to the end of the Great Room, and take the last door on your left. It will open to a spiral staircase that will lead you to a corridor. Walk through the corridor, and at the end you will see large double doors. Behind those double doors in the dining hall, in about one hour from now, the wizard will be having a banquet to marry the princess. Grab her and escape through the trap door at the back of the dining hall. From there, you will have to find your own way out of the castle and escape with the princess."

The prince, still looking shocked as ever, immediately began to put on the armor the guard gave him. "In return for your generosity, wise chief of the guard, I want you to find your way to a place called St. Mein. That is my kingdom. Ask for a man by the name of Captain Steven, who is captain of the guard there. Tell him what happened today and that I sent you. He will give you a new home. When I return from this place, I will look forward to having you as one of my chief guards. Should I not return, guard my kingdom as well as you have guarded this place."

As Samuel spoke, he could not help but feel a little sadness when thinking about his home, the place that was becoming more of a distant memory all the time. The chief guard nodded in approval and helped Samuel finish dressing.

"My prince, be careful. You are now my prince, and I will uphold your wishes. Rescue the princess. The wizard has been searching for two girls. His search has gone on for years, but he cannot find them. He keeps the reason secret; however, I know that one of the girls, the one they call Darby, is supposed to possess a power of love that no person has ever had. He wants to use that power to conquer the world by turning it into hate. Darby's sister Gabby protects them both. Should you not defeat the wizard and escape with the princess, he will focus all his attention on the girls, and the world will be doomed. All I can tell you is that if you exit the castle from the back entrance, head north from the castle. The girls are hiding four days' ride north in that direction. Fate will help you find them from there. Godspeed, my prince."

At the final words, the two gripped each other's forearms, shook, and parted. The chief guard left with nothing more than his tunic, pants, and shoes. Samuel watched as the guard quickly fled down the stairs. He admired the man and wished that they had met under different circumstances. But he had to focus on the mission.

As soon as the guard was in the woods and out of sight, something happened to the prince. All of the emotion, rage, and adrenaline that had been fueling him through the fight disappeared. The prince buckled to his knees, feeling every bruise, cut, and other injury hit him all at once.

Taking a few minutes to gain his energy, the prince stood tall, yet the castle stood taller. There was no turning back. He took one look back at the mountains he had crossed, drinking in the last few minutes of the sunset and reflecting on the one person who had kept him alive and going all these days: the princess. He closed his eyes as the sun slid off his face to be swallowed by the horizon.

With a deep breath, he stepped forward, put both hands on the enormous metal gates, and flung them open. Then he opened the gigantic wooden doors. The prince crept into the castle, taking in a large room lit with candles. He looked around for the door to the rear of a room that was the biggest he had ever seen. The walls rose fifty feet into the air. The ceiling arched another twenty feet above the walls. The doors behind him suddenly slammed. The clanking metal and wood echoed throughout the room.

CHAPTER X

The Rescue

SAMUEL whirled around to see if he had been discovered, but he was alone. The wind had slammed the door. The Great Room where Samuel stood was vast and open, and much dimmer now that the outside door was closed. The castle's interior was dark, illuminated only by feeble candles and the tiny amount of sunlight allowed in by the high, narrow slits of windows.

The walls were made of gray stone, not the warm, golden sandstone used to build the monastery. The gray stone, resembling ice, gave the castle a cold feeling. Instead of the graceful arches found in the monastery, the castle's interior bristled with sharp angles running the length of the ceiling and at the top of the walls.

Huge, ivory pillars in two rows lined the hall. Each pillar rose from the floor to the castle's ceiling. The pillars formed a sort of open hallway that ended at the back of the Great Room. Torches mounted on the pillars cast eerie shadows on the walls and floor as the flames danced; the open distance between them could easily fit a house.

The prince breathed slowly and deeply. Sharp pain pierced his lungs with each breath. He was sweating, bleeding, bruised, and winded. Samuel felt that he was nearly broken; only his longing to reach Kristina allowed him to muster the strength to carry on.

The prince slowly made his way down the corridor of pillars. He walked with a limp, for not only was he wounded, but the armor of the chief guard was heavy. The prince had never worn armor before, and he found it quite uncomfortable. He calculated the advantage it would have in close combat; he could easily push a man over now that he was almost twice his actual weight. As the prince walked, he searched for the door at the back left of the giant room.

Suddenly, a blue light glowed in the corner of the room. He moved off the path between the pillars and stepped to the left. He could see the shape of a softly glowing man standing at the end of the room next to a door. The man beckoned the prince to come closer, and so the prince went.

The prince kept the pillars on his right and the wall on his left. He did not want to take his eyes off the man. He also felt warmth in his presence, warmth that welcomed him and offered him a friendship rare in his journey.

As Samuel approached the man, he noticed the

thick robe that extended to the floor, covering the man's feet, and the staff in his hand that looked as if someone had taken the very trunk of a large tree and twisted it. Symbols in rows from top to bottom, the likes of which the prince had never seen before, glowed a dark emerald color on the staff. Samuel drew closer still and saw the man smiling as if telling him that all would be well.

Still panting from moving such a distance, the prince finally reached the man and spoke to him, his words echoing in the hall. "Who are you? I feel that I know you already. Have I dreamed you?"

The man stretched out his hand, which began to glow, and touched the prince's shoulder. Suddenly, every wound Samuel had endured began to heal. His cuts sealed shut; the bruises faded. The prince felt his energy renewed, as if he had slept through the night and eaten well.

"My dear boy, my name is Robert, and I am your friend. I have been watching over you since you were a child. You did not dream me, but I came to you when you were lost in the wizard's dream land. I brought you back to the world and broke his spell. I have been waiting for a very long time to meet the man who would free this world through love."

Recognizing Robert from the wizard's dream, Samuel embraced him. "I am so grateful for the blessing of healing you've bestowed upon me, as well as your rescue in the red lands. To see a friendly face in the wizard's castle is as welcome as it is surprising."

"You are most welcome," Robert beamed, stepping away. "All I have done is for love of the creator and this world, and you serve both."

"If there is anything I can ever do to show my thanks, I surely will find a way. You have been sort of a guide watching over me this whole time, haven't you? I knew after the dream in times of despair that there was a presence sustaining me. I thought it was my mother's presence, but it was you all along, wasn't it, Robert? You showed me the inner strength to get through the desert and the abyss and all the other times when I felt hope was lost!"

"Yes, Samuel, I have been watching over you this whole time. I have not been allowed to interfere directly when you were required to pass a test to proceed. However, I was able to offer you aid when you were under the wizard's spell and here in his stronghold. I have healed you from your wounds, and I am going to help you reach the princess."

"Is she near?" Samuel asked eagerly.

Robert nodded. "This door behind me leads to a hall and a stair; at the end are two large double wooden doors. Past them waits the princess. The wizard has arranged his wedding to her, and many guards attend the event. Use your armor to get past the guards and close to the princess. Once you are near her, grab her and escape."

Samuel felt very alone. "How will I escape, Robert? Once I take Kristina, every guard will know who I am."

Robert smiled and handed the prince a small, black, egg-shaped object. "The banquet hall has a large wooden door in the floor that leads to a tunnel. Use this weapon to distract those around you. It will spew forth enough smoke to mask your movement for a few moments. Get through the door in the floor with the princess, and I will meet you in the tunnel and guide you out of the castle."

The prince took the object from Robert, who smiled and then vanished, leaving the prince facing the door leading to the banquet hall. The prince opened the door and saw a spiral staircase that climbed many stories, so many that he could not see where it ended. Without further delay, the prince lifted his armor to adjust it, took a deep breath, walked through the door, and began ascending the staircase. It was a good thing that Robert had healed the prince, for the climb up to the top of the staircase was daunting.

One foot rising after another, the prince climbed the stairs at a good pace, careful to steady his breathing. While ascending, he thought to himself: If I'm going to have to do battle, at least I'll be warmed up and ready for the challenge.

Then his thoughts shifted to his dear princess, the woman he had not seen in what felt like an eternity. His heart quickened, and the thought of soon seeing her quickened his steps. He pictured her sweet smile, and her lips as ruby as ever. Her eyes above that smile reflected her inner beauty. The very thought of the princess banished all fear; anticipation of seeing his one true love drove him faster yet.

Suddenly Samuel came to the top of the staircase and saw a door. Upon opening the door, the prince heard music playing from the room beyond and saw the empty hall lined with tall, open windows. Their purple drapes, the biggest the prince had ever seen, danced in the wind.

Samuel closed the stair door behind him, walked over to one of the windows on his right, and pushed the drapes aside. He was hundreds of feet in the air. On both sides of the hallway was a steep drop to the rocky bottom of a valley. He also noticed how dark it was outside. When he had entered the castle, the sun was just about to go down. It was now completely gone.

The prince focused his attention on the end of the hall, where the two doors to the banquet hall were. He made his way down to them, and as he drew closer, his heart began to race. He wondered how long his borrowed armor would fool the wizard's guards. He would have to go straight ahead, taking each moment of danger as it came until he could reach the princess and bring her to safety.

The prince put his ear to the door and listened. He heard only basic chatter among the wedding guests and the soft music of violins and flutes. He stepped back, grabbed the handle of the door, and pulled it open.

As soon as Samuel set foot inside the room, he saw a table about one hundred feet in front of him. At the table, he saw the wizard standing and talking to a few people. To the wizard's left sat Princess Kristina.

The prince stood frozen as he stared at the love of his life. Relief at her safety washed over him;

though she was a hostage, she was still alive and well. Keeping her alive was all that mattered to him now.

He gazed at her, allowing time to stop. The movement of the people around him, the curtains that blew with the air, the subtle shifting of equipment from the guards standing nearby - everything came to a halt. His love for her was so great that time itself had no choice but to halt when his attention was on the fine features of the face that he cherished - the face he wished to hold and kiss at this very moment.

To the prince's surprise, he did not draw much attention when he entered the room. The guards posted around the room and the guards standing with their backs to the door he had just entered barely noticed him. Many of them glanced at him and returned to sharp attention, scanning the room and searching for any intruder. They even straightened their postures, as if they were recognizing a figure of high authority.

Samuel began to move through the banquet hall, his heart beating faster as he drew closer to the table. He walked toward the left side of the table to approach the princess from behind and not startle her. The wizard was engaged in conversation with other people in the room; so the prince used his distraction to close the distance between him and the princess.

The prince moved behind the table, closer to the princess. He looked to his left, toward the back of the hall. There on the floor was a small, wooden door built into the floor. That has to be the trap door Robert told me to find! The distance from the princess to the trap door was only twenty feet. However, if he was not careful and did not move quickly with the princess, he could risk never making it to his escape.

Turning his attention back to the princess, Samuel saw that she was fine and looked past her. The wizard was still engaged in conversation with his guests. As the prince drew within mere feet of the princess, she looked up at him, and his eyes met hers. The princess's mouth dropped open as she immediately recognized that the man behind the chief guard's armor was her one true prince, who had come to rescue her.

Kristina stared at her prince, unable to believe her good fortune. She wanted so badly to jump into his arms, but she knew that she must be clever and silent now. Samuel shared that unspoken communication – they were destined to be together. Their feelings were unchanged. Both were determined to leave this evil place together. In the middle of imminent danger, they shared a moment of joy, which was quickly replaced with the dreaded reality of the situation.

Samuel snapped out of the emotion that was overcoming him and gazed intently at the wizard, willing him to stay preoccupied with his guests. The prince slowly extended his hand to the princess, and she extended hers to him. The two had nearly clasped hands when the wizard suddenly turned around and pushed his arm out, hand wide open, in the direction of the prince.

"Back!" shouted the wizard.

A force the likes of which the prince had never felt picked him up off the ground and threw him across the room. The wizard's powerful spell felt to Samuel like an explosion.

Kristina immediately stood and gasped in fear, covering her mouth. The prince slammed against a nearby stone wall, sprawling as he hit. He then slid to the ground.

The prince stood up, threw off his helmet, and drew his sword, regaining his stance. He stood his ground; he was ready to defend his princess to the death. The prince knew there was little time. The guards in the room had seen that he was not their chief, and they drew their swords as well.

"How you ever came to defeat the best of my guards outside the castle is beyond me. How you ever survived the desert, the mountains, and the lost forest escapes me! You are quite determined, young prince. However, I knew you were coming all along. I let you walk into this little trap of mine," the wizard taunted. Then he extended a hand to the princess and magically bound her hands behind her back.

The prince sprang forward and jumped onto the banquet table. He shouted, "There will never be an obstacle so great that I cannot overcome it; my love for the princess is too great. You made a mistake, Ablewis, when you tried to put me under a spell. You underestimated the love I have for the woman you are now holding prisoner, and the love she has for me."

Then Samuel shouted to the room, "Your commander gave me this sword and armor. He changed his allegiance from the wizard to me! Prophecy foretells that this evil man is planning to use you to do his evil bidding across this world!"

The room filled with boisterous chatter. Heads turned as people searched each other's eyes for clarity and answers. Then, the prince turned back to the wizard. "As for you, wizard, you will not harm another person with your evil ways!" the prince shouted.

As he was shouting at the wizard, a guard began to creep slowly behind the prince. He drew a sharp dagger from his hilt and was about to swing at the prince on the table. The princess noticed him and shouted, "No! Samuel, look out behind you!"

Samuel quickly turned and with both feet jumped into the air, missing the slash of his attacker. The prince landed back on the table and kicked the dagger out of the guard's hand. This attack sparked a fight among the guards in the room. The guards on the left side of the room quickly ran toward the guards on the right side of the room, creating a large brawl as the townspeople in attendance began to flee the fighting.

The prince, landing on his feet and disarming the guard, jumped off the table and punched the attacking guard, making him fly back and rendering him unconscious. Then Samuel turned back to the princess. The wizard had both hands above her and was muttering some kind of incantation. With total disregard to physical danger, the prince charged to-ward the wizard. When Samuel got within arm's distance of the wizard, he leapt, throwing the whole weight of his body through the air to tackle his foe. As Samuel flew through the air, all of the sudden the wizard vanished.

Robbed of his target, the prince landed on the ground next to the princess. The wizard for now was gone, and the magical bonds imprisoning Kristina fell away. Standing up, she immediately wrapped her arms around Samuel.

At once, all time seemed to have stopped, and Samuel felt his empty heart burst and overflow with joy. No matter what may happen in the next few moments, he knew that right now he was finally at peace. The princess had brought Samuel peace, and for that he felt a new type of love for her grow inside.

Kristina embraced him quickly and then grasped his hand, tugging him towards the only door, leading to the stairs. "Hurry, Samuel – we must get away while the wizard's guards are busy fighting the guards loyal to the chief guard."

The prince noticed the guards fighting each other, some wearing the same type of armor he had been given and others wearing brass-colored armor. But the guards who seemed to be on his side were greatly outnumbered and were being defeated.

"No, Kristina – the creator has sent us help. Look there – there is where we go." Samuel showed her the square depression in the floor behind the banquet table. This was the secret exit Robert had said would lead out of the castle.

Without hesitation, the prince withdrew the egg-shaped object that Robert had given him, and smashed it to the floor. Once the object broke open, it spewed thick amounts of black smoke. As the smoke was filling the room, Samuel and Kristina raced hand in hand to the trap door.

Samuel could still hear the clanking of swords, accompanied by the growling of the men who were confused and lost in the smoke. Wasting no time, Samuel used his sword to pry the wooden panel upward. When he opened this layer of the floor, he saw an iron door with a large, circular handle.

The prince lifted with all his might, and the trap door slowly opened. The stale air flowing through their noses and into their lungs choked the prince and princess momentarily. After the stale air lifted, the princess took one look down the vertical escape path, where slippery, iron rungs could be used as steps to climb into the deep, dark hole.

"Follow me quickly," Kristina urged, swinging her legs onto the first rung. "I could not bear to be without you again."

Without hesitation, the princess began to climb down the protruding bars from the wall. As she sank out of view and into the darkness below, the prince followed right behind her. When he was eye level with the floor, he grabbed the inside of the large iron door, slammed it shut, and felt around the belly of the door until he found a locking mechanism. He locked it.

Then he began to descend the iron steps into the

unknown. He called into the darkness, fearing for the princess. "Kristina! Are you there?"

"I'm at the bottom, Samuel! It's about forty steps down. I'll wait for you right here," shouted the princess.

Samuel slowly descended the rungs to the bottom and planted his foot on solid ground. He could see that the only way to go was down a long corridor made of mud and brick. At the end of the corridor, something glowed softly. He could not tell if it was natural light or something else, but the soft glow was the only immediate source of light. Above him, he could still hear the clanking of swords and shouting of men. Below, all was silent.

"What is that glow, Samuel?" Kristina asked.

"I think that it is a messenger from the creator – Robert. He told me the way to escape and promised to meet us here," Samuel explained.

"Even if it is he, let's walk to him with our own light," Kristina suggested. "Whoever built this place would have left a light for himself. Let's find it."

Samuel ran his hands along the walls, and so did Kristina. As Samuel was taller, he soon found a large wooden stick with cloth on the end. He ignited it by striking his sword against the bricks on the wall.

Once the torch was ignited, he could see the corridor more clearly. Brown and grey brick stretched end on end for a long way, creating a tunnel of brick. As he walked, he grabbed another torch, lit it, and handed it to the princess. With one hand, each held a torch high; the other hands they clasped together as they walked.

After a time, the tunnel began to split left and right. The couple followed the light, whatever branch it chose. No matter how many turns they took, the soft glow kept a constant distance in front of them. They continued to follow the lighted path, hoping it would lead them out of the castle in time.

Finally Kristina spoke. "Samuel, why did you leave all of those years ago? I know you were troubled at our parting, but it was not a reason to leave."

"I could not stay any longer. I know I left you, Earabis, and many others behind without so much as an explanation. For that, I am truly sorry. It was just something I had to do. I needed to go and lay my childhood pain and present grief to rest. I had to find peace alone."

"For me there was no peace," Kristina said sadly. "I looked for you for the longest time, wondering if you were well or if I was ever going to see you again. No one had any word – no idea where you were – not for years."

The prince stopped in his tracks and turned to the princess. "Many days and nights I sat awake thinking about you, Kristina. I don't want you to think I forgot, not for one second!"

"Then why did you not return?" Kristina challenged. "Once you knew that the time my father had decreed I should be away had ended, why did you not look for me as I looked for you?"

Samuel looked into her eyes. "Finding peace took me longer than I expected. I am grateful for the time, for the hard work of searching made me able to endure the journey to find you. When I was ready to come back to St. Mein, I was prevented."

"What happened?" Kristina asked, worried.

"The wizard approached me disguised as someone I thought I could trust. He poisoned me, and I learned of his plan to kill my father and harm you. He threw me into some kind of spell, and I almost did not escape it alive." Samuel described to Kristina the weird, red world and the challenges he had faced.

"So the medallion I gave you really helped you?" Kristina realized, touching it where it gleamed around Samuel's neck.

"It brought me to myself again. You, the only good thing I could remember, saved me. Then Robert rescued me from the spell. Once I was free, I knew I had to save you. My father stood a great chance of dying; I was prepared to accept that. I would not accept the fate the wizard had in store for you!" Samuel declared.

"I never knew, my love. I am so very grateful that you came for me in time. The wizard was about to marry me, and I had no way of getting out. I knew you were coming for me, though," Kristina said. "I want you to know that even though I was worried, I never lost faith in you."

Samuel stopped in his tracks. He turned and looked deeply into Kristina's eyes. He wanted to so badly to kiss her, but he did not want their first kiss of true love to be in the belly of the wizard's castle. Instead, he cupped her neck with his hand

and slowly brushed her hair around her ear.

"Thank you. Thank you for never losing faith in me. I swear that when all of this is over, I will never leave your side again."

The princess placed her hand over his and leaned into his hand, telling him without words how much what he had said meant to her. Once the moment had passed, the two continued through the tunnel, searching for the end of it and the source of the light that guided them.

CHAPTER XI

The Escape

THROUGH the underground network of tunnels, the soft glow led Samuel and Kristina to a closed door. The glow passed through the door and disappeared out of sight, and there was nowhere else for the prince and princess to turn. Samuel stopped in his tracks, halting Kristina in her place, too.

Slowly he crept toward the place where the light had disappeared. Extending his torch in front of him, he approached the door. They could both see through the cracks that the glow was on the other side of the door, as if it were waiting for them to enter without fear of being harmed.

As the door was their only option, Samuel grabbed the rusted, cobwebbed handle and pulled the door toward him. Loudly it creaked, and the glow grew brighter as the door opened. Right in front of it, Samuel and Kristina saw a small platform surrounded by water.

Together, they stepped onto the platform and looked to the light.

Above the water appeared the same glow that had been guiding them through the tunnels. It soon became clearer as it hovered over a boat floating silently toward them on the water. The light resolved into a figure after a moment, and Samuel immediately recognized him.

"Robert!" Samuel shouted, his voice echoing through the large, watery chamber.

"Yes, Samuel, I have been with you this whole time," Robert smiled. "I am very pleased to see that you followed my advice and found the path to escape the castle. You have done well!"

"So it was you this whole time! I knew I recognized the glow. I even thought for a moment in the tunnel that I saw you!"

"It was I, indeed. I have been by your side the whole way from the last moment we parted at the spiral staircase, though you can only see me in the dark."

"I am certainly glad to see you now. But can you tell me where we are exactly? Our next step must be to get into this boat, because I can see nowhere else to go unless Kristina wants to swim with me. What do you say, princess?"

"I will pass on the swimming, Samuel, but you go right ahead. I'll sit here in the boat with Robert and cheer you on, though," Kristina smiled.

"So it's two for the boat, Robert," Samuel said with a smile as he looked at the princess.

They boarded the small boat and started to sail

210

through the underground cavern. The prince stood at the helm with his torch aloft, keeping a keen eye out for the first sign of trouble, while Robert took the rear of the boat, paddling and steering the boat. Kristina sat in the middle of the boat, her torch burning brightly. As they moved through the massive underground cavern, Samuel took note in great detail of his surroundings.

Far above the water soared cathedral ceilings and grand archways made of dark red brick. The archways rose in rows that seemed to stretch farther than the eye could see. The light from the torches glinted off distant stained glass windows.

The prince noticed the figures etched in the glass, depicting various scenes in each windowpane. They were high up, nearly touching the ceiling, and dim light shone through them at an angle, painting the small ripples in the water.

"I can see light coming through the windows. Do you know what part of the castle we are in, Robert?" Samuel asked.

"That light is not from outside, Samuel. It's not light from anywhere, really. You see, this cavern is like a fold in time. While you are moving out of the castle, there is no movement anywhere else in the world that you know; even time as you know it has stopped. This place is safe from the wizard, for it was built long before he took over this castle and started his reign of terror. Holy people used it in the early days to do exactly what we are doing now: transport people to safety."

"How old is this room?" Kristina asked in awe.

"Older than you would think," Robert answered reverently. "This castle is well over a thousand years old, and this room is the reason the castle was built. The windows that you noted tell the story of an age-old prophecy. They tell of a time when evil will menace the land. Then they speak of how true love will conquer evil, and evil will be no more."

As the three proceeded deeper into the vastness of the room, the prince examined the stained glass windows. He saw the story of a battle between good and evil represented through two central characters, one light and one dark. The character who represented light was going through different trials and steps in a journey.

First, the man of light was fighting a witch in a forest; then the man struggled for survival in the harsh conditions of a desert. The same man climbed a mountain where he faced great adversity. He battled a great winged creature and crossed a great abyss on a bridge like a chain.

Could this man be me? Could these windows really foretell the journey that I have been destined to fulfill all of my life? Samuel wondered. He remained silent and focused on the pictures in the windows.

The second to last window showed a battle with the seven guards at the gate. In this picture, however, he noticed something. Words appeared above the gate written in some ancient language that he did not know.

The prince asked Robert, "Can you see the window to our right - the one up in the distance with the castle gate? Do you know what those words written above the entrance mean?"

"I do. They say 'only righteousness shall pass' - only he who is truly righteous of heart, mind, and soul is destined to pass through the gates and defeat the evil one," said Robert.

"You defeated the guards and passed through the gates," Kristina smiled. "You are that righteous man, Samuel."

"I hope that I am," Samuel smiled back. As he focused again on the windows, his smile faded. As the group was passing the last window, the prince noticed that the man of light was kneeling on the ground and holding a woman in his arms. The woman appeared lifeless, though the sun shone bright in the background.

The prince refused to look at Kristina, though he could feel her eyes on him. She cannot die. These pictures cannot tell our story. All the same, he had a terrible feeling that he could not avoid the fate shown in the windows. The significance of life and death fell on him like a cold, heavy hand on his shoulder.

...

Slamming his fist on the table, the wizard barked orders to his men. "Find me whoever is still alive that was guarding the castle gate tonight!"

Men hurried about the great room at the top of the castle. The wizard knew that the prince had gone into the belly of the castle, and he was sure that Samuel would not make it out alive. The wizard headed to an altar room where he performed his magic spells. He wanted to show the prince that no matter where he may run, the wizard would always have him in his grasp.

Once in the altar room, the wizard opened a large glass book. The spells within were etched into pages of glass bound by magic. The wizard put the book on a podium in the middle of the room, raised his hands, and started breathing slowly and deeply.

As he meditated, certain words began to glow green until all the words the wizard desired were illuminated in the greenish hue. The wizard then began to speak loudly, his voice echoing off the wooden walls in the altar room.

One fly appeared. Soon, a dozen more joined it. Within moments, the entire altar room was full of flies. When the room could be filled no more, the wizard shot his arms out straight in front, as if pushing the cloud of pests forward. The flies zoomed out of the altar room through all of the cracks in the rock-covered floor. In an instant, they had funneled out of the room and disappeared.

"There, Prince Samuel, now you will feel my wrath," the wizard said darkly.

Ablewis left the altar room and returned to the great hall, where he called a meeting with all of his generals. Though his tone was fierce and his information was limited, his objective was clear. "Find Prince Samuel and Princess Kristina and kill them! They will not escape!"

Once he was done talking, the generals in attendance at the meeting quickly went their separate ways to carry out the wizard's orders. As the wizard was about to leave the great hall, a soldier came running up to him.

"My lord! There has been an attack on the guards at the gate. Four are dead, and three are missing. One of the missing is the captain of the gate himself!" the soldier gasped.

"Missing! More likely he has deserted! Prince Samuel was wearing his armor in the banquet hall. Let all know that if the captain of the gate is ever found, he is to be executed on the spot!" shouted the wizard.

"Yes, my lord!" replied the soldier. Instantly he raced to obey his master.

...

Suddenly the prince heard a loud buzzing sound in the distance. The sound grew louder with each second, starting behind the group and quickly filling all directions.

Then flies started buzzing everywhere and landing on the travelers in the boat. The flies got so bad that Samuel and Kristina had to breathe through cloth pressed to their noses and mouths. They swatted frantically at the insects while Robert tried hard to control the boat so that it would not tip over into the dark, murky water. As the struggle with the flies worsened, it was getting increasingly harder to breathe.

Then Samuel caught a glimpse of Robert trying to pray or perform a spell; the prince was uncertain of which it was. Robert lifted his staff and held it horizontally above his head. The staff began to glow bright blue. The center of the blue light was white, so bright that the prince could not stare directly at it. The flies started to ease in their attack as the light increased its radiance. Then there was a bright flash of light followed by a loud explosion.

BOOM! The light shot across the entire arena, killing every fly in its path. Once the light finished working, the flies that had been attacking the three fell down like rain. The light itself seemed to embed in the very walls of the room, lending a soft luminescence to the whole area.

In this new light, it became very clear that the cavern where they sailed was actually an old church.

The prince could see holy writings on the wall, like he had seen in the monastery of St. Mein. Nostalgia gripped the prince, and for a moment, he felt safe. He embraced, only for a moment, the same safety that had comforted him as a boy.

The prince's memories quickly faded when he noticed a blue light in the distance. Robert was steadily guiding the small boat to this light. The princess was calm, her eyes fixed on the light in the distance. She was possibly reliving memories of her own, or maybe just contemplating her freedom. As the prince was about to ask her, Robert spoke.

"In a moment, we will have to stop. I will be able to take you no farther. I cannot tell you what you must do. All I can say is that you must have faith if you want to leave this place."

The prince sat in silence as the boat came to a halt against a small wall that seemed to be holding the water in the room. To his left and his right, the wall stretched into complete darkness. The wall itself only rose a foot above the water line. From the brick wall, the prince saw that there was a gap engulfed in total darkness. This gap stretched about ten feet until it ended at a wall that rose to the top of the room. The blue light was on the wall, where it faded and lent life to a golden door. The door itself glowed, lighting up the area around it and showing whoever would like to pass through its way that he would have to pass one last test.

The prince stood up and went to the edge of the boat, where he stepped on the thin, brick wall. Only two feet thick was the wall itself, so the prince had to be extremely careful and not lose his balance. He looked at the door, studied the surrounding area, and returned to his seat. The prince then looked up at Robert, hoping the kind man would give him yet more guidance. Robert, however, just remained silent, staring away from the door.

"What are we to do?" the princess asked. "We cannot go back the way we came, and the only way out of this castle is through that door."

"I know," said the prince. "Robert has brought us this far, and the only thing he told me before he took his current vow of silence was that I had to have faith. So what does that mean? Does that mean we just wait here, and somehow the door will open and let us across that gap? I just don't know."

"Robert, is there anything else you can tell us about this door?" Kristina asked.

When Robert remained mute, Samuel stood up on the boat and grabbed him by the cloak to get his attention. But the moment Samuel's hands touched the cloak, Robert disappeared into the darkness, his cloak falling into the water.

"I guess we are on our own," the prince said with a hint of despair in his voice.

"We are not alone," Kristina said, her eyes blazing. "The creator is with us." She stepped off the boat and onto the wall, just as Samuel had before. She looked straight at the door, her gaze demanding the door to open.

"What are you doing, Kristina?" the prince exclaimed.

"Robert said that if we were going to leave this place, we had to have faith. I'm having faith." Before he could stop her, she lifted her leg and took a step into the darkness.

As her weight came down on her foot, she landed on a solid surface. Opening her eyes wide and taking a deep breath, she steadied herself on the invisible platform. Samuel's face went from a look of horror to a look of total surprise.

Kristina had faith, and she took a leap. This leap would lead both of them to freedom.

As Kristina took her second step and planted her feet on the invisible platform, she turned back to the prince, stretched out her hand, and beckoned him forward. Samuel stood, took the princess's hand without hesitation, and followed the princess to the door. When they reached the door, Samuel pulled on the handle and opened it.

Bright light, green grass, and trees burst into view. Without further hesitation, Samuel and Kristina exited the underground room and fled outside. Faith had freed them and led them to safety.

...

As the wizard walked the halls of the castle, he eagerly watched his army prepare for battle. He was sending every last man to hunt for the prince and princess, who had artfully escaped his grasp. He would do everything in his power to prevent them from fulfilling the prophecy of his doom.

As the army prepared, the wizard returned to the

altar room. He needed to cast a spell on the prince while he was still in the castle. Should the prince find the secret door in the belly of the castle, the wizard would be able to track him after the prince left the castle.

Whispering, Ablewis enchanted the door that would grant the prince freedom. When the prince grasped the door handle, he would touch an invisible resin that would allow the wizard to find the prince after two days' time.

Ablewis leered at the glass book. You may think you have escaped me, Samuel, but you have not. I write the end of this story, and in the last chapter, you die and I win.

CHAPTER XII

Cleric Jeremy was in his study, reading by dim and flickering candle light. Within the past months, his days had passed quietly. He often sat with his thoughts, wondering where Prince Samuel was and if he would accomplish his task in fulfilling the prophecy. He missed him as badly as he might have missed a son, if he had had one.

As he sat lost in his thoughts one day, a bright light interrupted him, filling the room. After the light diminished, Summer and Laci were in the room with him.

Seeing them, Jeremy jumped from his seat, startled. Who are these creatures of light? What message do they come to bring? he wondered.

Before he could speak, Summer floated up to his face, panting. "Are you Cleric Jeremy?" she demanded.

"Why yes, yes, I am. But who are you, and what are you doing here in the monastery?"

"I am Summer, and this is my sister, Laci. Prince Samuel sent us to find you. He almost has the princess, and they need your help."

"Samuel! He is still alive! Thank the creator," Jeremy exclaimed in joy.

"Yeah, yeah, the creator is the one who sent us! Now get your things. We have to hurry, because last time we saw Samuel, he was at the castle gate about to fight a lot of very mean men in ugly suits," Summer urged.

Without hesitation, Jeremy grabbed his cloak and led the girls into another room; at its rear was a holy shrine dedicated to the creator. In the center of the room was a podium that held a rather large book made of stone. There was room enough for eight people to stand in a circle around this book so that many could follow along and listen to the words while one person read.

As Jeremy ushered the two fairies toward the book, he slowly opened it and started turning the thin stone plates of its pages. The lettering looked quite odd to the fairies. Laci noticed that the letters were not written in ink. They were written in sand that stuck to the stone as if it was a part of the page.

"Why are those words written in sand? Was it just easier to make words from the stone itself?" Laci asked, intrigued.

"No, my dear. You see, a book exists in this world that has great power. That book is made of glass, and long ago it was lost to the very wizard Samuel is now facing. The only way the monastery found to combat the wizard, should he ever use the book, was to create something that was the opposite of glass: stone and sand. Good will always fight evil with an opposite. Sometimes a greater kind of evil is used to fight evil, but that always brings about grave results. So in this way, we are using the gifts of knowledge that the creator has given us, keeping evil out of the equation."

Laci stared at the pages, taking in the fine detail and the beautiful method that was used to craft the letters. After a few moments passed, Cleric Jeremy opened to a page that had a circle etched in the top of it. "This page," he explained to the girls, "is a portal page. I can transport myself, along with whoever is in my presence, to within one hundred feet of the prince."

"So this portal page can transport anyone, and anything for that matter, to where the prince is?" Summer asked.

"Yes, that's true. Why? Are you thinking of bringing along anyone else?"

"Yes! Earabis! Prince Samuel said we needed to return with him. Plus, he may be able to offer more protection for the prince," Laci explained.

"That is a good idea, indeed, because Earabis actually returned not too long ago. He has been in the stables resting. Until you two showed up, he was our only sign that the prince was still alive and continuing his journey," Jeremy agreed.

Jeremy immediately summoned one of the junior

clerics to bring Earabis into the shrine room. After an hour or so, Earabis arrived, already saddled and bridled. He seemed to sense what was about to happen and started to stomp his feet and shake his head, causing his long mane to sway. The light reflected softly off his brown coat as he stood in front of the fairies.

The fairies were astonished at the magnificence of the steed. He was every bit the horse that Samuel had described over nights spent at the campfires in the mountains. After the brief introduction of Earabis to the fairies, Cleric Jeremy had the fairies slip into his cloak pockets, and then he loudly chanted the words in the book of stone. In an instant, a bright flash shone out of the book, followed by a loud explosion.

The junior cleric that had brought Earabis into the room was still outside the door. At the sound of the explosion, the cleric ran in, startled, and frantically looked around for Cleric Jeremy. To his astonishment, there was no sign of him, the horse, or the two fairies that had accompanied him.

...

Outside Ablewis' castle, Samuel and Kristina ran farther, faster, and for longer than either could have thought possible. They had no idea of time or distance. The only thing they knew for sure was that they had exited the castle around noon. When they stopped to take their first break, the sun was slowly setting.

After leaving the castle in its belt of woods, they crossed a field, which seemed to span an eternity. After the field, they climbed down a steep cliff through a maze of rocks. Several times the prince and princess almost lost their balance in trying to gain a foothold.

After the cliffs, they crossed a swamp, which eventually led them into a forest. As the trees grew thicker, the prince began to scout out an area where he and the princess could stay safely for the night.

Neither one knew exactly what direction they were heading. The princess was following the prince. The prince was following a strong feeling that was guiding him. He could not be sure whether he was leading the princess to safety or to her demise.

The prince knew that his instinct had served him faithfully in the past. There was no reason not to trust it at this point, especially since he had nothing more to go on. Besides, going away from the wizard and Darniem in any direction had to be good in the end.

It seemed he was all alone on this task of getting her to safety. The creator had come through for Samuel a number of times during this journey; so why should the creator have to help Samuel further? Samuel had risked his life and that of many others to come and find the princess. Failure at this moment was not an option.

Samuel let these thoughts slowly fade as he searched for a secluded area in the dense forest that would provide ample protection and cover from any enemy forces that could have picked up on their trail. Samuel spotted a thick covering of vines and grass over the bottom part of a large tree. He guided the princess there and told her to rest for the night.

For a time, the two sat silently as the darkness consumed the forest. As the light slowly faded, the sounds of all creatures inhabiting this area came to life. Crickets, birds, frogs, and the distant howl of a wolf echoed through the woods. As the initial sounds of life in the forest resonated and then slowly fell in sync with one another, the prince and princess slowly relaxed, leaning their backs against the tree where they sat.

Samuel loosened his armor and put it to the side. He put an arm around the princess. The princess reached up by her shoulder where Samuel's hand lay, and she grasped it, pulled it tightly around her, and tucked her head in his shoulder.

She put her head on his chest, listening to the sound of his steady beating heart. Oh, how she had longed to hear this sound again! After all the years of wondering if he was alive when he was hiding in the woods, after being held captive by the wizard and spending days in her mind entertaining an unknown fate, the princess finally knew peace.

But Kristina could tell that Samuel was not at peace.

Though his arm circled her shoulders, that arm was stiff, and his body was rigid. His head moved at the slightest sound. The hand she did not hold rested on the pommel of a sword.

"Samuel," Kristina said softly, bracing herself when he jumped at the sound of her voice. "What's worrying you?"

Samuel shook his head. "It's nothing. Try and get some rest. We'll leave at dawn."

"Do you know where we're going?" she asked.

He frowned, impatient and offended. She could see the ridges in his brow by moonlight. "We're going away from the wizard. Isn't that enough?"

"No," Kristina told him, sitting up. "My Samuel wouldn't be content to flee. My Samuel would know where he led me and what he was meant to do. My Samuel would talk to me instead of treating me as a burden. Who knows? Perhaps I could help you instead of being a worry to you."

"You're not a worry to me," Samuel assured her quickly. "I just – I'm only following an instinct. I can't explain it. That instinct led me to you; so I've learned to trust it."

"Tell me about how it led you, Samuel. Maybe there is a message in your journey that I can understand, hearing it," Kristina urged.

Samuel told her that he was sorry for leaving the kingdom without saying so much as a decent goodbye. He told her that the temptation in the forest, the harsh days and nights in the desert, and the cold days in the mountains were only possible to survive because of her. It was always her. After his tale ended, Kristina turned to him and patted his chest.

"What are you doing?" Samuel asked, surprised.

"You have something for me - the pendant the

witch gave you. She said to give it to your true love. Were you saving it for someone else?" Kristina teased.

Blushing, Samuel took the pendant off his neck and placed it over the princess's head. "I couldn't save it for anyone else. You are my only true love. You know that."

"I know," Kristina told him. "And you are mine."

Something seemed not quite right about the pendant around Kristina's neck. Somehow, he had expected a sign or a key to the wizard's defeat when he obeyed the witch's instructions. However, he could not become too distracted now.

"Did you see in my story where we are to go next?" Samuel asked her.

Kristina frowned in the darkness, touching the smooth, purple pendant. "I saw three things. First, we must stay together, no matter what. We are both vulnerable apart. Second, we must find the girls from your dream. They need us, and the creator is leading you towards them. Third, help and direction will come when we need them, and not a moment before. So we may rest well tonight without worrying about our direction. The creator will make sure that we go where we should."

"Those are three true things," Samuel told her. He had known all she had said before, but hearing her say what she had learned lessened the burden he had felt all day. He no longer felt alone leading.

All the same, he could not relax his guard. The princess slowly fell deeply asleep, buried deeper into his arms as the night passed on. Though she lay there with him, he stood guard as a sentry would over the most prized possessions of a kingdom. For she was dearer to him than anything or anyone else in the world.

Late into the night, while the moon was still high in the sky, the prince looked into the deep, dark forest, scanning the area for intruders. The sounds of the forest had quieted as most of its residents slumbered. Looking left and right, Samuel suddenly caught a glimpse from the corner of his eye of a glowing blue object in human form.

From his angle, the glow appeared blurry. He focused directly on the blue glow, and it was gone. Shaking his head, he wondered if he was slipping into sleep; so he stood up, gently laying the princess on the ground. He covered her with the only shirt he had and stepped out from his hiding position. As he walked slowly around the tree, he bent his knees to keep a low profile. He moved methodically, placing one foot directly in front of the other so as to minimize his tracks in the area.

As he finished making a complete circle around the entire tree, he was about to go back into the hiding position when a blue glow appeared a few feet from him. It was not a bright glow but rather a soft hue. The glow slowly began resolve into a human form, and as the glow solidified, Samuel's mother stood directly in front of him.

"Mother!" Samuel exclaimed with great joy.

"My son, keep your voice low; enemies wander these woods," Kathleen admonished. "But do wake your princess. I should meet your bride."

Samuel parted the curtain of vines and brush that hid Kristina and woke her, laying his finger on her lips to make sure she would be quiet. Then he brought her out to Kathleen. "Mother, this is Princess Kristina. We are going to be married as soon as we return."

"Blessings on you, child," Kathleen told Kristina. "If my son has chosen you, then the virtue within you must equal the beauty I can see."

"Thank you, Mother," Kristina smiled. "I'm grateful to see you."

"Mother, so much has happened," Samuel told her. "I want to thank you for the two companions you sent with me. They were very loyal and provided much help in my journey."

"That was my pleasure, son. I knew you were going to need some help, and those two were perfect for the job. Besides, Summer likes your sense of humor!"

"That she does. She has one of her own; that is for sure. She just would not let that whole thing go about me being eaten by a bear," Samuel said, smiling wistfully. "I hope she is all right."

"She is, my son, and you will see her again. She and other friends will join you soon. But first, you may wonder why I have come to you," Kathleen began.

Samuel felt the echo of his earlier despair returning. "Mother, I am so lost out here. I have no idea where we are, and I fear for our lives. I am being guided by sheer instinct alone. All I could think of when I left the castle with Kristina was to get her as far away from that place as possible. Now I am in a land that is unfamiliar, and I have no way of knowing how far the wizard could be from my trail."

"Son, ever since you set foot outside the castle, I have been by your side. Every step of the way, I have been whispering in your ear that you needed to keep moving. I know you could not hear me, but it was the only thing I could do. And it seems you have followed my voice. A mother's voice can always be heard through her child's heart, you know. The wizard has not enough magic in all of creation to distort or control that kind of power."

"I knew it! I felt this strong urge to keep moving, no matter how tired I was feeling. I kept thinking that if I can just keep moving until nightfall, I will be able to let Kristina rest while I came up with a sounder plan of escape," Samuel said.

Kathleen smiled lovingly. "I want you to know you have done well, but your journey is not over. You still have two other girls to save."

Samuel turned to Kristina. "It's just as you said. The creator sent me those dreams on purpose!" Excitedly, he asked Kathleen, "Was one younger than the other by a few years? And does the older girl have blonde hair? I had a strange dream about them while I was out in the desert. I could not make sense of the dream; however, I did feel a connection. And then Kristina said that they needed us."

"Yes, Samuel and Kristina, you have to find those two girls. Protect them at all costs, with your lives if you must. Their names are Gabby and Darby.

Gabby is the older one, and Darby is her sister. Darby has a special gift inside her that the wizard wants more than anything. This gift she possesses would give the wizard absolute power over every living thing in every realm imaginable," Kathleen explained.

"But how do I find them, Mother? If the wizard is searching for them, should he not have an upper hand in getting to them before I can?" Samuel asked.

"That I cannot say. I know he has been looking for them for some time, many years at that. I do know that he had their parents killed long ago; so the girls will no doubt need your protection," Kathleen replied.

Kristina vowed, "We will protect them. We will not let the wizard capture or destroy them."

"You are both good hearts and good souls," Kathleen told them. "The creator is with you."

When she finished speaking, she raised her hands above her head and lowered them to the ground slowly. A ball of bright light appeared, and Samuel and Kristina raised their hands to cover their eyes because the light was too bright to view directly. As the light dimmed, the pair lowered their hands and saw a picture of a cabin in the woods. Next to the cabin was a field of dried-up crops, and in the distant background was a mountain.

"Follow your current route. You will come to a stream crossing about an hour's walk from where you are now. When you get to the stream, face north and continue walking. Do this, and you will come to a large, open field. On the other side rests a cabin which will look desolate from the outside, because it is protected with a strong blessing from anyone who seeks to harm these girls. However, your hearts have proven righteous, as you have been tested along your journey. So you will be able to see the cabin as it is, and you will be able to see Gabby and Darby as well.

"Gabby protects Darby fiercely. When you get there, be very kind to both girls, and ask Gabby if you can rest in the cabin. I fear you will not rest long, though, for the wizard may be very close when you arrive. Be ever watchful and guard them," Kathleen instructed.

As she spoke her last words, she hugged her son and future daughter and faded back into the forest. By now the sun was showing signs of defeating the night's moon, bringing birth to the morning - nautical twilight. Samuel looked around momentarily from where he stood. A peaceful feeling compounded by a sense of confidence grew in his soul. He knew the mission was not over yet, but he had more faith than ever in his instinct and the forces of good that had been aiding him during his journey.

A smile came to his face as he realized that, should the fairies succeed in their mission, he would be seeing not only his old friend Cleric Jeremy, but Earabis as well. Samuel turned to the princess, who was smiling serenely at him. Both of them knew that they had to get moving. They were now in a race against time. If the wizard got to the girls first, all would be lost.

After such an encouraging visit, both felt full of hope and purpose. Samuel thought Kristina's smile was more beautiful than the morning sun. The princess put her hand on Samuel's. This is how the two exchanged good mornings to one another. They were both happy to be with each other and were grateful for the chance to live yet another day.

"Here is your shirt, kind sir! Thank you for it; the night was chilly," Kristina said as she handed Samuel his shirt.

"You are welcome. I would rather stay and talk and find a decent breakfast for us, Kristina, but we have to get moving."

Kristina nodded in agreement. "The girls need us. We'll find something along the way."

In no time, they covered all tracks they had made into and out of the camp. And as daylight approached, the two made their way from their campsite and through the thick of the forest. As they walked, they began to talk about everything that had happened over the years.

Kristina told Samuel about how, after he disappeared, she spent many long days and nights studying. She told him about how she wondered where he had gone and each night would pray for his safe return. Samuel in turn explained what he did in the forest for all of those years: how he honed his swordsmanship, learned survival skills, and met Ablewis. The two walked through the woods for only a few hours before they finally reached the stream that Kathleen had mentioned.

By then, the sun was a quarter of the way up in

the sky. So Samuel decided it would be best if they moved with great urgency from the stream until they came to the edge of the tree line. When Kristina and Samuel finally saw the field, they stopped for a moment. In the distance, Samuel spotted a cabin. There was no sign of trouble, yet he still had to be cautious.

Samuel took the princess' hand and began to cross the field. It would seem that there was still hope in the seemingly impossible mission.

...

Before long, the wizard received word from his generals that his army was prepared and ready to hunt down the prince. The army did not consist solely of men, who were lured to serve the wizard by his evil influence and empty promises. His army also contained demonic creatures with wings as well as undead warriors whose flesh was no more - the wizard's magic held their bones together.

The wizard instructed his generals to form the army so that he could inspect the ranks before he set out with them to find the prince. While the army was forming, the wizard returned to the altar room with the glass book. After reciting a spell, the wizard beheld a vision.

The prince and the princess crossed a field, heading toward a cabin. In the background was a mountain peak that the wizard recognized. This particular peak was shaped like a backwards C. He knew that this mountain peak was west of his castle and that the field where he saw the prince could be no more than a day's ride from his castle.

Could it be? the wizard thought. Could the girls really have been hiding so close to my castle all of these years? It would be the perfect cover, because every time the wizard had sent a search party to find the two girls, he always started in other realms. He'd assumed that their parents would have hidden them as far from the wizard's castle as they could.

Slamming his fist in frustration, the wizard hit the podium with such force that the glass book fell to the ground and shattered into pieces, along with the vision he was currently seeing. But the wizard was calm, because he realized he did not need the book any further. The trap he had set for the prince had worked.

When the prince had touched the door to leave the castle, a blue glow that was invisible to Samuel had clung to him, revealing his location to the wizard when the wizard chose to look. The wizard had no further use for the book of glass.

He strode to the courtyard of the castle, where the army waited. Then he stood in front of them and made it known that not one would return to the castle until the girls were captured and the prince and princess were dead. His orders were clear and cold.

Once he had the girls in his possession, he would not need to use any other spells. The powers that Darby held would supply enough power for him to turn all of the light in this world into darkness. He would indeed be the supreme ruler of every living and dead thing imaginable.

The wizard basked in this thought for a moment, cracked half a creepy smile, and then shouted, "RIDE!"

Anthony Farina

Chapter XIII

The Girls

Approaching the crest of the field, Samuel and Kristina finally saw the cabin and rushed to the front steps. Samuel took Kristina's hand as they slowly climbed the cabin steps, ensuring they did not alarm the inhabitants. Once at the door, Samuel looked around one last time to make sure he had not been followed, and then he knocked.

After he knocked, Samuel waited patiently, glancing behind him again for any signs of pursuit. Slowly, the door cracked open. A little girl stood at the cabin's entrance – a girl about the age of twelve with fine strands of blonde hair and brown eyes that sparkled with the day's sun. She looked at Samuel cautiously at first, but then a warm smile spread across her face.

"You're him, aren't you? You're Prince Samuel," Gabby said with certainty.

"Yes, I am Samuel, and this is Princess Kristina,"

Samuel said politely.

"Darby has been talking about you; she has even drawn pictures of you. She is a really good artist. Oh, and I'm Gabby, by the way. We have been expecting you; please come in," Gabby said, opening the door farther.

Slowly walking inside, Samuel looked around the place while Kristina observed Gabby closely. The girl's clothes had grown tight and were badly patched. Poor, motherless dears, Kristina thought tenderly. We must do all we can to help them.

"Samuel, Kristina, won't you come in and sit down? We have a lot to talk about," Gabby invited.

The two guests moved to a couch in the main room and sat next to a fire. Gabby went into the kitchen to get some tea for them. When she left the two alone, Kristina turned to Samuel.

"We must help these girls," Kristina told Samuel. "They need parents, and I think that the creator means for us to care for them. That must be why we're here. They cannot stay here, so close to the wizard, and they cannot stay alone forever. We will keep them safe."

Samuel pressed Kristina's hand gently and nodded. "During this whole journey, I have been fueled by two things: faith and love. My love for you is what brought me through the worst of the journey. My faith has brought me many blessings, such as two fairies, the messenger Robert, and dreams like the one I had about Gabby and her sister. Faith was my compass when I had none. It means more to me than I can say to see faith and love guiding you, too," Samuel said.

Kristina looked Samuel in the eyes and smiled, glad that the man who had her heart was worthy of it. She then wrapped her arms around him and held him tight.

"You two look tired," Gabby noticed, standing with a tray of tea in the doorway.

"Yes, we are. We have been through a lot to get here, but we are just happy everyone is safe," Samuel said.

"I can see you are a good man, Samuel. Darby is sleeping now, but she has taken a liking to you. She says she dreams about you a lot. She says that you're a man who will protect people, no matter what type of evil may be near. Here, drink this tea; it's from the calla leaves out back. It will give you strength," Gabby said, passing the tea.

"You make a beautiful tray of tea, Gabby, but there are only three cups. Is there no one else here to take care of you?" Kristina asked.

"We don't have parents. They died a few years ago. Darby has a hard time understanding what happened, but I think she is dealing with it better. The wizard was looking for us; well, he was mainly looking for Darby. That's what my mother said, anyway. She said Darby was born with a special gift, and that gift could destroy all the evil in the entire world. She also said that if Darby should ever be captured by the wizard, the world would be thrown into darkness till the end of time."

"And you protect her from that fate," Kristina sympathized. "That's a heavy burden for you to shoulder alone. Is no one here to protect you? What has kept you from falling into the wizard's hands during all this time?"

"One day, before my parents were killed, my mother asked the creator for a special blessing. Her blessing has protected us. She said that the blessing would make us invisible to the eyes of the evil one and all who follow in his ways," Gabby explained.

"What a wonderful mother you had," Samuel told them. "I had a wonderful mother, too. She sacrificed herself to give me life, even though she knew that my life meant her death. I have missed her every day of my life. I know how you must feel."

"You poor girls - the hardships you have had to endure over the years! Not having parents and living a solitary life in hiding must have been so hard. My heart goes out to you," Kristina said.

The princess left Samuel's side and sat next to Gabby, putting an arm around the girl. Her brown eyes sparkled with the light that shone through the windows. She smiled the warmest smile, one that spread to everyone in the room.

"Who is this?" a small voice said in the doorway.

Samuel and Kristina stood, exchanging glances. They knew that the second girl was Darby, and they could see immediately that she was special. She radiated love and peace.

"Hello, I am Samuel, and this is Kristina. We were just sitting here talking to your sister; I hope we did not wake you," Samuel said.

"Oh no, you didn't wake me. I was having a dream

about a bear. I heard voices; so I came down here to see who was in the house. We don't get many visitors, and it is nice to have company," Darby said while rubbing her eyes.

The pendant that Samuel had put around Kristina's neck started to glow, and the princess took it off. It began to feel warm in her hands; so she gave it to Samuel, who held it for all to see.

Darby's eyes lit up and smiled when she looked at the beautiful gem. The prince noticed her smile and extended the pendant toward Darby. As he did, it grew brighter still. Darby took the pendant from the prince and, as she held it, light flashed from the pendant. Then the gem turned back to its dormant color.

Kristina gasped in delight. "She is meant to have that pendant, Samuel! I may be your true love, but Darby – Darby is pure love itself. Put it around her neck."

The woman from the woods' voice echoed in Samuel's head. Her words about giving the pendant to true love all made sense now. The creator had protected the girls because one of them held the only weapon that could defeat the wizard: love. The weapon was not the pendant itself; it was only a compass to point to the chosen one gifted to carry true love and hope for the land.

Everyone in the room stared in silence as Darby put the pendant around her neck. The silence was abruptly interrupted by a loud blast, accompanied by a bright flash of light outside the cabin.

The prince drew his sword while standing up, instantly ready to defend the princess and the girls. "Stay here," ordered Samuel as he left the room and went outside to see what was happening.

As he opened the door, his facial expression went from being watchful and guarded to a look of pure joy. In front of the cabin stood his loyal friend Earabis, who was carrying Cleric Jeremy. As Jeremy dismounted the horse, the prince sheathed his sword and ran to them.

"Earabis, ole boy - you're alive! You made it!" the prince exclaimed. "Cleric Jeremy!" the prince shouted as he moved in to give him a big hug. "There is only one way that I know you got the message to come and find me, and it must be that two little pixies fulfilled my orders."

As Samuel finished speaking, Laci and Summer floated out of Jeremy's pocket and yelled, "Fairies!"

"Yes, yes, I know what you are," said Samuel, as the two floated up and kissed him on the cheek. Samuel then moved back to Earabis and patted the head of his golden brown steed. "It is good to see you, my friend. Our journey has been long, and I cannot tell you how grateful I am that you have arrived," Samuel said with a warm smile.

"Samuel, it is good to see you as well, but we must go inside," urged Cleric Jeremy. "Is this the place where the girls are hiding?"

Samuel nodded to the door behind him. "Yes, they are inside with Kristina."

"Kristina!" Summer said excitedly. "It's about time we get to meet this girl that you stormed a castle for!"

"Exactly, Summer and I left you at the castle gates, Samuel. We did not know what your fate would be, but we had faith that you would somehow bring Kristina to safety. We hurried as fast as we could to tell Cleric Jeremy about what was going on, and we got here as fast as we could," Laci said.

"They did just that, but let us get inside. Samuel, we need to hide Earabis somewhere out here; can you place him close by?" Jeremy asked.

"Sure, there is a place out back where I can put him. There is water and food for him as well," Samuel said.

Samuel walked Earabis around to the back of the cabin. "Eat your fill and rest well, my friend, for I fear the worst of this whole journey lies ahead of us in a short time." Earabis nodded and began to eat the lush grass. Samuel returned to the front of the cabin and led the three guests inside.

As he entered, he found Gabby, Darby, and Kristina waiting in the room where he had left them. The fairies floated inside and immediately went to Gabby. "This must be Gabby," Summer said as she floated around her head in circles. Gabby's eyes chased Summer as she moved.

Laci floated in front of Darby and sat on her nose for a second. "This must be Darby!" she said excitedly. "You two girls are really special, you know."

Darby laughed as she tried to swat Laci from her nose. Laci was too quick and moved away. "Wow! Fairies do really exist!" Darby said as she stared in awe at Summer and Laci floating around the room.

"Yes, we most indeed do exist. However, some people get us confused with our annoying cousins, the pixies," Summer said as she moved up to Samuel's face and stuck her tongue out.

Darby laughed at the sight of Summer toying with Samuel. Gabby was smiling, too, because she had not seen her sister smile in a very long time. For once, the two girls did not fear being captured, and Gabby's thoughts were at peace.

"Girls, this is Cleric Jeremy; he is a very dear old friend of mine who taught me a lot, starting from the time when I was your age. He has given me much guidance over the years," Samuel said.

The girls waved to him and smiled. "Pleased to meet you, sir," Darby beamed.

Jeremy bowed gallantly and then moved over to give Kristina a hug. "Your parents are very worried about you, but they have the utmost faith in Samuel. I saw them two days ago, and they are awaiting your return. Everything in Ferdinand is fine, and I must say that it is good to see you alive and well," Jeremy said to Kristina as he embraced her.

"I have been so worried about them. Thank you for letting me know they are okay. I do miss my home very much. I can't even begin to tell you how relieved I am to be here right now instead of being in that terrible castle with that wicked man. Samuel fought so bravely to rescue me," Kristina said fondly, smiling at Samuel.

Samuel stood back and grinned at everyone. He did not know what the next day would hold, but for now he was happy. He had not felt like he had been in a home since the day that he'd left St. Mein, five years ago. Today he felt more at home than he ever could have thought possible.

It was not because he was in some man-made structure that looked like a house. Rather, it was because home to him were the people he had carried with him all of those years in the wilderness, the people that he turned to in his heart when the desert got too hot or the mountains too steep. The people in this room were his home, including the two girls whom he had met only a short time ago.

As everyone conversed and got acquainted, the morning grew into the afternoon, and it was decided that they should all eat. Laci and Summer floated away from the group for a moment and began to converse among themselves.

"Laci, do you think it would be an abuse of power to use our magic to bring a feast for everyone here?" Summer asked.

"No, not at all. The creator actually told me once of the importance of having everyone around a table for a meal. He said it brings everyone together. He also said that when it comes time that all of us are together, he would grant me permission to use magic to create a buffet of food for them," Laci explained.

"What are you two talking about over there? How I should be eaten by a bear? Or are you planning some trick?" Samuel said, laughing.

"You being eaten by a bear would only be followed by me calling you Sabrina!" Summer laughed.

"Okay, pixie, whatever makes you feel two inches taller - go ahead and keep talking," Samuel joked.

The rest of the room looked a little confused as Summer and Samuel teased each other. "I will explain all of that over dinner, everyone. For now, why don't all of you wait right here while Summer and I prepare a surprise for you? Darby and Gabby, would you like to come and help? We could use some good ideas," Laci said.

Gabby jumped up and down with excitement. Darby's face lit up, because she was still trying to grasp the reality of talking to a fairy. She nodded yes with a smile, took her sister's hand, and together they followed Laci and Summer into the kitchen.

While Darby and Gabby and the fairies went to prepare the meal, Samuel, Kristina, and Jeremy all stayed in the main room and conversed. "Jeremy, the girls are in danger. We have to get them back to St. Mein and put them under the protection of the monastery. There is no way the wizard would dare attack the kingdom," Samuel said.

"You're right, we have to find a way to move them back there quickly. The problem is that once they leave this cabin, the wizard will know where they are. They are only protected as long as they are in this house, unless the wizard has found a way around the blessing, of course. If he has, then he most surely is on his way here right now," Jeremy explained.

"Samuel, Earabis is here. Why don't you use him to get the girls back to safety?" Kristina inquired.

"I am sure there is a quicker route back than the one you initially took here."

"Never. I came this far to get you, and I will not leave you. I know I must protect them at all costs, but I am not leaving your side. Who knows what will happen if the wizard captures you again? He may send you some place I can never find. Losing you for good would end my world, Kristina; I just cannot take that chance," Samuel pled as he looked at Kristina.

She saw how his eyes were saddened at the thought of leaving her. "I know, Samuel, and if there were another way, I would not want you to leave me, either. I just do not see much of a choice right now; we have to get those girls to safety," Kristina said.

Samuel gently caressed Kristina's cheek. "Remember what you told me last night? We must stay together. We must help the girls. And we trust the creator to send help and direction when we need it."

"I agree with Samuel, Kristina; he cannot leave you after everything he has done to save you from the wizard," Cleric Jeremy said. "However, maybe there is a way we can all leave here together. There is safety in numbers, and I think that between all of us, we make a pretty strong force."

"So we go together. We must break it gently to the girls, though. They have known no other home, and they have only just met us. We will have to think carefully not only of how we leave safely together, but also of how we convince the girls to come with us," Kristina reminded them.

The three sat in silence for a few moments as they contemplated the ways to get everyone back home safely and together. Moments later, all three started to smell the most delightful aroma wafting from the kitchen. Laci floated into the main room and announced to Samuel, Jeremy, and Kristina that dinner was ready.

As they entered the room, all stood in awe of the meal on the table before them. Darby's mouth watered at the sight of the chocolate pies and warm breads. The meal included fruits from every realm, roasted pheasant, lamb, and potatoes cooked to perfection with other vegetables.

Gabby almost broke down crying at the sight of this feast, because she could not remember the last time she was able to enjoy such richness. She remembered briefly how she used to enjoy feasts like this with her parents when they still lived here. Those were good times she held dear to her heart.

After everyone had enjoyed first helpings, Kristina rose at her place and looked around at the table. "I think that it is time we discuss with the girls what we would like to do. We don't have the details settled yet, girls, but Samuel and I have something very important to ask you."

Darby sprang out of her chair and rushed to Kristina. "Please don't leave us! We will be no trouble at all if you will only take us with you."

"Yes, please let us come," Gabby pled. "We've been waiting for you so long, and it would be awful if you went away and left us here."

Samuel leaned back in his chair and laughed. "So much for convincing them, Kristina! Yes, girls – we want you to come with us and live in my castle. Kristina and I will be married, and you'll stay with us. You'll be our family, just the same as if you were born our daughters."

"It's the best news ever," Darby sighed. "I was going to offer to do your dishes if you'd let me come!"

The feast resumed then in friendly laughter. Everyone talked and joked as they ate. Night fell as they sat around the table and got to know each other even more. The hour finally grew so late that Samuel declared it was time for everyone to get some rest.

"I'll stay up and take first watch. Tomorrow we are going to begin the long journey back to St. Mein. We will need our rest, for it is a long journey indeed. Jeremy, will you take second watch? I just want to be sure that Kristina and I were not followed by anyone. Getting the girls back to St. Mein is the top priority."

"Indeed, Samuel, I will get some rest and relieve you in a few hours."

"Samuel, I'll be happy to stay up with you, too; we fairies really don't need to sleep much at all," Summer said.

"Sure thing, Summer; it will be good to have some company. But no making bunnies appear!" Samuel teased.

"All right, Samuel - no bunnies, I promise!"

The group started to get up from the table and

go their separate ways to find a place to sleep. As Kristina was walking away from the table, Samuel gently took hold of her wrist. Kristina turned, meeting his gaze and staring at him for a long moment. Neither said a word; they just looked at each other.

Kristina's body turned toward Samuel's, and she grabbed his other hand. They did not need to speak, because they both knew what the other was thinking. They wanted this journey to be over so that they could live in peace with each other.

Samuel wanted to speak the words, "I love you." But his mouth only moved slightly, and silence stretched between the two.

After a few moments, Kristina moved close to Samuel and wrapped her arms around him. "Whatever happens tomorrow, I will follow you. I will follow you to the end, no matter what. You are my prince."

"And you are my princess; you always will be," Samuel said as he took a step back from Kristina, all the while holding her hands. "Will you go upstairs with Darby? Sit with her and watch over her tonight. Do not leave her side, no matter what. I will be downstairs, and periodically I will go outside to check on Earabis. Should the creator will it, we will have no trouble tonight, and we'll be on our way at first light."

Kristina nodded while dazzling Samuel with a brilliant smile. She then turned and went upstairs to accompany Darby and Gabby. Meanwhile the fairies were cleaning up the table and Cleric Jeremy was in the main room sitting down and saying a prayer. Samuel walked in, and Jeremy looked up from his prayer.

"We will be all right, Samuel," Jeremy assured him. "The journey back is a long one, but once we start, we should be able to move quickly enough to make it back safely to St. Mein without being detected by the wizard."

"I am afraid that he may already be on his way here," Samuel confessed. "This whole journey, it seemed like he was one step ahead of me all the time."

Jeremy clapped Samuel's shoulder firmly. "We have the creator on our side; we cannot lose. Have faith, Samuel, for with faith all things are possible."

Samuel nodded his head and started walking toward the door. "I'll go take a look around outside and then come back in. I want to make sure everything is secure before we turn the lights out in the cabin. I know that some sort of spell has protected the cabin; I just have this bad feeling that we are being watched tonight."

Samuel walked toward the door, opened it, and stepped outside. He stood on the porch of the cabin for a few moments, letting his vision adjust to the night. He breathed in deeply, letting his senses adjust to the scent of the area. After a few moments, his ears were able to hear better through the echoes of the night.

Samuel walked around the cabin and glanced into the field. He saw no sign of anything that portended danger; so he moved around to the back of the cabin, where he found Earabis. He walked to his friend and patted his mane. "If anything alerts you tonight, my friend, do not be afraid to make noise. I will come out of the cabin at a moment's notice." Earabis grunted as if he were confirming the prince's orders.

Samuel walked around the remaining area and headed back into the cabin. He sat down by a window and looked up at the night sky. His thoughts would keep him busy for the next few hours. He knew that the fate of everyone he loved, along with the fate of the world, rested on his shoulders.

He thought about all he had endured to this point: defeating the witch in the woods, crossing the desert, nearly freezing to death in the mountains, rescuing Kristina, and finally reaching the girls. His journey had indeed been blessed by a higher power; his survival alone was proof of that.

Faith was what he needed at this point, just like Jeremy had suggested. "Have faith, Samuel." The words echoed in his head. Samuel stared deeper into the night sky as the hours passed, all the while searching for faith in every corner of his soul.

CHAPTER XIV

Final Battle

amuel, why don't you go get some rest?" Jeremy suggested. "You have been up for hours, and I am more than capable of taking over watch until the sun comes up."

"That sounds like a good idea, Jeremy. I'll head upstairs and lie down for a bit. Wake me up at first light," Samuel said as he stretched his hands above his head and let out a silent yawn.

He walked upstairs and saw an open space with two beds. The princess slept soundly, with Darby curled up next to her. The two must have developed an immediate bond for the child to trust her in such a short time. Gabby was asleep soundly in the bed adjacent to Darby's. Samuel found a spot on the floor next to the only window in the room and fell asleep using his arm as a pillow.

In his dreams, he saw Kristina smiling at him. Across the barrier of sleep, his conscious mind glowed, and his heart fluttered. Her smile was always a light in the darkness to him.

Then, the light around her faded as an unseen force was pulling her away. The emotions in his dream became dark and fearful. The peace of deep sleep was slowly turning into a nightmare.

He looked closer at Kristina, her smile turned into sadness, and she let out a loud, painful cry. Her life was being taken from her. In the next instant, she fell to the ground motionless. She gazed at Samuel, and the life in her eyes faded into an abyss. A bright light flowed from her body as her spirit ascended.

"NO!" Samuel sat up quickly. The light from dawn shining on Samuel's face helped him to understand that he had just been dreaming. Kristina was right by his side.

She had heard him moving around and tried to wake him just moments ago. "Are you okay? Your whole body was shaking, and you had a look of terror on your face, even though you were sleeping."

"Yes," Samuel said, breathing heavily. "Yes, I am okay. I just had a bad dream."

Samuel did not realize that he was holding Kristina's hand, as if he was trying to confirm that she was really alive. It was hard to grasp that his fear had been a false reality, conjured up by the thoughts of worry and fear that he had been burying during this entire journey. He stood, shaking off the last of the terror.

"It's dawn now. We should let the girls rest just a bit more, but then we need to get going," Samuel said.

Kristina nodded in affirmation. Both of them headed downstairs to find the fairies cooking breakfast for the crew. Cleric Jeremy was in the main room, still checking the area.

"Good morning to the two of you. All has been quiet, Samuel. The fairies got up early and started cooking. Nothing like a hearty meal before a long trip!" Jeremy said happily.

As he finished speaking, Gabby and Darby were walking down the stairs. "Is that bacon I smell? That is my favorite food!" Darby said excitedly.

"It sure is, Darby. We thought you might like this little treat from us. We have a long journey ahead; so Summer and I prepared you two a nice meal," Laci said as she set the table.

All sat down to eat a glorious breakfast. Samuel explained to everyone about the journey they were about to take and how they would need to move quickly to get back to St. Mein safely.

"Have you girls ever ridden a horse before?" Samuel asked.

"No we haven't, but I have always wanted to," Gabby remarked.

"Well, today is your day to ride one. Outside is my friend Earabis, one of my best friends. He has been out there all night. You will be riding him all the way to St. Mein. The rest of us will be walking right by your side."

"Bacon for breakfast and now a horse! This is the

best day ever!" Darby said. Her expression made the whole room erupt in laughter. It would seem that the group was naturally drawn to each other, a trait that would ease the journey home.

"Yes indeed - he is one of the best. And speaking of my horse, I am going to check on him and get him ready for our journey. Everyone else, finish your breakfasts and pack for the journey. We will leave within the hour."

After Samuel gave instructions, he got up from the table and excused himself. He went outside and found Earabis. He checked the saddle and reins, ensuring all was secure. After a few moments, Earabis started to move around. Samuel started to tug at him. "Easy boy, what is it?"

Earabis was shaking his head forcefully, trying to free himself from his reins. Samuel could almost hear King Sal's voice teaching him to see with his ears and hear with his eyes. Earabis could not speak, but Samuel heard what he was saying all the same and turned around to look toward the cabin. When he turned, he saw a hideous creature just feet from him, preparing to jump and attack him.

The creature lunged forward, giving Samuel no time to react beyond jumping aside. But while the creature was in mid-air, Cleric Jeremy approached from the side and slammed a staff into its midsection, knocking it onto the ground and rendering it unconscious. Samuel looked at Jeremy in disbelief.

"I can never repay you for that. What is going on? I thought we were hidden from the wizard's creatures," Samuel said.

"I heard rustling out here and came to see what was going on. Just as I feared, we have been discovered. This creature that just tried to attack you is a scout. More of them will follow in no time. We have no time to travel to safety. You must warn the girls and keep them inside. I'll untie Earabis and get him ready. We are about to do battle with the wizard's entire army. Now go!" Jeremy exclaimed.

Without hesitation, Samuel ran as fast as he could to get into the cabin. He opened the front door and slammed it shut behind him.

Kristina came running up to him. "What is going on, Samuel? What happened outside?"

"We have been spotted. I do not know how, but Jeremy says the creature that attacked me was a scout, and the rest of the wizard's army will be here in a short time. We don't have time to leave. You must lock the girls and yourself in this cabin," Samuel instructed. "Summer, place barrier spells on the windows and doors. You're staying in here. Laci, you come with me outside. Jeremy, Earabis, you, and I will have to defend this cabin. Should the wizard arrive, we must keep him at all costs from entering this place."

The girls ran up to Kristina. "We're scared; what should we do?" Gabby asked.

"Go upstairs and hide. I'll help Summer lock everything up down here. When we are done, we will come upstairs and stay with the two of you," Kristina ordered. "Samuel, I want a word with you."

Impatient, Samuel stepped into the kitchen with

Kristina so that they could speak privately. As Kristina approached him, he saw the worry in her eyes and softened. "Don't worry," he told her. "I'll protect you. You'll be all right."

Kristina frowned and shook her head. "We shouldn't be separated. Remember? We're more vulnerable apart. Either you should come inside with me, or I should fight outside with you. We belong together."

"No," Samuel disagreed vehemently. "Jeremy and Earabis and the fairies alone can't defend this cabin. They need me. But I can't have you out there. You haven't been trained to fight. I'll worry about you and get distracted and be hurt. Please, Kristina – trust me. Stay inside."

"I don't like it, Samuel," Kristina told him. "It feels like we're making a mistake. I know you think you're saving me, but I just know that we will be in more danger if we're apart."

Samuel shook his head like a dog shedding water. "I won't accept that. I've been in battles before. There is no way I am letting you near such danger. Your duty is inside, keeping the girls calm. I'm sure of it."

Kristina sighed. "I'll do as you ask because of the love I have for you. Be safe, and fight quickly so that you can come back to me."

"I will," Samuel promised. He wanted to kiss his true love before the battle, but worry goaded him out of the kitchen and outside before he knew it. He listened to Kristina bolting the front door, and then he set his face toward the forest, where the creature had emerged.

Just then, Samuel heard a loud roar. Sprinting around the cabin, he saw Cleric Jeremy and Earabis fending off a creature that looked like a giant cat with horns. Its fangs hung over its mouth in a ghastly and frightening way.

Jeremy did not waver in courage as he stood his ground against the beast. He struck his staff at it to knock it off balance. Jeremy displayed a strength that Samuel had never witnessed during the life of their friendship. The creature fell backward, nearly tripping over its own feet at the force of Jeremy's blow.

Samuel stood in awe as he watched Jeremy do battle with the creature. A moment later, he noticed three darker, scaly creatures approach from the field to the right of him. Earabis noticed them as well and immediately rushed to his masters' side.

Samuel did not hesitate. Drawing his sword and charging in their direction, he and Earabis collided with all three creatures. The creatures fought in an uncanny motion, their maneuvers difficult to anticipate. They seemed to bend the laws of nature as they moved with ultra-fast speed, yet their arms twisted gracefully as they closed in to strike Samuel and Earabis.

Samuel deflected blow after blow of the three creatures with great force. Slashing to and fro, Samuel was finally able to land the sharp edge of his sword on the arms of two of the creatures. Earabis raised his front hooves and connected with one of the creatures to Samuel's left.

The third creature slipped behind Samuel to attack him from the rear. Samuel noticed the creature's movement on his blind side out of the corner of his eye. Samuel thrust once more at the creature to his right and quickly flipped his sword, grabbing the handle. Driving the sharp edge of the sword behind him, Samuel subdued his attacker.

By this time, Earabis was finishing off the other creature. Turning his attention once again to the creature on his right, which was still swinging its arms wildly, Samuel immediately disposed of him with two quick slashes: one to the left and one to the right.

Once Samuel and Earabis had finished fending off the attackers, Samuel turned to see Jeremy still doing battle with the cat-like creature. By this point, Jeremy had injured the cat enough to gain leverage on it. He quickly dodged a swipe from the cat's massive claw, regained his balance, and struck the cat with the rounded end of his staff. The cat shrieked loudly in pain. As the last vibrations of sound left the cat's mouth, its eyes closed, and it fell to the ground, still.

"If this is just a hint of the wizard's army, we are going to have our hands full," Samuel said, breathing heavily.

"Do not fear, Samuel; the creator has blessed us in more ways than one," Jeremy reassured him.

Just as Jeremy was speaking about a blessing, Laci floated out of the front door and up to Samuel and Jeremy.

"Summer and Kristina have finished locking the house. They are upstairs with the girls trying to hide them," Laci said, scanning the ground and noticing the fallen enemies at Samuel and Jeremy's feet. "Wow! That is one big cat! You guys have had your hands full. Well, it looks like you're going to need a little more help. Samuel, place your sword on the ground."

Samuel obeyed and stepped back from his weapon. Laci waved her wand over it, and with her eyes closed, she started to pray. Thin blue and red streaks traced down the center of the sword, weaving together in an intricate pattern. A flash of light appeared and then extinguished.

"Go ahead, Samuel; pick it up," Laci ordered. "The sword is now unbreakable. Should you become overwhelmed during this battle, concentrate on your faith in the creator. Your faith will give you the strength of a thousand men. Without faith, though, you will just be wielding a normal sword."

Samuel picked up the sword; he gazed deeply in wonder as he took in the beauty of his new tool. He then brought the weapon down to his side. "I will use it with all my faith until my last breath. Thank you for this wonderful gift at a most desperate time," Samuel said, nodding his head in gratitude to Laci.

No sooner had Samuel lowered his sword than everyone crouched - their attention quickly turned to a vibration in the ground. The trees in the distance on the opposite side of the open field started to shake violently. The ground began to vibrate more intensely, as the trees were still shaking violently.

"It sounds like the world is going to end! There is no way I'm going to miss this!" Summer shouted while she floated up to Samuel.

"All right, Summer, but if things get too bad, you head right back into the cabin and protect the girls and Kristina," Samuel ordered.

"Will do, Captain Samuel!" Summer said, saluting. Summer still managed to lighten her companions' moods in the most desperate of times.

Suddenly, the rustling trees exploded with creatures of all shapes and sizes. They were running as fast as they could. There was no way for anyone to count the mass of enemies engulfing their position. The only words Samuel could mutter were, "Hundreds - there must be hundreds of them."

Laci and Summer quickly floated to the sky, about ten feet above Samuel and Jeremy. Simultaneously raising their wands, they shot bolts of light forth, exploding charges into the crowd of minions that charged toward Samuel and Jeremy. A large group of creatures flew up into the air, back to the tree line.

Once the smoke cleared from the explosions, more creatures charged forward. But the explosions caused a little room between the attackers and the group.

"Stand your ground! They must not enter the cabin!" Samuel shouted to all.

Mounting Earabis, Samuel began to charge into the group of creatures that were headed straight for the cabin. Earabis charged forward with such power that any creature which came close enough to touch the steed was thrown back to the ground ten feet or more. This act of bravery startled the enemy, sending fear through the forces that would descend upon the cabin. Though Earabis and Samuel were able to take on the brunt of the initial force, a large number of creatures slipped by them, heading straight for Jeremy.

Standing firm with his staff, he battled each creature as it approached him. Their intent was to kill. Jeremy's intent was to maim, and Jeremy did just that. Thrusting the staff into the chest of one creature, driving the other end of his staff to the ground and throwing another creature off balance, Jeremy moved fluidly through the crowd of enemies.

Still in the sky, Laci and Summer floated around the battlefield, blasting light from their wands to dissipate the enemies. In the midst of the fighting, Summer noticed one of the creatures sneaking onto the porch of the cabin. She immediately left her position of attack and headed straight to the door. Pointing her wand at the creature while it was in mid strike, preparing to knock the door down, Summer blasted it with all her might.

A cloud of smoke exploded where the creature stood, and as it cleared, Summer began to laugh. "There! That is what you get for trying to break into the house! You will now live out your life as a cute bunny!" Summer turned another one into a cat. She laughed as she floated in circles upward and back to where Laci was.

Jeremy was still striking with all his might; piles of creatures lay at his feet. He was beginning to feel tired from battle. Quickly subduing another attacker, he sprinted over to the crowd that formed around Samuel.

He could see Samuel had dismounted and was fighting close to Earabis. Earabis would need room to kick his strong legs. Samuel moved in a half circle around a small group of enemies, hitting each creature only once and then moving to another. His sword would slash a leg or an arm, only to be met by another attacker. As one creature started toward Samuel from his blind spot, Jeremy jumped in at the exact moment and tackled the creature.

"Jeremy!" Samuel shouted. Turning his attention away from the group he was fighting, he came to Jeremy's aid and kicked the creature that was on top of Jeremy. The creature rolled off Jeremy and onto the ground. Reaching out his hand, Samuel said, "Thanks, old friend, but we need to fall back, closer to the cabin doors."

"Agreed," Jeremy said.

"Laci! Buy us a few seconds so that we can get to the cabin door!" Samuel ordered.

"You got it," Laci shouted. "Close your eyes; this is going to blind everyone!"

No sooner did Laci finish saying this than she raised her wand, and a light as bright as the midday sun engulfed the entire area. Samuel and Jeremy moved back to the cabin while keeping one arm covering the tops of their eyes. Earabis followed suit. When the bright light faded, every creature in the area moved around as if in a dazed spell. When they reached the front of the cabin, Samuel noticed a bunny sitting at the front door.

"Summer must have found some humor in all of this," Samuel said, cracking a smile.

But the evil creatures attacking him suddenly gained ground and started to close in on Jeremy and Samuel. There were a little less than half remaining at this point.

"Are you up to finishing this, old friend?" Samuel said, looking at Jeremy.

"Indeed! Let's send these creatures back to where they came from!" Jeremy shouted as he raised his staff.

The three fought side by side for what seemed like an eternity. The fairies used their powers to subdue more creatures while Earabis and Jeremy fought alongside Samuel. Samuel began to feel hope arise from deep within - a hope that said they were going to make it out of this alive.

"Samuel! Look! They are running away. There are only a few of them left now!" Laci said as she hovered farther into the air to get a better view.

The group battled a few more creatures, and then the rest began to fade back into the woods.

"Yay! We did it! We won!" Laci exclaimed.

Summer and Laci began to dance in the air. Samuel and Jeremy just leaned over, catching their breath, Earabis still close by.

"Do you think that was it?" Samuel asked.

"I do not know. I sure hope so," Jeremy remarked.

As the girls were dancing in the air, relishing

their victory, a black cloud engulfed them. The two started to cough, and then they fell to the ground.

Samuel rushed to their aid. "Jeremy, can you take them inside? I believe we have another battle to fight."

Jeremy picked up the fairies and rushed them inside.

"What happened to the poor dears?" Kristina fretted.

"It must be Ablewis," Jeremy guessed.

"Will they be all right?" she asked.

"Yes, they will be. He just incapacitated them momentarily. They should come around momentarily," he said. "I need to head back outside; keep an eye on things!" Jeremy yelled as he ran out the door.

As Jeremy leapt off the cabin steps, he rushed to Samuel's side. Suddenly, from behind, the defenders heard the sound of marching, men chanting in cadence, and the beating of drums. Samuel and Jeremy turned around, facing away from the field, and gazed into the woods that surrounded the back of the cabin, about three hundred feet away. To the left of the cabin stretched the massive woods. To the right lay the open field, where the blast of smoke came from.

"Do you remember how I told you to have faith? And if you did, the creator would come through for us?" Jeremy asked.

"I do," Samuel answered. "I remember well. My faith has been with me through this whole journey. What is coming through those trees, Cleric?"

"Just wait, you'll see," Jeremy replied.

As the marching grew louder, men in armor began to emerge from the woods. Ranks too numerous to count filled the entire forest that encircled the cabin. Leading the men on horseback, Cleric Kerwin emerged from the woods and headed straight to Samuel and Jeremy. Once by them, he dismounted and embraced Jeremy.

"Your plan worked like a charm, old friend! Once you cast the spell from the altar room, I immediately began to get the army of St. Mein ready to march. Within hours, the men were ready to go," he explained. "We marched all night and took the most direct route here. I do hope we are not too late for battle?" Kerwin said as he turned his attention to Samuel. "Samuel, my dear boy! It is good to see you! I have brought the armies of Ferdinand and St. Mein."

As he finished talking, the armies came to a halt in even ranks and formations; they stood ready and disciplined, waiting for their next orders. The armies of St. Mein were in light blue armor. On their breastplates, they each wore a symbol unique to the Kingdom of St. Mein: two ravens flying above a man. The man wore a black cloak. He carried a staff in one hand and a book in another.

The armies of the Kingdom of Ferdinand wore green armor. The symbol on their chest was a sun rising over a field of crops. Regardless of the different types of symbols, both had an inner meaning that pointed toward peace and justice. This was one reason why the Kingdoms of St. Mein and Ferdinand had always gotten along well.

Within moments of the armies' halting, a loud horn blared from the woods that surrounded the field, opposite where Samuel, Jeremy, and the entire armies of Ferdinand and St. Mein were. The horn called forth the angry screams of men, and then the army of the wizard erupted onto the open field. The two armies were now only one thousand feet apart from one another. The men in the wizards' army wore red armor. The center of their breastplates depicted fire raining down on earth, symbolizing the destruction they intended to do to the whole world.

"Well, Samuel, looks like we are not finished yet," Jeremy remarked.

"This ends now," Samuel said as he gazed straight at the approaching army.

Without a moment's hesitation, Samuel started walking toward the wizard's army, sword raised in hand. His walk turned into a run and then into a full-out sprint. He moved so quickly that Jeremy and Kerwin had little time to react.

"Charge!" sounded Kerwin with a loud roar.

The armies of St. Mein and Ferdinand began to advance, following Samuel. All the while, the wizard's army quickly picked up pace. Should the creator be watching from above, it would have looked to him as though two landmasses were about to collide. The sheer number of men involved in this battle was epic.

In the lead with both his armies to his back, Samuel took aim at a single evil soldier and charged with all his might. He was aiming for a man with a spear. Though there were hundreds just like this particular one, Samuel chose to unleash his fury on this one. He kept running as fast as he could. Within moments, he was in striking distance of the enemy. Taking a giant leap in the air, Samuel raised his sword above his head with both hands. Coming down from his leap, he brought his sword down in front of him, and when he made contact with the soldier's armor, he nearly split his breastplate in two.

The soldier fell to the ground, dead. Samuel stood up quickly and began to swing, block, and parry every enemy that approached him; there were many. At this point, the two armies collided. SMASH!

A loud, metallic sound screeched throughout the whole land. Men screaming, swords clanging against swords, and hand-to-hand combat ensued. The number of men that fell to the ground in the first few moments was such that anyone around who could take notice of anything but fighting for his own life could have mistaken the vibration for an earthquake.

The fighting lasted for hours. Though it would seem that the two kingdoms were having trouble gaining ground on the enemy, they did not allow the enemy to gain any ground toward the cabin. A stalemate would ensue for at least another hour.

Treetops exploded with winged beasts. Razor-sharp claws protruded from the ends of their feet. The beasts blackened the sky due to their sheer numbers. Swooping down into the onslaught, the screeching hordes picked up soldiers from the armies of St. Mein and Ferdinand alike. Samuel, still fighting off foe after foe, was quickly able to dodge one of these beasts by rolling to the ground, just in time for one of the creatures to miss grabbing him.

The numbers of those fighting for good soon diminished, and the ground force was closing in fast on the cabin. In a little time, nearly half of the two kingdom's total force was demolished. Those who met their fate with the winged beasts would find themselves being flown through the air and dropped to the ground from a great height.

Bursting through the cabin doors, Laci and Summer emerged, wands pointing up to the sky. They floated high above the ground and proceeded to chant. As their chanting grew louder, the sky began to consume the light. Bolts of lightning rained down from the cloud-covered atmosphere. The bolts precisely struck the winged beasts flying around the air. All but one beast remained in the air after the lightning barrage. The beasts that were struck fell swiftly to the ground.

Laci and Summer conjured up another storm of lightning bolts to finish off the remaining creature. As the bolts came down, they were quickly deflected from the beast, scattering the electric force into the air. The creature was able to pinpoint where the lighting was being summoned from and made haste in approaching the fairies. As it came in closer, Samuel took notice of the situation and ran quickly in front of the fairies.

As he was running, keeping his eye on the airborne attacker, he stopped in his tracks. He knew who the rider was. It was Ablewis, the wizard.

He had no time to digest the reality that he was about to come face to face with his nemesis. Wasting not another moment, Samuel took hold of his sword, as to throw a spear. When the creature got close enough, he launched his sword into the air, aiming straight for its heart.

The sword flew straight past the fairies, causing them to turn and see where it came from. The sword continued its direction and stuck right into the breast of the creature. As it was struck, it raised its neck, let out a loud screech, and spiraled to the ground. The wizard, holding onto the beast, was able to cast a spell to ensure that the beast did not crash into the ground. It floated instead and came softly to a landing spot.

The battle raged on. Samuel quickly searched the ground for another weapon. Picking up a sword from a fallen soldier who wore the crest of St. Mein, Samuel ran to where the wizard had landed.

He saw that the spot he needed to reach was halfway between the cabin and the trees where the enemy had first approached. Knowing that he would leave the cabin unprotected, he decided to seize the opportunity to confront his arch-enemy. Samuel ran with all his might, swinging his sword to the left, then the right, as he deflected attempted blows by the oncoming attackers.

The crowds between Samuel and the wizard served as a minor blockade. Samuel's determination to seize the moment coursed through his veins, giving him the strength and courage that he had been seeking throughout his entire journey. He was not afraid. Fear had left along with all doubt about his capabilities or the question of whether the mission would be carried out with great success.

Crossing one more hurdle of foes, Samuel made it to his destination on the battlefield and wasted no time in attacking the man who sought to destroy the world. The wizard saw Samuel in just enough time to pull the hero's sword from the chest of his winged pet. As he did so, he grinned. What better justice could I ask than to defeat him with his own weapon, he thought.

Running toward the wizard without saying a word, Samuel jumped into the air, sword raised, and let out a loud cry as he sliced the air, attempting to connect his blade with the wizard.

The wizard deflected the first blow, starting the epic battle of good versus evil. The wizard blocked blow after blow. In return, Samuel deflected each of the wizard's attacks with his sword. Left, right, up, down, the two enemies dueled in combat, each attempting to strike the other down on the spot. From the intensity of the fight, they knew their strikes were not meant to wound. Each blow was meant to kill instantly.

"You are not leaving here alive, Prince! I will have your head before this is over!" boasted Ablewis.

The wizard then raised his hand as if to cast a spell at the prince. As he thrust his arm forward, Samuel raised his hands to block the oncoming attack. A moment later, Samuel realized that nothing had happened. The wizard repeated the movements again with his hands, but no magic was conjured. The prince remained unharmed.

The prince seized the moment of confusion and advanced close to the wizard, swinging his sword into the air to land the final blow. With a loud cry of anger, Samuel swung at the wizard with all his might. The wizard looked up at Samuel, and as he was about to meet his fate, he realized that Samuel's sword was restraining him from using his magic.

The wizard immediately dropped the sword and began to disappear from where he was standing. However, he did not dematerialize quickly enough, for Samuel was able to slice his cheek just before he was gone. Following through with his strike, the prince fell to the ground and landed on his knee. Jeremy rushed to his side.

"Hurry, Jeremy, he cannot be too far. If he disappeared, there is no telling where we shall see him next," he gasped.

"We are holding our own for now, Samuel; the wizard's army may soon have the best of us. I'll regroup the armies, and you head back to the cabin," Jeremy instructed.

"Use Earabis to rally the troops. Once organized, bring everyone up to the cabin so that we can defend it. Earabis!" Samuel shouted.

Charging through the ranks, Earabis approached Samuel. The horse had received no wounds, proving his worth in combat.

"Earabis, take Jeremy around the field; protect him at all costs," Samuel instructed.

Jeremy jumped onto the horse, and the two took off through the battlefield. As the war raged on, Samuel could hear Jeremy shouting to the armies.

Samuel turned around and began to fight his way back up to the cabin. As he approached the front, the fairies were blasting away at any attackers in sight. Samuel ran up and began to offer aid to his loyal friends.

Samuel noticed during the fighting that the enemy was attacking only those present outside the cabin. It would seem that none of them could see the actual cabin, even though the spell the wizard put on Samuel and Kristina had brought them to this place. Whatever the cause, Samuel knew that he could use this blindness to his advantage while the battle ensued.

He would keep a watchful eye out for the wizard, letting his guard down for not one moment. The girls were well hidden inside, along with his one true love, Kristina. Should he somehow make it out of here alive with Kristina, he would kiss her.

All of the days and nights that he had grown up getting to know her, he had never once tried to kiss her. One of his greatest fears in life was that he would perish without ever having the chance to tell her and show her how he truly felt, how she was the source of his strength during the entire journey.

These thoughts gave Samuel a deepened strength to stay the course. He must see the girls to safety once and for all, and he needed to defeat the wizard to do so.

Once this was done, he would kiss his true love. And this kiss would be greater than the ones in any stories that were in the fable book Kristina used to read to him while they sat under the tree by the lake at the monastery.

Samuel was ready to dare any danger for her, for she was his Foreververse.

Anthony Farina

Chapter XV

Forever Verse

While war raged outside, Gabby and Darby remained hidden in an upstairs room, deep within a closet. Kristina hid in the room as well, pacing between the closet door and the middle of the room, all the while listening to the sounds of armor colliding with armor and sword striking sword. She feared for Samuel with every blow she heard.

She remained out of sight for fear that the blessing that was cast upon the cabin to conceal it would diminish. She knew that if it were, she and the girls would stand little chance from a concentrated enemy invasion of the cabin. She took no chances and stayed out of sight from the windows.

Her patience and nerves were growing weary as time passed throughout the day. Hours went by, and the three remained safely hidden from the foes outside. As screams of the dying along with the horrific sounds of battle could be heard all around the cabin, inside there remained nothing but silence.

The very silence was like an exquisite torture to Kristina. She had no way of knowing whether Samuel still lived. She had no idea whether she would have to escape the besieged cabin with the girls alone and raise them by herself while she mourned her lost love. The possibility of life without Samuel yawned before her in unbearable emptiness.

As the sun began to crest the tree line, intent on retreating for the day, memories of Kristina's life began to flood her mind like an uncontrollable tidal wave. She remembered the first time she met Samuel near the pond back at her beloved monastery. Thinking of the sweet hours and days that had followed, her heart began to beat faster, and a smile stole across her face in the darkest of hours.

Reading the fable book underneath the tree, a cherished place where she and Samuel would spend many hours, solemnly giving him her medallion, laughing and sharing stories about each other's families - these memories kept her warm when she needed comfort most.

Pondering all of the times she had spent with the prince, she realized that at this very moment, he was risking his life for her, just as he had been all along. Far too many emotions had swept through the princess over the past few days since her rescue at the castle. She had been spared little time until now to understand the depths of Samuel's love for her.

His search for her equaled in danger what her search for him had cost her in time and devotion.

They truly loved one another as partners. They had kept their childhood promise to find each other, and the understanding of the love they shared was precious to her.

The man who fought an army outside the windows would stop at nothing to see her and the two girls, whom he hardly knew, to safety. To Kristina, this kind of sacrificial love made Samuel a true prince, even more than his royal birth. He possessed all of the traits in his heart that were required to carry out the benevolent duties of a good ruler.

An understanding of her own heart told her in the same way that she was a princess - not just because of her royal birthright, but because she too would stop at nothing to protect him and the two girls who held the fate of the world in their small hands.

There was still one more thought eating away at Kristina's consciousness as to why she felt like a princess. This particular thought crept out of the dark recesses of her mind and uncovered itself, making known to her soul the reason why she held this title. It was Samuel's love for her.

All along, she had been the driving force for him to survive and complete his mission of rescuing her. He, too, had been her strength to stay alive and not lose hope in the darkest of times. This was what it truly meant to be a princess in the world.

Beyond the birthright given her and the ruling of a kingdom, being a princess gained meaning through the completeness she found in the love she and Samuel shared. They ruled one another's hearts –

the most sacred and important trust of all.

Kristina began to smile more widely than she ever had. At this moment, she realized that true love had been with her from a very young age. This type of love never died, and she possessed this priceless, immortal treasure for her own.

...

Nearby in the shadows, an evil royal guard and a group of ghastly minions surrounded the wizard. At first he could not see the princess, for the cabin disguised her. However, his magic allowed him to locate her essence. He initiated a spell that would draw her out of whatever hiding the creator had provided for her.

Once he located her, everything made sense to the wizard. Samuel was guarding the one place the wizard could not see. And inside was not only that sweet princess of his, but the two girls he sought as well. He could sense their presence, as well as his own victory.

A sharp grin split the wizard's face. He knew the kinds of weak people who believed in love and virtue. Kristina would not stay hidden for long.

The princess's love would draw her to Samuel, who had been so frightened for her that the fool had not even given her a weapon. His fear neutralized Kristina as a danger to him and made everyone fighting for her vulnerable.

The very separation Samuel had meant for Kristina's protection would make her vulnerable to the wizard. All he had to do was wait.

...

Suddenly, the noise of the battle outside height-
ened. Shock crossed Kristina's face as she remembered that the one man who had brought her such
joy and inner wealth could possibly lose his life at
any moment. "Samuel!" she cried.

"What's wrong, Kristina?" Darby asked.

"I'm afraid for Samuel, and I hate being away from
him. I should be doing something, not hiding from
danger!" Kristina exclaimed.

"Samuel only wants you to be safe," Gabby told
her. "He loves you, and he wants to protect you."

"That's true," said Darby slowly. "I just don't
know if that's true love."

"What do you mean?" Kristina asked, sitting down
beside the open door of the closet where the girls
hid.

"You two are supposed to be together. Mother
used to tell us that loving someone meant loving
all of them. You're brave, just like Samuel, but he
doesn't love that part of you. He's afraid that if
you're brave, like his mother was, he'll lose you
like he lost his mother. True love accepts all of a
person without fear," Darby said. "Samuel's fear
keeps him from loving you truly."

Kristina thought over Darby's words, and she knew
that they were true. "But what do I do now, Darby?
I should have insisted that I come with Samuel, but
I didn't. And I don't even know how to fight, even if

I had a weapon! I want to be brave and help Samuel defeat the wizard; I just don't know what I can do."

Darby held Kristina's hand. "Right now, you and Samuel are obeying fear, not love. But love is the only thing that can defeat the wizard. What does love tell you to do? What would you do if there were no armies outside?"

Kristina did not even need to think. Samuel had almost kissed her several times during their escape, but he had drawn away at the last moment. More than anything, Kristina wanted to go to Samuel and kiss him – to feel his arms around her and share their first kiss.

"I would go to him and kiss him," Kristina answered. "But how would I reach him in the middle of a battle? And what will I do afterwards without even a sword to defend myself?"

Darby smiled. "Love defeats the wizard. That's all I know."

"I know something else," added Gabby. "The creator makes a way. The creator hid us for years. He helped us provide food for ourselves the whole time. He showed us that you were coming. If you obey love, then the creator will take care of the rest."

"That's right," Darby approved. "Love and faith together – you have to have both."

Kristina leaned forward and hugged both girls. "Thank you both so much. You've reminded me of the truth when I most needed to hear it. I'm so grateful that we're going to be a family. I couldn't ask for better daughters."

"We love you, too, Kristina," Darby told her, kissing her cheek.

"We couldn't ask for a better mother," Gabby agreed, kissing her, too.

Kristina stood up with her hand on the door. "I have to do what I can to hide you while I'm gone. Once I leave the cabin, I don't know how long the creator's blessing will last. But if the creator tells you to come to me, listen and obey him. You may have some part to play that I can't guess. Pray that the creator guides my steps, dear hearts."

"We will," Gabby promised. Darby nodded agreement.

At once, Kristina closed the closet door, walked across the room to the beds, and pushed a bed against the doors. It would serve as one last defense for the girls should enemies break through.

"Girls, I leave you in the hands of the creator," Kristina said. "As soon as I can, I will return."

Though she moved quickly, time seemed to move slowly for Kristina. Her body was operating at one speed, her mind another. She went down the staircase and straight to the front door. Pausing only a moment, she opened the door to see Samuel in combat with numerous enemies. The minions of the wizard that he fought towered over him.

She watched as he swung his sword hard and fast, slicing the air. The enemy could not help but to pause in awe at the ferocity of one man who stood against many. Knowing he was vastly outnumbered, the prince continued to fight for his life and that of the princess.

Kristina stood in a state of shock and awe as she watched her hero do battle with the forces of evil. The very ferocity of his fighting drew her closer. She continued to open the door and lifted a foot to step onto the porch of the cabin.

•••

The wizard could sense Kristina's essence strongly now; she must be coming out of hiding. The wizard could tell that the creator had placed a strong blessing on the cabin, because he would not be able to see or touch Kristina until she had stepped away from the cabin.

The wizard's next move was to send the brunt of his force close to Samuel. He could now see why Samuel had fought in the same spot for the last few hours. He knew that Samuel was protecting something, and that secret was about to be revealed. The wizard's plan was working; he would soon have all he required to rule the universe.

The wizard, however, lacked one essential quality: the capability to understand true love. This great weakness threatened his plan. But in his blind cruelty and insane thirst for power, he could not see his own weakness.

•••

Samuel fought even harder as time wore on. He did not notice that Kristina was just about to leave the steps and security of the cabin and touch her feet to the ground. Harder every moment, he fought the onslaught of the wizard's forces. Cleric Jeremy remained right at his side, fighting wave after wave of attackers. The fairies blasted the unsightly creatures, focusing their might on the minions who approached Samuel and Jeremy from their blind side.

Meanwhile, Kristina moved closer. As she set foot outside the cabin door, her presence glowed. Then she appeared, as if out of thin air.

Ignoring the strong feeling of fear at the sight of the enemies in front of her, she determined to go to the prince. Moving down the cabin steps, one foot at a time, Kristina continued to draw closer to her beloved prince. Kristina stepped off the cabin and onto the ground. Regardless of the dangers all around her, her pace remained slow and steady. Love guides me, not fear, she reminded herself. Only love defeats the wizard.

Keeping her eyes only on Samuel, she proceeded. The wizard could see her clearly now, though she did not see him. Love quieted her fear at all the battle that ensued, for her only focus was Samuel.

For a moment, the princess felt hope. This hope ignited a feeling deep within her, one that she had never known before. Suddenly, she found herself within feet of her prince.

Dark creatures began to surround her, forming a circle and blocking Samuel from her sight. When she lost sight of him, fear began to overtake her. She could not see Samuel; she could not even see the cabin anymore.

Turning her head to the left and right, she

searched for a way out. Kristina grew frightened and started searching frantically for Samuel or Jeremy – for anyone friendly, any hope at all. All she could see was the crowd of monsters around her.

Now that she was on the ground, the cabin that had been blessed by the creator came into full view for all the enemy to see. The wizard ordered his entire army to descend upon the cabin and find the girls inside. The blessing had vanished.

The remaining soldiers from the armies of Ferdinand and St. Mein were down to about a quarter of their original strength. They continued to fight what enemies they could, knowing the cabin was now vulnerable. Both armies held off the brunt of the remaining enemy forces; however, a large group of the enemy still pressed forward to wipe out Samuel and Jeremy for good.

Jeremy noticed the enemy's change in tactics and ordered the fairies to come with him. "Samuel, get Kristina and the girls out of here! Earabis, the fairies, and I will buy you as much time as we can, but I am afraid this is the end, my friend!" Jeremy shouted as he rode into the oncoming force that slipped by the two armies.

The fairies followed Jeremy. Samuel could see Earabis raising his hooves, the fairies blasting away, and Jeremy leading a desperate charge into an overwhelming enemy force.

Samuel still did not realize that Kristina had left the safety of the cabin. There was too much confusion on the battlefield for him to see her.

Samuel prepared to face a group of about ten of

the wizard's deadliest allies. The creatures stood eight feet high, covered in dark, shaggy hair, and had tusks that protruded from their mouths to the tops of their heads. They were charging full speed at Samuel. With only about twenty feet between him and his attackers, Samuel took a deep breath and held tight to his sword. The sword began to glow blue as he concentrated all his might from his hands and into the hilt of his weapon.

The first beast launched at Samuel, jumping into the air and swinging with his tremendous claw to take Samuel out with one swipe. Samuel dodged the attack and countered with a swing to the stomach of the beast. The beast hurtled over him and fell to the ground.

Another creature of the same type approached. This one held what looked to Samuel like a small tree. The creature started bashing the ground, intending to pack Samuel deep within the dirt. Samuel quickly used the creature's repetitive attack method against him.

Samuel dodged the first two swings, and upon the third strike slamming into the ground, Samuel moved out of the way and then placed his foot on top of the tree-like weapon. He used the enemy's weapon as leverage to stand on. Once on the tree limb, he stepped up and slammed the butt of his sword into the beast's skull, knocking the second creature unconscious.

But there were still too many creatures to fight. Each one that Samuel slew took a great deal of his energy away, making the prince extremely tired.

Three more beasts met their fate before something caught the corner of the prince's eye.

Before he knew entirely what he had seen, an old dream returned to Samuel in a devastating flash. He saw a battle, a princess, a crowd of enemies – and he was going to die. A wicked man was going to seize him and chase him. Terror seized him for a moment before he shook it away.

He quickly turned all the way around to see the princess surrounded by the forces of the wizard. He left the remaining crowd of beasts and headed straight to the large gathering that surrounded the princess.

Without hesitation, he forced himself into the center of the circle where she stood. Exhausted and outnumbered, Samuel felt death approach for the first time in his life. Death brought a cold feeling to Samuel's bones. His body immediately began to ache for the warmth of life again.

Samuel tried to rationalize during the midst of chaos that fear brought these feelings to him. But he could not help but think that all hope was about to be lost if he did not act quickly. He could not fight all of the enemy horde. There were too many, and they were too strong. He could not save his friends. They were outnumbered, and they would soon meet the hands of death as well.

Time froze, and everything he loved about Kristina flashed across his mind. He remembered the way she smelled, looked, and felt as she held his hand for the first time. He remembered the times they rode horses through the fields. He remembered the love he felt for her daily as he faced the most dangerous parts of the world to rescue her. Finally he reached the ring of monsters surrounding her and fought his way through.

"I love you, Samuel!" Kristina exclaimed. "I love you forever!"

"Grab my hand!" shouted the prince.

Kristina grabbed his hand. The prince pulled her through the crowd of enemy beasts and guided her back onto the porch of the cabin.

"Kiss me!" Kristina said.

"What?" Samuel exclaimed.

"Just kiss me!" Kristina insisted.

In an instant he pulled her close and kissed her. As her lips touched his, time stopped. The prince knew that this woman was his true love, and the princess felt the same emotion rush through every fiber of her soul. She held no part of herself closed. All the light of love and faith and joy within her blazed with unimaginable power.

As their Foreververse opened before them, the princess radiated a great force of energy. The force swept through the immediate area and all of the land. As quickly as light crests the morning horizon and banishes the darkness on the earth that it illuminates, so too did the light from the princess shine on all things, living and dead.

The creatures the wizard had conjured at once turned to dust as the light touched them. The wizard cried loudly in pain and fell to his knees, his whole figure shrinking and withering and growing feeble. He became so weak that he was unable to pick himself up. His magic was gone.

But so was the light shining from the princess. Empty of all the goodness and strength within her, she lay still and unmoving in Samuel's arms. With a primal shock of grief, Samuel recognized the picture he had seen underground in the stained glass windows of the wizard's castle. He and Kristina had won the day, and it had cost them everything.

The remaining soldiers on the battlefield stood silent and in awe of what had just happened. Reverence hushed them. Then four of the soldiers of St. Mein walked over to the wizard and dragged him to where the prince and princess were.

Samuel's men brought the wizard to him, stopping ten feet away and dropping the wizard to the ground. Kristina lay in Samuel's arms, lifeless. Samuel buried his head in her chest as tears like rain fell from his face, yet he made no sound.

Kristina's love for Samuel had been so great that her love had destroyed the entire army that remained of the wizard's forces. But destroying the wizard's magic had cost the ultimate price of her life.

Samuel lifted his head from her chest, cleared his eyes, and scanned the battlefield. Everyone that had fought with him, all those who fought for good, remained alive, but all the ones who would see the world turn to darkness, the entire army of the wizard, had all turned to dust. The wizard looked as if he had aged a millennium.

Samuel's sadness quickly turned to anger as he focused on the wizard. The wizard was responsible for all of the death here today, good and bad. Samuel lay Kristina down gently, drew his sword, and walked over to the wizard, locking a hardened gaze on his nemesis.

Samuel's steps were heavy as his feet slowly pounded the ground. At each step toward the wizard, his anger grew. Grabbing the wizard by the throat, he lifted him up, raised his sword, and pointed the tip at the wizard's belly. He would gut this villain just as Ablewis had murdered King Sal. He would take the wizard's life as surely as Ablewis had taken Kristina's life. Within moments, Samuel would have his revenge.

"Go ahead, boy - do it. Embrace the hatred and anger you have for me. I took everything from you, and nothing you can do to me can bring your princess back!" the wizard rasped.

Samuel's mouth remained closed, lips tight with fury. Breathing heavily through his nose, he stared into the wizard's dark eyes. Samuel wanted so badly to run his sword through the wizard.

"Samuel! Stop! Don't do it; this is what he wants – to corrupt your soul!" Jeremy warned.

Breathing harder and tightening his grip around the wizard's neck, Samuel deepened his gaze into the wizard's eyes. He fought for control of his anger. He fought to remember goodness and the dictates of the creator.

The wizard laughed maniacally. "What are you waiting for, Prince? Do it! Exact your revenge!"

With a loud cry, Samuel squeezed the wizard one last time, throwing him to the ground. "Never. If I take your life, then I become just as you are, and all that was sacrificed will be for nothing!" Samuel barked.

Samuel took one last look at the wizard and turned around to where Kristina lay, her body still motionless. Samuel walked over to her, knelt down, and held her once more. He had no more strength to give for the good of the world. He was empty inside, the gates of his Foreververse eternally sealed against him by the death of his true love.

Darby walked out of the cabin, Gabby right by her side. She walked slowly up to Kristina and knelt down beside her. She, too, sobbed for the death of one who had sacrificed so greatly. Gabby stood by Darby, one hand on her shoulder. Darby's tears fell onto Kristina's face.

As more tears began to fall, a dim light started to glow from the pendant Darby wore. Samuel noticed this and stood up. He took a few steps back to let Darby have her moment. As Darby cried, she heard Gabby whisper to her, "It's going to be all right. You can do what the nice man in white told you to do."

Darby kissed Kristina on the cheek and stepped away. To everyone's surprise, she walked straight to Ablewis, who was still shaking and laughing and coughing on the ground. She stooped to touch him on the shoulder, and he shrank from her touch as if she burned with fire.

"Ablewis, your doom has come upon you," Darby announced in her sweet, high voice, loudly enough for all still living to hear. "This is your judgment: you are going to become a good man. You will know the evil you have done and mourn for it. You will see the kindness you might have done and long for it. You will reach for the mercy you denied to others, and it will be shown to you. Beware, Ablewis – the creator bids you to enter the fires of unmaking and remaking, and you will enter."

Darby's pendant flashed purple fire, and the fire wound into golden chains that bound Ablewis hand and foot and neck. He cried aloud as they touched him, and then he was struck silent. The brightness quickly faded, and all in the area bowed their heads in awe and respect of what had just unfolded.

Turning to Cleric Kerwin, Darby extended a hand to the silent Ablewis. "The creator charges you with the cure of this man's soul. It is not an easy task. Do you accept it?"

"I do, lady," Cleric Kerwin said, bowing. "I will be his mentor and his friend to the end of his life." He led Ablewis slowly and gently to his own horse and helped him to mount. Then Kerwin led the horse away.

Samuel stared at Kristina, and in an instant, hope came back to his soul in full force. "Darby, the pendant – you can bring her back! If you could make the wizard good, you can do this. Please – I beg you. I cannot live without her."

Tears fell from Darby's eyes. "I have a message from the creator for you, too, Samuel. I don't understand it, and I wish it was different. But it's what he says."

"No!" shouted Samuel. "The creator has to give her back to me!"

Shaking her head as she continued to cry, Darby said, "The creator told me that you have to bear your grief for the sake of other loves. You have to trust him. I'm so sorry, Samuel!"

A robed figure appeared in their midst. Samuel recognized him immediately. "Robert! How did you get out of the castle? And why didn't you come to help earlier?" Samuel questioned.

"Samuel, you have done well. Kristina was the key to defeating the wizard. Her love for you destroyed his evil magic, which he fueled with his hatred for this world. Once his powers diminished, I was free to leave the castle that was my prison.

"I have known Ablewis for over a thousand years. Long ago, when he was young, his lust for power fueled his search for magic. He wanted nothing more than to rule the world with it and make every living thing submit to his will. His magic became so powerful that no other forms of magic could stand against it.

"True love displayed at precisely the right moment in time was the only thing that could free the world, and the wizard, from the bond of magic he held. I am here to comfort you in your loss and to deliver the righteous dead to their reward."

Robert lifted his hands over the battlefield. Wind began to blow, wind mixed with light, like a white, glowing hurricane. Samuel could see it erasing the piles of dust that had been the wizard's minions. The broken bodies of his own brave soldiers faded from his sight, too.

While that bright wind still blew, Robert tenderly picked Kristina up and held her in his arms. Samuel saw what he intended to do – he was taking Kristina into that bright wind. Tears fell again from his eyes.

"In the castle, the windows I saw - they were a telling of what was to come, were they not?" Samuel asked.

"That is correct. The windows were the foretelling of a prophecy. The wizard built his castle over that place, which used to be a most holy site of worship to the creator. By doing so, he was able to keep the secret prophecy hidden for a time," Robert explained. "But all is fulfilled now."

"I can't bear for her to be gone forever," Samuel sobbed.

Robert smiled gently at him. "Who said anything about forever?" As Robert spoke his final words, he, along with Kristina, walked into that bright wind and disappeared. The wind ceased then, leaving only trampled crops and muddy earth to show there had been a battle.

Shortly after this moment, Samuel turned to Gabby and Darby, who stood alone. He opened his empty arms, and the girls rushed to him. The remaining armies gathered around the three. Jeremy came to his side, along with Earabis. The fairies floated up to Samuel and sat on his shoulder.

"Girls, how would you like to come and live in a kingdom where you will never have to live in fear or on your own ever again?" Samuel asked the girls.

"Would we! It has been too long since we have had parents to watch over us. Do you still want us, even though Kristina is gone?" Gabby asked.

"Of course I do," Samuel told them, hugging them tight. "You are the meaning of the creator's message to me. I have to bear my grief for the sake of other loves. You are my other loves, my daughters. You are my princesses now."

"Princesses!" Darby exclaimed. "I don't know how to start being a princess, and neither does Gabby!"

"You'll learn," Samuel smiled sadly. "How about we get you two home first? Then we can begin your training, and we will become a family. How does that sound, my princesses?" Samuel asked the girls.

"It sounds like a good dream," Gabby said with a

smile.

"It sounds like the best thing in the whole, wide world," Darby agreed, hugging Samuel's neck.

Samuel stood up, arms around his new daughters, and faced his remaining army. "Captains of Ferdinand, let us all return to our kingdoms. We will live side by side in harmony and keep peace in our land!" Samuel shouted.

All cheered in agreement. Men shook hands with one another in recognition of a new brotherhood between the kingdoms. Soldiers do not shed blood together without becoming brothers, and this battle against evil had sealed the kinship between them for generations.

...

Samuel returned home with Darby and Gabby, who were given a place in the kingdom to dwell in peace and happiness. Samuel announced his father's death and took the throne in his place. He never married, but remained faithful to his true love for the rest of his life.

Cleric Jeremy returned to his duties as abbot of the kingdom and ensured that all religions and beliefs were welcome within the kingdom's boundaries. He also oversaw the education of the future queen of St. Mein, Princess Darby.

Captain Steven ensured that the Kingdom of St. Mein remained strong and well-defended against any new evil that should arise. Knowing that he was growing old, he trained the former captain of the guard from Darniem to lead the army and safe-guard the kingdom in time. Captain Steven also trained Princess Darby in the queenly arts of riding, fighting, and commanding an army.

Captain Steven also sent men to Cleric Kerwin to guard the place where he and Ablewis lived. To the day of the wizard's death, he never again lifted a hand or a thought against any man. When Ablewis died of old age, Kerwin buried him and returned to the monastery.

Earabis lived out his days in the lush green fields, riding the same trails he had traveled at the time of Samuel's youth. Laci and Summer visited him often when they came to see their friends at the castle of St. Mein. Those visits weren't always pleasant.

Though Samuel treated Darby and Gabby with love, Kristina's loss haunted him. He missed her every day, and Robert's last words to him seemed like a cruel taunt.

He tried to be a good father to the girls. Remembering the sorrow of his youth and the father who could not bear to see him because of the loss of Queen Kathleen, Samuel made sure to dine with Darby and Gabby every day and listen to their stories of friendships and misunderstandings and school lessons. Rising above his own great grief to love his daughters was the hardest thing Samuel had ever done.

To ease his aching heart, Samuel turned to wine. And as Darby grew older and more able to rule, he slipped away to the wilderness for weeks at a time and lived in the place he had lived when Kristina's father had taken her from him. There Samuel hunted and fished and drank and wept. Nothing he did made him forget his love or his pain.

When Darby reached the age of eighteen, she was wise and beautiful and just and compassionate. She was ready to rule the kingdom. Samuel crowned her queen and lived as her loyal subject.

To pay homage to her foster father, who had braved so many dangers to rescue her and defend her from the wizard, Darby smoothed the path he had traveled, removing the obstacles that the wizard had placed in Samuel's way.

She ordered a path to be made through the lost forest. Men cut a great swath through the forest and built a gravel path through the place the witch had lived. They used the trees to build shelters along the way from St. Mein through the forest.

Next, Darby tackled the desert. She caused stone houses to be built at intervals of a day's ride, and at each house, she ordered a well to be dug and trees to be planted. Never again would anyone burn with thirst and heat for days as Samuel had.

Then Darby ordered a trail to be marked across the mountains and shelters to be built along the way. She made sure that each one held stone jars of water and dried food for travelers, as well as stacks of kindling for fire. Never again would a traveler lie blue with cold and near death at the mountain's heights.

At the great abyss, where the road turned toward Darniem itself, Darby ordered men to make a bridge. The first men who reached the abyss saw that the dragon which had guarded the place had turned into a great, solid rock, though the chain of his imprisonment still stretched across the chasm. Builders used the wide, strong chain in its anchor of transformed dragon to anchor a strong bridge of wood and stone.

The road was so well made that the people of St. Mein began to use it for pleasure and for trade with Darniem and the kingdoms beyond. Connected to the rest of the world for the first time by the queen's highway, the people of Darniem grew kinder and more industrious and virtuous. Over the generations, the land of Darniem changed so vastly that the wizard would not have known it for his own.

One change Darby did not make. She left the cabin where she had been hidden as a child exactly as it had been on the day she left with Samuel. It was too sacred to change.

The whole land grew fertile and enjoyed many generations of great peace. Darby ruled the kingdoms with Gabby right at her side, and for her part, Gabby never let any harm come to her dear sister. Jeremy and Steven advised the queen and helped her make the kingdom into a place of plenty and harmony for all of its subjects.

When Darby was twenty-five, Samuel came to her throne room to bid her farewell. "I have always wondered what became of the wizard's castle," he told her. "I mean to see it again while my legs can still carry me."

Darby knew that Samuel didn't want to see the

wizard's castle half as much as he wanted to stand again in the place where he had last held his living sweetheart and lost her. Being wise and kind, she did not say what she knew. "My heart goes with you, my dearest father. I hope that you find what you seek and return safely to us."

"You are a good queen, Darby – a better queen than I ever was a king. I am glad to see you on that throne. Whether or not I return, the creator has done well by the Kingdom of St. Mein," Samuel told her, kissing her hand.

"The creator has done well by me, too, Father. I know he will watch your steps as you go." Darby blinked away the tears that rose to her eyes. She had a feeling that she was telling her beloved father goodbye forever and that she would not see him again until she rose in death to join the creator himself. However, she did not want to burden her farewell with those words between them.

Samuel shared her feeling, though. When he left the throne room, he sensed that he was leaving it finally. He wore the clothes of an ordinary traveler, and he took only what he needed to sustain his life in a small sack he carried across his shoulder. Leaving St. Mein, he saw its fertile fields and pleasant vines with satisfaction. It was blessed, and he could leave it in peace.

His journey now was so different than his journey of years before. The forest was only a forest with no witch lying in wait. Samuel felt nothing within it beyond gratitude for its shade and quiet streams. He stayed in the shelters Darby had caused to be built, and he blessed her wisdom.

Likewise, the desert was hot and hard to cross, but the wells and stone houses at spaces made the hardships bearable. Without the weight of worry that he must hurry to save the princess, he could see its beauty, too. He breathed the clean air and felt the sweat leaving him like a cleansing.

When he reached the mountains, he stared at them in awe and wonder. They were majestic and terrifying. No snake barred his way. No enemy hindered him. Just as the desert had scrubbed him clean, the snows of the mountain anointed and freshened him. And thanks to his loving daughter's goodness, he crossed with warmth and food and shelter.

Reaching the abyss, Samuel saw the new bridge that reached across the chasm. Across it, he could see the shape of the beast he had caused to sleep with the help of the red flower. Samuel crossed the chasm easily, and when he looked back at the land he had crossed, he felt that it was a land he had never known and would never again see.

From the bridge, the journey to the wizard's castle took very little time. Samuel arrived to find a bare ruin, open to the birds and the beasts. No man guarded it; no man ruled it. Samuel found the door by which he had escaped so long ago and retraced his steps to the underground cavern, the old church, and its mysterious windows.

Inside, Samuel stared at the images of his life for hours. He saw his own birth and his mother's death. He saw his brief, sweet love story. He saw his exile to the wilderness and his confinement in the wizard's spell. He saw his journey to save Kristina, and the battle, and her death.

There the windows ended. Samuel stared at the glass picture of the woman he had loved until the light faded from the windows entirely. Then he retraced his steps in the dark to the distant door. He was not afraid. All evil had gone from the castle a long time ago.

Samuel slept under the stars in an empty field. And in the morning, finding the rest of the way was almost too easy. The little cabin stood plain and small for all to see, as any reason for its concealment had ended the last day he had seen it.

He went inside and saw Darby's childish drawings still pinned to the wall of her bedroom. Her hand had traced his young face holding a sword aloft. She had also drawn him with a woman, clearly Kristina, in wedding clothes. They stood on clouds, holding hands. Samuel took the picture of him and Kristina and left the room.

Samuel stayed in the cabin for days, sleeping in the room downstairs that Gabby and Darby's parents had shared. He pinned the picture Darby had drawn to the wall of that room and looked at it often. He did not drink; he had not brought any drink with him.

Though he did not quite understand why he stayed, Samuel could think of no other place he wanted to be. His life seemed to have led him to this place. It was the last picture in the story of the stained glass windows – beyond it had been nothing else.

On occasion, Samuel sat on the cabin's front steps remembering the battle he had fought and what had come after it. Twenty feet in front was where it had been – the bright wind that had taken his army and his future bride. He stood in the same place where he had seen her go, and he remembered Robert's last words: "Who said anything about forever?"

On the third night of his stay, Samuel lay in his bed and thought again of Robert's words. He sat up suddenly, gasping with the pain of the memory. He could swear that his heart was tearing in two as he saw again the bright wind rushing through the clearing, taking the dead to the creator.

He fell backward, staring out the bedroom doorway, which had filled with light. The light seemed to grow larger and brighter until it swallowed the whole wall, as if the sun in the sky had come to earth and touched the cabin. A door opened in the sun, and the face he loved best peered through it.

"It's you!" Kristina exclaimed. "I've been waiting for you to come. Let me help you up."

Samuel backed away from the vision. "It can't be you. I watched you die. I'm only dreaming again! In the morning, you'll be gone." He hid his face and sobbed.

Cool, strong arms slid around him, and he felt the give of the mattress as someone sat beside him.

"I'm not a dream, you know. I'm your own Kristina, who loves you. Open your eyes and look at me if you don't believe it," she invited.

He opened his eyes. Close to him was Kristina, and she seemed solid and real and as young as she had been the last time he saw her. He looked down at his tough, old hands and felt embarrassed. "Even if it was you and not a dream, we don't belong together anymore. You're young and beautiful as an angel. But me – I'm old now. I've had a hard life. I tried so hard to forget you that I think," he looked away from her, "I think I might have finally done it."

"No, you haven't," Kristina insisted. "You remember me. I know that you do."

She reached a slim, pale hand towards his neck and held a gold chain in her fingers. From it dangled the medallion of Raphael, which she had given him long ago. At her touch, it glowed golden, dazzling his eyes until he lifted them to her.

"Is it really you?" he asked. "Have you come back to life after so long?"

Kristina stood and faced him. "I am more alive now than I have ever been – and so are you, my beloved, at long last. Look at yourself."

Samuel looked down at his hands, which were smooth and brown and boyish. He felt suddenly light and full of energy, ready to run a race or ride a horse. He laughed with the joy of it.

A thing like a shadow stretched out on the bed behind him. Samuel did not regard it. Kristina stretched her hand to him once again, and this time he took it and stood. Side by side, the two of them faced the door in the sun and looked through.

Beyond the doorway, he could see a garden of flowers, a tree by a lake, and a small house, big enough for two. Two horses pawed the earth near-by, anxious to run and carry riders. And sudden-ly, the time Samuel had waited to rejoin Kristina seemed like a breath, like a moment – like it had never happened at all.

"Welcome home, love," she smiled, and she kissed him. The first kiss they had shared in the midst of pain and death could not compare to this one, on the threshold of light and life. Samuel felt his soul knit to Kristina's, as he knew hers was knit to him. When he opened his eyes and gazed at her, he knew that he lacked nothing. Peace and con-tentment enveloped him.

If this is death, he thought, I have been wrong ever to fear it.

Then, with Kristina beside him, he stepped into their Foreververse, never to leave it again.

-The End-

ACKNOWLEDGMENTS

•••

Over the course of the seven years it has taken to write this single piece of work, the number of people I wish to thank could easily outnumber the pages in this book. My daughter, Darby, was the inspiration for this novel, but a few others stand out:

- My life-long friend, Kristie Naglich, has inspired me to overcome more obstacles in my life than I can give her credit for.
- My nieces, Summer and Laci, who have always had an interesting dialogue as sisters, served as comic relief for this work.
- My mother (who I did a good job describing in this book) is one of those mothers who cares more for her children than for her own life.
- Robbie Grayson who continually gives me renewed support and a chance for my work to be known.
- Robbie's wife, Sharilyn, made the impossible happen with this work, because I am not the best at following the rules of fiction and fantasy. Great job by the way... still!
- Jackie Nickle, your artwork captivates the minds of the readers as much as the story itself does! We made a great team working on this for over a year, and the labor has paid dividends.

Forever Verse